COLD LAKE

DAVID WOLF BOOK 5

JEFF CARSON

D0369308

CROSS ATLANTIC PUBLISHING

DAVID WOLF SERIES IN ORDER

Dedicated to my family, friends, and readers who have given their generous support. Without you I'd be ...

CHAPTER 1

Sheriff David Wolf looked up and saw the line of trucks and SUVs thundering down the dirt road at five-alarm-fire speed. Letting up his bodyweight on the wriggling animal underneath him, he hissed in pain as a hoof glanced off his knee. The dust from the slowing vehicles washed over the volunteers inside the cattle pen, and then moved on to envelop the rest of the crowd gathered on the surrounding lawn.

"Who the hell is that?" Deputy Tom Rachette squinted and waved his hand.

"MacLean," Wolf said.

The calf bleated, protesting the ropes expertly lassoed around its head and hind legs. The two men controlled their horses, pulling the ropes with practiced precision.

Rick Welch, third-generation owner of Triple T Ranch, quickly shaved the calf's right rear haunch and a volunteer weekend cowhand approached with two smoking branding irons.

"God damn it," Rick mumbled through clenched lips, waiting for the cloud to pass.

Luckily, a light morning breeze dispersed the dust, and the air became breathable again.

The unplanned break over, Wolf sagged his weight onto the animal and held tight. At six foot three and two hundred pounds, he'd always carried a muscular physique with little effort, or, in the case of his years as an army Ranger, with tremendous effort, but now that he was almost forty-one years old, his muscularity hid the fatigue within that came after rigorous activity. The morning's work had his shoulders and abdominal muscles screaming for mercy. As sheriff of Sluice County for the past three years, he was lucky if he managed to break away three times a week for weight lifting, and the cardio ... well, he figured his cardio was living in the mountains of Colorado.

He'd lost count of how many calves they'd done so far, but he knew there were plenty more to go. Even with the second and third team of horsemen and volunteers working just as hard inside the pen, it was going to be an all-day job that might go into tomorrow.

Deputy Tom Rachette, a fit young man in his mid-twenties, seemed to sense Wolf's slowdown and squatted next to him, gripping the calf's hind legs and stilling the animal for good. Rachette was shorter than average, but in Wolf's estimation, the deputy was built like a bull, and he had tenacity and strength rivaling that of most larger men.

"Thanks," Wolf said through gritted teeth, a fresh twinge of pain shooting through his lower back.

Triple T Ranch had the largest herd of cattle in Sluice County, and it was a community operation to get the cattle branded every year. Wolf hadn't missed the event for seven years running, and Margaret Hitchens, town real-estate agent and self-appointed chairperson of the Wolf-for-Sheriff election campaign, had turned the branding into a rally for votes, complete with food and games for the entire family outside the cattle pen.

Margaret had seen to it that the *Sluice Sentinel* had run announcements in the three weeks leading up to the event, and nearly every display window and cork board in Rocky Points featured one of Margaret's come one, come all invitations. Over fifty men, women, and children had shown up.

And now there were a few more uninvited ones.

"Okay!" Rick shouted.

The ropes slackened. Wolf slipped the loop over the rear hooves and he and Rachette jumped up, clearing out of danger.

"Sheriff Wolf!" a deep, jovial voice called from the other side of the fence.

Wolf turned with little enthusiasm toward a rising commotion.

A videographer scrambled with a tripod and camera, and an army of still photographers darted this way and that, kneeling and climbing into photo-opportunity positions.

Wolf instinctively glanced at Margaret, who was already out of her lawn chair and charging towards MacLean, a suspicious crease on her brow beneath her cowboy hat.

"What's this?" she demanded.

MacLean looked over at her like she was an attacking rabid dog, then smiled pleasantly.

"Margaret, I heard about the cattle-branding and thought I'd volunteer." He raised his voice for everyone to hear over the mooing. "That is, if you'll have me."

Photographers snapped photos. The videographer panned from MacLean to Wolf.

Margaret scoffed and walked away.

Wolf walked to the fence with an outstretched hand caked with dried mud.

MacLean knotted his hand with Wolf's and shook vigorously. His smile was confident, his steely eyes either ignoring or oblivious to the cool reception of every person surrounding him.

The cameras whirred and clicked.

Releasing Wolf's grip, MacLean hopped over the fence with considerable grace for a fifty-five-year-old. His brand-new work boots stomped down on the dusty earth and he bent down, grabbed a handful of dirt, and rubbed it across his chest, leaving a skid mark on his expensive white button-up shirt.

"Mr. Welch!" MacLean boomed, marching toward the owner of the Triple T Ranch with his now dusty hand.

Rick fumbled with the branding irons, leaving MacLean holding out his hand without a partner to shake it. Finally, they shook and MacLean beamed a smile framed by his perfectly trimmed silver goatee.

The photographers pounced.

Wolf heard a ping on the fence and a collective gasp. He turned in time to see a photographer's head whipping back as he landed on the ground. The camera-wielding man's smooth-soled shoes were no match for manure.

The guy bounced up without hesitation and snapped some shots.

Wolf turned on his heel and plucked Sarah from the crowd.

Standing in front of her chair to get a better look, she met Wolf's gaze and smiled.

They gravitated toward one another at the fence line. He watched her and took a cleansing breath, feeling a jolt of energy. The combination of the crisp air and watching her move was better than ibuprofen or any other pain reliever. As far back as high school, when he'd met his sweetheart turned wife, turned ex-wife turned—whatever it was they were now—she'd always liked to dress the part of a cowgirl, and with her worn jeans, frayed hat, button-up embroidered denim shirt, she wore the look just as well as she had back then.

They met at the fence and she handed him a water bottle.

"Real nice of him to show up," she said. "What an asshole. No wonder this guy's winning. Good God, there's like ten photographers. Is he shooting another commercial?"

Wolf drank the cold water and let the sun warm his skin. It was clear blue skies with visibility as far as it got to the north and south, with pine-tree-covered mountains socking them in to the east and west. The dung-scented air was warm with a steady cool breeze, making it biting cold in the shade, typical of early June in the middle of the Rockies.

Sarah's jeans stretched against her thinly muscled leg as she propped a boot on the fence and she smiled up at him.

"You look like a dust bunny. Here,"—she reached through the fence and ruffled his hair, sending a cascade of dirt onto Wolf's shoulders—"let's unveil that gorgeous dark hair of yours for the cameras, and let's wipe your face. It looks like one of those cattle pooped on it."

Wolf closed his eyes and let her delicate hands do their brusque work. "I think one of them did."

"—Wolf?"

He turned around at the sound of his name.

MacLean stood with Trevor Lancaster, the undersheriff of Byron County. Lancaster was Wolf's age—younger, taller, and more muscled than his boss. Wolf couldn't help notice the way the man raked his eyes up and down behind Wolf, taking in Sarah's figure with unreserved curiosity.

Besides Lancaster, all eyes were on Wolf.

"What's that?" he asked.

"I said," MacLean yelled over the cows, "why don't you and I mount up and rope one of these calves? Show 'em how it's done?"

MacLean was oblivious to the glares he received.

"I don't think you or I could show any of these men

anything they haven't done themselves over fifty times already today."

MacLean's smile wavered for an instant, but he shrugged and walked toward a horse and grabbed the reins from the dismounted cowboy. The sheriff of Byron County climbed on with expert speed and grabbed the lasso off the saddle horn.

Wolf turned back to Sarah and handed her the water bottle.

She smiled and winked. "Go get 'em, Sheriff."

Wolf looked at Sarah's beautiful Colorado-sky-blue eyes, her tanned face flecked with tiny circles of sunlight passing through the holes in her cowboy hat, and at that moment thought he could wrestle down a bull with his hands. Then when he tried to think of the last time he'd thrown a lasso and came up with no memories, his confidence came down a few notches. With a sigh he turned around.

"All right, Sheriff Wolf!" Margaret Hitchens thrust a fist into the air and tried to rally some cheers from the crowd.

Travis Chapman hopped off his Mustang and gave Wolf the reins. "You got this?"

"Nope," Wolf said, climbing up without hesitation. The beast beneath him twisted and bucked, and Wolf managed to keep his seat, though barely.

Chapman finally calmed the Mustang down and handed up his coiled lasso.

Wolf took it, let out some slack, and twirled it in a slow circle, getting his bearings with riding a horse and twirling a lasso—two actions alone he hadn't done in years.

"You be the heeler?" Sheriff MacLean winked at Wolf.

Wolf smiled. Roping the heels meant he'd have to lay the lasso loop as a trap in front of the moving calf's rear legs and then snag the legs as it moved through the loop. Though looping either the head or heels was no easy task for the unpracticed, the former was the more difficult task. Successfully heeling a calf was something he'd seen the men today fail to do on numerous occasions. They were professionals. Wolf, most definitely, was not.

"Sure," he said, getting the feeling that this politically masterful opponent of his had just roped him.

MacLean turned and pursued a calf without hesitation, tossed the lasso and snagged its head in a swift fluid motion. He yanked the line and stopped his horse. The calf twisted, turning its hind legs toward Wolf.

Wolf rode into place, feeling wobbly in the saddle as the huge Mustang accelerated.

He twirled the rope above his head, at an angle towards his left shoulder, like his father had taught him all those years ago. Then he rode up alongside the left hind leg, just like he remembered, letting the loop grow with each twirl. He watched the calf hop, the hind legs leaving the ground in a steady, predictable rhythm. And then he threw.

And he whiffed.

"Come on Wolf!" someone yelled from the crowd.

"You can do it sheriff! Waaahooo!" Margaret Hitchens's voice was easily picked out of the silence.

Wolf tried again, missing the mark one more time, and then again. This time the toss was good, but he was late pulling the slack.

"You gotta flatten your toss!" MacLean said.

Wolf chuckled to himself as he reeled in the rope. *I've gotta flatten your face.*

Amid a deafening uncomfortable silence, Wolf missed again.

"All right," MacLean declared. "I'll take the heels. You got the head."

Ah. Okay. Easy enough, Wolf thought. He felt like he was

thirteen all over again, tossing a rope at a wooden dummy with his father barking at him.

"Okay, you got this!" Deputy Rachette started a renewed wave of banter. "Come on, Sheriff!"

"Yay, Sheriff Wolf!"

Wolf took a deep breath, twirled the rope above his head, this time keeping a nice bend in his elbow with each revolution. He picked an easy target: a calf that was standing still, unobstructed in the confusion of moving cattle.

The rope hit the rear half of the animal and dropped to the ground.

MacLean laughed. "Okay, let's give back the pros their horses. We could be here all day!"

Wolf ignored him. He whipped back the rope and stretched the loop out, twirled it over his head twice and tossed it. Sailing through the air, the loop went over the head of a brown-and-white spotted calf and landed around its neck. He pulled back, tightening the slack, and then wrapped the rope around the saddle horn. He steered his horse the opposite way, whipping the calf around and presenting the hind legs to MacLean.

"Hey! Now we're talkin'!" MacLean yelled.

A split second later, Wolf's rope yanked back incredibly hard—too hard—almost sending him off the saddle as the Mustang twisted back. At that second, he saw the calf in the air, both hind legs securely roped and pulled back, the animal poised to land on its side.

"Whoa!" Wolf pulled up on the reins, but too late—the calf was stretched inhumanely thin, and just when Wolf thought he had ripped the animal in half, the Mustang stopped and backed up a few steps.

MacLean wasted no time turning and dragged the calf backwards towards the men with the branding iron.

Wolf followed, keeping total slack in his rope, more than a little relieved that the calf was struggling against the tow.

As the men branded the calf, MacLean sat tall with a self-satisfied grin plastered on his face.

Once again, Wolf felt bested by this man, in an arena he was unfamiliar with.

Being appointed sheriff of Sluice County, just like Hal Burton before him, and Wolf's father before Burton, Wolf had never had to pander to the masses, never had to act a part; he'd simply shown up for work and done the best job he could.

Now that the smaller Sluice County was merging with its neighbor to the south, Byron, things were changing. Big time. Down in Rocky Points, just a block and a half from the station, a three-story monstrosity of a municipal building and new sheriff's office, complete with state-of-the-art jail cells in the basement, was going up in record time. And with the new structure came something even bigger. An election. And a campaign. *Multiple* campaigns, because the people of the newly formed Sluice–Byron County were voting not only for a sheriff but for other seats in the new county government too.

It was now spring and the election would be held in mid-summer by special order of the governor of Colorado. With the political atmosphere like a mosh pit at a thrash-metal concert, Sheriff Will MacLean seemed to be at home amid the chaos.

Wolf wondered just how MacLean planned on cutting and pasting all this video footage, what exactly he was going to do with all these photos.

No doubt something awe-inspiring, just like the rest of the man's campaign for sheriff had been thus far.

Wolf felt no awkwardness when it came to mountain living. But the pixels captured through those lenses said otherwise. That's all that mattered. The airtime on television that

MacLean's campaign could buy would undoubtedly show the people otherwise.

"And that," Margaret Hitchens yelled, "is Sheriff Wolf's attitude towards his job in action. Never give up! Never give up!"

A lone whistle pierced a smattering of applause.

Wolf felt his face go red as he jumped down and handed over the reins.

"Sheriff Wolf!"

Rachette had his cowboy hat off, waving it in the air with one hand and holding a radio in the other.

Deputy Patterson stood next to him with excitement painted on her face, and not because of the recent action. She held her radio, too.

"What's up?" he asked as he reached the fence line.

Patterson climbed two slats of the fence and leaned toward him.

"We have a dead body," she said. "Correction: almost a dead body."

CHAPTER 2

Rubber boat fenders squeaked against the wood of the marina docks as wake waves rolled in.

Wolf raised his face to the sun, letting it inject some warmth into his skin while the breeze sucked it away. He knew the lake had been named for a temperature inversion found at roughly fifty feet beneath the surface of the water, but as he zipped his jacket to his chin he thought that Cold Lake was living up to its namesake.

Taking a deep inhale through his nose, he whiffed gasoline, vinyl seats, and dead fish, a combination that brought back memories of bass fishing with his father.

Lime green in color, the boat in front of him was nothing flashy, just a middle-of-the-line family model with a powerful outboard motor that five to ten grand could buy. What lay inside on the stern floor, however, was anything but ordinary.

The hypnotic movement of the sphere in the black plastic bag slowed as the wake of the passing boat dissipated. Then a combination of waves lifted the back end and rolled the bag over for an instant, revealing a mouth and nose through a tear in the plastic.

Rachette let out a soft whistle.

Stepping off the dock and onto the rear seat, Patterson snapped on her rubber gloves. She was five foot one and a year younger than Rachette, and she had a granite physique that was maintained with strict diet and exercise. Unlike Rachette's stocky build, she was thin and wiry. As she moved with quick precision, the boat barely swayed under her negligible weight.

With wide blue eyes and bobbed dark hair, she was the definition of cute, and could lull the opposite sex into leering, but as Wolf watched her grip the plastic bag without hesitation and look inside the rip, he, just like everyone who met Heather Patterson, was reminded of the fearless fire within.

The teeth within the disembodied head were yellow, unnaturally large-looking from receding gums. The lips were like mangled worms, and the nose was snow white and waxy, like it had melted flat against the face.

Rachette stepped into the boat after Patterson, keeping his distance with his second step.

Wolf turned at the sound of boots coming down the dock.

Sheriff MacLean stepped next to him and watched Patterson work.

"Eye sockets look mutilated," she said. "Gouged with a knife."

"Jesus." Rachette backed into the space next to the driver's seat.

"That's beyond disturbing." MacLean zoned out for a moment and turned to Wolf. "Listen. I've got a thing tonight. Congressman. Attorney General. Commissioner. DA. I can have Lancaster stay if you need, get another few deputies up here."

Lancaster stood motionless behind his boss, a head taller than MacLean, clearly staring down at Patterson's backside and not the grotesque item she was prodding.

"No thanks," Wolf said.

MacLean shrugged and then squinted one eye. "Deputy Patterson, right? And Rachette?"

"Yes, sir." Rachette nodded politely.

Patterson nodded and snapped some photos with her Nikon DSLR camera.

"You two are going to be interviewing for the new Sheriff's Department next month, correct?"

"You two carry on." Wolf stepped backwards and walked up the dock toward the marina. "MacLean, Lancaster, follow me, please."

"I'll see you later, Deputies," MacLean said, taking his time turning and walking after Wolf.

Lancaster trailed his eyes up and down Patterson one more time and walked after his boss.

Wolf escorted them under the tape and over to their SUV, which sat in the newly paved parking lot of the lake marina.

"I'd appreciate it if you didn't bully my deputies."

MacLean frowned and took off his sunglasses. "Bully? I'm not bullying your deputies. I'm trying to open a discussion with them about their future. I would think you might be open to that."

"Is that what you're doing?" Wolf looked at Lancaster. "And you: Deputy Patterson is a fifth-degree black belt, so you keep letting those dead eyes of yours wander like that and I can't guarantee your safety."

Lancaster nodded with a sneer.

"And Sheriff, the election hasn't happened yet," Wolf said. "The Sluice–Byron County Sheriff's Department doesn't even exist for another month. You might want to remember that. You guys have a nice fundraiser tonight."

Wolf patted him on the shoulder.

MacLean looked down at the spot Wolf had touched,

smiled and put his sunglasses back on. "Have you heard about my event?"

"The fundraiser? The one you just told me about on the dock?" The lake they stood next to, though being the third largest in Colorado, could not contain Will MacLean's ego.

"I was serious back there. I have Congressman Blake coming. Commissioner Heller, the retiring commissioner of *your* county." MacLean ticked off his fingers. "The DA. The ADA. Your old boss, Burton, he's confirmed."

The last name stung Wolf. But he figured if Burton was going, it was for the Scotch and food, not for support.

"If you'd like to join reality and come down to Ashland tonight, it's going to be quite a party. I sent you an invitation."

Wolf turned and walked away.

"See you Monday night," MacLean called after him. "Hope you can prepare all those talking points with all this new action going on."

Wolf sucked in a calming breath with little success.

CHAPTER 3

"HERE." Oliver Chevalier tapped his fish-finder screen and pulled back the throttle. "This is the spot."

The boat coasted, riding up as the wake passed underneath it, and then bobbed in the water. Wolf's ears rang in the relative silence of the idling motor and his skin tingled as the cold rushing air became warm and still.

"Right here." Oliver looked pale. "You can see the depth change underneath us. Starts at one hundred and thirty feet, give or take, then it drops off to three hundred feet plus." Oliver tipped a paper cup vertical and sucked down the last drops of his coffee, then poured another helping from his metal thermos with shaking hands.

Wolf gazed at the screen, seeing the precipitous drop off underneath them. He rubbed his hands together to build warmth.

"Should have felt it this morning," Oliver said. "It was damn cold. Every year you forget how cold it still is, all the way into June."

"Where did you pull up the bag?" Wolf asked.

Oliver Chevalier shivered and shut his eyes. "Yes. Sorry. We were trawling the deep parts with this downrigger. Looking to catch some lake trout. Caught one"—he raised his eyebrows —"big. Huge. And then later, I snagged something, and I realized I'd run too far. I knew I'd probably snagged the boulders where it turns shallow. Then I turned around and pulled up that bag. Billy was makin' fun of me about it. He grabbed it and brought it in, and then he dropped it and started yelling. I still remember that sound. A head dropping into the boat."

Oliver stopped talking and took another sip of coffee. He set the cup down, walked to the front of the boat, knelt on the cushion and vomited over the side. The loud grunt of his expulsion echoed off rock cliffs looming over the western shoreline in the distance.

"Oooookay," Patterson said, turning towards Wolf and Rachette.

Wolf studied the fish finder. "You come here a lot?"

Oliver wiped his mouth. "Yeah, the boulders are a marker for me and Jed. We usually start here and troll north and south. It's our spot."

The screen of the sonar device was split, with a multicolored image sliding by on the left, and a black-and-white image on the right. "Can you tell me what we're looking at here, Oliver?"

Oliver looked over at him and wiped his chin. He wobbled over and leaned over the display.

Wolf caught a whiff of Oliver and held his breath.

"Bottom's at one hundred thirty-four feet indicated by that number—you can see the boulders there—then the bottom drops out from under at that bright-white patch. They say it goes down to four hundred plus feet. The down-imager won't go that deep. This right here is the lowest point between that island," Oliver pointed to a low-forested island to the east, "and the shore there." He pointed to the west to the cliffs.

"So you thought you snagged one of those boulders?" Wolf tapped the screen.

Oliver stood up and nodded. "Well, yeah. Had to be. There's nothin' else down there. Of course, it wasn't a boulder." He lunged back to the front of the boat and bent over, his grunts echoing once again.

Wolf, Rachette, and Patterson huddled in the back of the boat and Wolf studied the surrounding landscape. To the east was a wooded island the size of a football field. Opposite the island to the west, there was a steep wooded embankment with a line of cliffs above that that stretched to the north and south. The granite cliff line varied in steepness, and the cabins on the rugged shore hugged the back of their properties up to the precipice. Wooden staircases zigged and zagged down the rocks, teetering on stilts, down to the shore where docks jutted out into the water. Behind it all, thousands of acres of virgin forest and snow-veined rocky peaks shone in the mid-morning sun.

Rachette lowered his voice and tapped the screen. "Yeah. I *hope* those are boulders."

CHAPTER 4

"WHAT ARE you guys going to do for jobs?" The search-and-rescue rookie talking to Rachette was grating on Deputy Heather Patterson's nerves.

"Do you have to re-apply?" Tall, muscular physique, and a nice set of eyes, the guy was cute and meant well, but he was poking the bear. Either he was a quasi-moron or he knew what he was doing and trying to rile them up, and that made him an asshole.

No, Patterson thought. The guy was a dumbass rookie who didn't know when to shut up. The apologetic glance from his superior told her as much.

"Yep. Gonna have to re-apply," Rachette answered, unfazed by the guy's upfront question. "Bullshit. But necessary bullshit, I guess. They say there should be minimal cuts. I'm confident we'll have our jobs in the end."

"Good luck," the rookie continued. "My sister works for the town of Rocky Points and she says that MacLean's a real dick, but he's gonna win. I guess he's been coming into town, walking around like he already runs it. Made my sister get him a cup of coffee across the street, like she was some sort of—"

"Can we talk about something else?" Patterson glared.

The rookie blinked. "Yeah. Sure."

Patterson turned and looked at Sheriff Wolf sitting out in one of the ASIS rigid inflatable boats.

Her boss stared at the western coastline in deep thought, up at one of the houses on the cliffs. She followed his eyes to the house on the hill, and then ran her eyes alongshore left to the next property, which must have been a good half-mile away to the south. Then she looked past it to a bend, where the tip of a dock protruded from the shoreline pines, aluminum edges gleaming in the sun.

Patterson took a deep breath and closed her eyes. The fishy lake air smelled exhilarating. She'd always liked spending time near or on freshwater, whether kayaking the Roaring Fork near Aspen growing up, or the time she'd spent right here at Cold Lake, waterskiing behind her uncle's boat. The sound of lapping waves against boat hulls triggered memories of fishing with her father, uncle, and brothers. The whooshing air against her face on the boat ride over had triggered vivid memories of sitting next to her late grandfather, who used to sit on top of the chair back and let his wispy comb-over flap in the breeze. She remembered doing the same, peeking over the glass, the wind rushing up her nose and over her hair.

"Hey, uh, Deputy?" Oliver Chevalier cleared his throat. "I really have to use the bathroom. Like. Now. Number two."

Patterson opened her eyes.

"Hey, Sheriff?" Rachette said into his radio. "We gotta take Mr. Chevalier in."

Wolf looked over and held up a thumb. "Okay, let's get someone to take him into the marina in his boat. Whoever does can stay on shore and wait."

"Copy that." Rachette looked at Patterson with raised eyebrows.

She nodded at the rookie. "You take him in. We'll stay here." Her tone left no room for arguing.

The Sheriff's Department fleet boat pulled alongside Oliver's boat, and as Patterson and Rachette climbed onto the solid 1987 model equipped with two powerful outboards, Patterson felt like her legs were shaking. She realized it was her racing thoughts. It was what Rachette and the rookie had been talking about—their uncertain future.

Because it was clear as day. In the end, Sheriff David Wolf was not going to win the upcoming election for sheriff of the merged counties. Her Aunt Margaret had told her as much in confidence. But it was no secret, not to anyone. Wolf was dead in the water.

She looked back at Wolf. He was staring again at the lake's edge, immersed in the case, on another dimensional plane. She'd seen him look like that before, and it was a sight to see. A formidable sight at times. She'd never witnessed such sheer determination in anyone. But in the two years she'd been on the force, she'd also seen that he was a ruthless realist when he needed to be. That is, he was quick to see when determination became delusion, and he would act accordingly, with sometimes dizzying speed to cut losses.

So what was he thinking about with this election? What was his plan? At the moment it seemed he was ignoring the inevitable outcome. He'd been appointed to the job of sheriff of Sluice County last time. Elections something he was clearly not comfortable with. Or good at.

And now Rachette and Patterson were being put in a tough situation. They were loyal to Wolf, that was never in doubt, but were they supposed to ignore MacLean? Were they supposed to be standoffish?

"Patterson." Rachette slapped her shoulder.

"Jesus. What?"

"What's going on with you? I said they're back up."

Patterson turned back to Wolf's boat and saw that the divers had surfaced.

Rachette leaned a hand on the side of the boat. "Holy crap."

Each of the four divers carried at least one black plastic bag. Two of them had two bags, one in each hand.

Wolf pulled one dripping bag over the side of his boat, and Patterson could see that it was similar in shape and size to the head at the marina, but these bags had another something inside —a rectangular sag that streamed water as they were lifted. The stony clank on the boat's hull told her they were bricks. Probably stuffed inside to keep them submerged.

The late spring sun suddenly felt hotter and she rolled up her sleeves.

"Six." Rachette said. "Six more." He stood up and looked at the inky water. "Dang, there could be a lot more than that down there."

A whining engine came around the corner of the island and cut down to an idle, then continued crawling into the cluster of boats. It was the Sluice County Chief Medical Examiner, Dr. Lorber. At six foot seven, his pole-thin frame was easy enough to spot, swaying with the wake like a pine in the wind, sticking up head and shoulders above the others in the boat next to him. His ever-present assistant, Dr. Joe Blank, was with him, looking cold as he rubbed his hands.

There was a sharp whistle and the boat turned toward Wolf and the emerged divers.

Lorber's boat slid by, the Mercury outboard engine gurgling as the water frothed behind it, and Patterson held up a hand to him. Lorber pointed a long finger and nodded.

"Nice 'stache," Rachette murmured.

Lorber had shaved his usual five-day beard into a bushy caterpillar mustache, but that's where the grooming stopped.

His uncombed hippy-hair was as long as ever, flapping against the center of his back in the breeze.

"Is that jealousy?"

"Psh. I could grow a 'stache like that in a week."

"You'd be happy if you grew a map of the Galapagos Islands on your face after a week."

Rachette glared at her, but had no comeback.

CHAPTER 5

WOLF GOT up from the bench seat of the ASIS inflatable as it slid alongside the SCSD fleet boat. He steadied himself as the pilot gave a quick burst in reverse and held out a hand to Patterson. Climbing aboard, the boat rocked under his weight.

"What's the news?" Rachette asked.

"The news is, we've got at least eight bodies down there. They just pulled up six heads. Add that to Chevalier's catch this morning and we've got seven. Then there's an extra bag down there. No head accounted for with that one. It could be a full body inside.

"Everything's wrapped in plastic. Same as the heads, they're weighted with bricks inside." He pointed down and made a circle with his arm. "Apparently they're spread out, covering at least a hundred feet diameter area."

"So there could be a lot more down there?" Patterson asked. "Visibility can't be that good down there."

"We'll find out. They're doing more sweeps with the sonar. It's going to take a while."

"Good Lord." Rachette gazed at the western shoreline. "There's some sick bastard living over there."

"Not necessarily," Patterson said. "Said sick bastard could have come from anywhere. All we know is, this is his preferred spot for body dumping."

"Then someone over there must have seen something," Rachette said.

A sharp whistle pierced the air.

"Hey!" Lorber waved a long arm above his head. "You've gotta see this!"

Wolf turned the key and started the engine, then flipped the button for up-anchor. The winch at the front of the boat whined and the thin, wet cable spooled in.

Lorber stood impatiently for a moment then barked an order to his pilot. Their engine bubbled to life and they sped over, easing up beside.

"Look at this," Lorber said.

Wolf snuck in next to Patterson and Rachette and peeked overboard.

Lorber bent over a bag with a slit in it, revealing a face on another head.

Wolf stared into the past. "Nick Pollard."

Lorber nodded. "Yep. I'd bet my hair on it."

"Who's Nick Pollard?" Rachette asked.

"An old missing-persons case." Wolf's gaze locked on the waxy face.

The sight sparked recognition in Wolf's mind, and he was more certain than ever they were correct. The facial hair pattern poking out at them was unique—impressive growth for a seventeen-year-old kid—and it was a visage that the residents of Rocky Points at one time knew well.

"How old of a case?" Rachette asked.

"Twenty-two years." Wolf said.

"He looks more recent than that, doesn't it?" Rachette frowned. "Are you sure?"

Patterson cleared her throat. "The cold water at that depth would have slowed autolysis, or when the body's enzymes within the cells go into post-death meltdown."

Lorber tilted his head side to side, as if to say, *at least partly right.*

Patterson continued. "The almost perfect preservation of the face is due to the formation of adipocere, otherwise known as saponification, which is the formation of a waxy substance that ends up coating the skin. It's formed by the anaerobic bacterial hydrolysis of fat in tissue. Cold, wet environments are perfect for production."

"I love Science Fridays," Rachette said.

"Spot on, Patterson." Lorber looked at Wolf. "I'll check dental records. Probably went to Dr. Unruh in town back then. Shouldn't take more than tomorrow morning, probably this afternoon."

Wolf nodded. "Make it as quick as possible. There were reporters at the marina. But I'm not going to jump the gun and tell the Pollards just yet. The facial hair is right and it looks like Nick Pollard, but I wouldn't bet my hair on it. I'll wait for you."

Lorber nodded.

"So, who was this guy?" Rachette asked.

"A case my father never solved."

CHAPTER 6

WOLF WAS the most exhilarated he'd been in years as he sat across the table from Sarah. Candlelight danced on her face and made it look like she had a spark in each eye, or maybe it was that she shared the same feeling.

"Excuse the interruption," the waiter said in a low voice as he placed a basket of bread in front of them.

Wolf leaned back, making way for the food. He felt like he'd come up for air after being submerged in water, like the divers today after sitting at thirty feet for decompression, only he'd been submerged in something much better with Sarah. He realized that from the moment he'd picked her up from her house and smelled her perfume as she'd climbed in his truck, he'd been buried in the present. Time was passing one elevated heartbeat at a time.

He gazed out the floor-to-ceiling windows of Antler Creek Lodge, marveling at the pink painted western sky gouged by peaks. The late spring snow that clung in spots outside were like blankets of orange sorbet in the fading light of the sunset.

The fragrance of fresh bread pulled his gaze from the windows to the table.

"Thank you." Wolf nodded to the server as he left.

Sarah tore a slice of bread in half and bit into it. "So, are you ready to talk about today yet?"

Wolf tore his own piece and chewed the soft, warmed goodness. "I'd rather not ruin our first date in years."

She sipped the wine, keeping her eyes on his. "Just tell me. After that exit this morning? And I can see that it's on your mind. What happened?"

Wolf took a sip of water and leaned forward. "We found some dead bodies today."

"Oh my God. At the lake?"

"In the lake."

"Some bodies? Plural?" Sarah's eyes bore into his. Her breathing was clearly escalating.

Wolf checked the neighboring table to his right. The couple were smiling at one another, distracted in conversation.

He simply nodded, not wanting to go into details.

"Jesus," she whispered. "Like, a serial killer?"

Wolf nodded.

Her eyes glazed over and she sat rigid.

He regretted telling her now. The spark in her eyes had been doused by fear.

"Where on the lake?" she asked.

He reached over and squeezed her hand.

She flinched and then relaxed. "Sorry. My God, though. That's so crazy. A killer right here? I can't think of any missing people. Are they Rocky Points citizens? Have you identified anyone?"

He squeezed her hand again and flicked a glance to the neighboring couple. They had gone silent, reaching for their drinks. Both startled by Sarah's last words, clearly wondering if they'd heard correctly.

Wolf and Sarah sipped their wine, waiting for the couple to resume their discussion.

When they did, Wolf spoke just above a whisper. "We identified one of them. Do you remember Nick Pollard?"

"Yeah, of course. You found *him*?"

Wolf shrugged. "Looks like it. We'll be sure tomorrow."

"My God. All this time, and he was in the water?"

Wolf narrowed his eyes. "What do you remember about it?"

"I remember he went missing on the Fourth of July. They were all saying he went up to the lake and never came back. He went up to see ... ah, I forgot her name. But some weird girl, used to be homeschooled? Remember? Lived on the western shore? Everyone was saying that her dad killed him."

Wolf pulled his eyebrows together. "How do you remember all this while I didn't recall any of it?"

Sarah smiled. "I don't know, Sheriff Wolf. How didn't you? Oh wait, because you were doing two-a-days in Fort Collins, trying to impress the CSU cheerleaders with your tight spirals the summer after our senior year."

Wolf smiled. "Ah. Right. I had already impressed the right cheerleader by then."

Sarah smiled sheepishly and looked down.

The past, damn it. Wolf had learned recently that talking about their past with Sarah was a sure-fire way to ruin the moment, and he'd just done it again.

"Anyway," Wolf said. "I'd rather not talk about it anymore. It was a tough day, and I'm excited to be here with you."

She looked up with a resigned smile. "Okay. But you have to keep me posted." Her eyes turned mischievous. "Seriously, though." She let go of his hands and leaned forward on her elbows, creating a gap between her breasts that Wolf wanted to dive into. "I thought that fifth toss of yours today was going to rope that calf. The way it barely hit him in the ass and then hit the dirt?"

Wolf blinked. "I will murder you."

She laughed that deep, throaty laugh of hers he loved, and then took a sip of her white wine.

He smiled wider than he ever liked to in public, and then brought his own glass up to his lips and tasted the exquisite Argentinian white. It was sweet, and as he swallowed it warmed his entire body. It had been a long, mentally taxing day, and he could not think of a better way to wash the dirt off his thoughts than with a swig of wine and the most beautiful companion Wolf had ever known.

They locked eyes and stared at one another, and Wolf knew that his ex-wife shared the same sentiments. They both knew something special was happening between them. For the first time since their divorce, since years before that actually, they felt the spark between them again. And for the first time, they were moving on from the past without looking back. It was more than a spark, Wolf thought—it was a warming fire that was ignited by the friction of their souls. Or something. Wolf checked himself and took another sip of wine.

"How's the new place?" Wolf asked.

She nodded. "Good. Great. Jack seems to like it. I think he likes being away from my parents for the first time in years. And, of course, I'm not there all day." Sarah took a distracted sip of wine.

Wolf squeezed her hand. "He's doing all right."

She closed her eyes and nodded. "It's just, he's getting so angry sometimes. And do you know what he told me when I said you and I were going out tonight? *So?*" She frowned and shook her head. "*So?* What kind of response is that to us finally going out on a date—something he's been hounding me about for years?"

Wolf shrugged. "Teenagers."

She bit a fingernail. "Do you think he's doing pot?"

"No." He squeezed her hand again. "Hey, let's just enjoy this dinner. Jack's doing fine. I'll see what's bothering him this weekend. He probably just doesn't ..." Wolf let his sentence die. He was going to say, *He probably just doesn't want to get his hopes up too much*, but that mirrored Wolf's own thoughts too closely to voice out loud.

"What?" she asked.

"Nothing," Wolf said with a smile. "Dinner. I could eat that horse I was riding today."

He felt the touch of her bare foot rubbing the inside of his knee, which sent a tingling wave through his body.

"Salmon for the lady," a voice said as the waiter materialized from thin air. He pushed the steaming plate in front of her.

She leaned back with a reddening face, as if she'd been caught in the act by the waiter, and clasped her hands. "Thank you."

"And the filet."

Wolf watched a three-inch-high cylinder of meat slide in front of him, and the steamy aroma of steak, garlic mashed potatoes and asparagus made his mouth flood.

"Thank you," he said.

He paused when he looked up and saw a flicker of horror in Sarah's eyes as she looked past Wolf. He followed her gaze and saw an elegantly dressed man waving at her from the bar at the front of the restaurant.

She waved back, pasting an unconvincing annoyed look on her face.

"Who's that?" Wolf asked.

"A client." There was no hesitation in her voice. "Geez, that looks good." She gawked at Wolf's plate.

Wolf cut a sliver of meat and held it out to her.

Ignoring the piece of filet mignon bobbing in front of her face, she looked into the distance once again. There was a small widening of her eyes. She put her knife and fork down and looked at her lap. Smoothed her napkin.

Wolf took the bite and studied her, knowing the man was now on his way over. He cut and forked another piece, and then put it in his mouth.

"Sarah." The man stepped next to their table with an upturned palm thrust at her.

She looked up and feigned surprise and then placed her hand into his. His large hand enveloped hers and he began pulling her up.

"Come on, I need a hug. It's been so long."

"Oh ... okay." Sarah stood up and raised her arms awkwardly while the man dove in for the embrace.

Wolf leaned back and put an elbow on the table, observing.

The man had mid-length wavy dark hair that was impeccably combed, and he wore a dark suit and an expensive white shirt over a muscled physique. The top button of his shirt was open, revealing a gold necklace around a thick, tanned neck. His watch was a platinum Rolex with a black face and there were no rings on his fingers. A good-looking guy by no stretch of the imagination, Wolf thought, and clearly the man had a big wallet.

The man's giant arms enveloped Sarah's slender body, his big hands splaying flat on the bare skin that was exposed by the slinkily cut dress.

The hug was a second too long, awkward for Sarah, who began pulling away.

As they separated, the man brushed the fabric the whole way from her ribs over her hips, past her panty line, which was *not* there, and then finally drew his meat hooks to his side.

Wolf stood and slapped the man's back, hard enough for a

hollow thump to echo through the dining room, silencing the nearby tables.

"Hey, there. I'm Dave."

The man whipped his head around with wide eyes, like he was suddenly in a fight.

Movement and gasps of astonishment came from behind Wolf, and when he looked down he saw that his chair had careened into a woman's back.

"Oh, I'm sorry ma'am."

The woman looked up at him with exasperation and turned back around to face her husband, who was now glaring up at Wolf.

Wolf slid his gaze back to their visitor. "And you are?"

One side of the man's chiseled mouth rose and his eyes softened. "The name's Carter. Carter Willis." He extended a hand. "It's a pleasure to meet you."

Sarah sank down into her chair and took a sip of her water.

Wolf came into the handshake with knuckle-crunching force, but found the man's huge grip too hard to dent. The shake lasted the same awkward amount of time as the hug had, and then they let go.

"Well, see ya around, Carter," Wolf said.

Carter looked down at Sarah and blew air from his lips. "See you around. Nice to meet you, Sheriff."

Wolf watched the man stroll away and sat down.

Sarah was board-stiff, her face drained of color.

Adrenaline coursed through Wolf's veins, rendering the meal in front of him unappealing, but he dug in anyway.

The rest of the meal was eaten in complete silence. The couple next to them were even sucked into the abyss of awkwardness, eating without speaking, keeping a wary eye on Wolf and Sarah, then refusing the dessert menu and leaving as fast as possible—a cadence Wolf and Sarah followed closely for their own dinner.

After settling the check, they walked out of the restaurant and into the cold thin air on top of the mountain.

"I don't know what that was in there."

"That's right," she said. "You don't." She held her gaze in front of her, her feet crunching along the wet rocky earth of the ridgeline toward the waiting snow cat.

Scott Reed, Deputy Patterson's boyfriend for the past year, saw them coming and smiled, then let his face drop when he saw Wolf and Sarah's mood.

The cat and gondola rides were spent with a wedge of silence between them. The car ride was the same, and as Wolf turned onto Beacon Light Road and toward Sarah's new three-bedroom, three-bath overlooking the east side of town, the monotonous silence was shattered by the beep of Wolf's phone. He picked it up and read the screen.

It was a text from Dr. Lorber that read: *Nick Pollard confirmed with dental records.*

"What's that?" Sarah asked, an edge to her tone.

With a frown, he dropped the phone and pulled over. The tires scraped to a stop and he turned toward her.

"What did I do so wrong? A scumbag comes up to our table, obviously eyeing you up, gropes you right in front of me and then I'm supposed to take it? Supposed to be grateful to meet the guy?"

She shook her head. "You think that's what happened?"

Wolf blinked. "Something else happened?"

She leaned her head back, closing her eyes in exasperation. "That man, Carter Willis, is an interior designer that we worked with for one of our projects in Aspen. He's one of the best." She looked at him. "And he's also gay."

"Yeah right. The guy all but grabbed your ass."

She opened her mouth and closed it. "I knew this was too good to be true."

"What was?"

"This. Us." She twirled a finger. "We had our run, and every single time it looks like we're going to make a good go of it again—every single time since you went off in the army, mind you—something goes wrong. We throw some wrench into the gears of our relationship, or some gay guy comes up to our table at the worst possible moment and ruins the whole mood. Or some ... bitch from the FBI comes and sleeps with you for months. Or ..." She stopped talking and shook her head.

"Or you tell me you cheated on me with some guy when I was in the army, so whenever I see some guy like that give you a groping—a *friendly* hug, sorry—I can't help but wonder if I'm meeting that guy."

"David!" Her voice rose to a yell. "How many times do I have to apologize for my mistake?"

Wolf gripped the wheel. "Maybe Jack knows something we don't."

"Yeah. Maybe so."

Wolf put the truck in gear and drove.

CHAPTER 7

WOLF PULLED down the sloping driveway and stopped in front of Sarah's house.

"Good night."

The passenger door slammed shut before he had a chance to respond.

His headlights reflected on the front bay windows, and his heart skipped when he saw that Jack was inside, squinting, watching the situation unfold with a front row seat.

Christ, it was Friday night and he was fourteen years old. Wasn't he out with his friends?

His son's grim expression said it all. It was as if he was watching a bad movie scene again—his mother turning her back on his father, their relationship a hopeless mess, and his dream of his mother and father getting back together, so he might one day have a regular family, evaporating into mist once again.

It was heartbreaking for Wolf to see all that in the course of one glance.

Jack strolled along the inside of the window toward the front door and greeted his mother as she stormed inside, and then looked out at Wolf.

Wolf shut off his headlights, rolled down his window. "Hey."

Jack lifted his chin and stepped out onto the pavement in his socks. "Hey."

"Whatchu up to? Not out doing something tonight?"

Jack flipped his head to one side to move his bangs out of the way. "Brian's downstairs. We're playin' vids. I was just getting some food for us in the kitchen and saw you pull up." He looked back toward the house. "Nice date for you and mom, huh?"

Wolf looked at his son and pulled his mouth into a line. "Oh yeah, you guys have that football camp tomorrow up in Vail. That's why you aren't out at a movie or something."

Jack nodded, looking up into the sky at nothing in particular.

Wolf nodded. "Well, be careful, all right? You've grown a foot since last fall, but that doesn't make you invincible." He poked a finger into Jack's ribs. "You're a freaking stick."

Jack slapped Wolf's hand away and smiled. "I'm bulking up."

Wolf smiled. If it weren't such a harrowing experience for Jack already, Wolf would have laughed out loud at the audacity of his son's transformation as he underwent puberty, springing up from five foot nothing to over six feet tall during nine months and acquiring the voice of Barry White. And Jack *still* complained about pains in his legs. The kid was going to surpass Wolf in no time.

"I'm not going to be able to make it up to the camp. Sorry."

"Yeah, I heard about the bodies at the lake. It's all over the news."

Wolf frowned. *Damn it.* That had been a quick reaction by the media, and he still hadn't told the Pollards about Nick's body. Hell, he'd only just confirmed the body's ID. He looked at the glowing clock on his dash and wondered if he should be acting. But it was late. Almost ten p.m. He would talk to the Pollards first thing in the morning.

"Dad?"

Wolf turned to Jack. "What?"

"Nothing." The disappointment on his face told Wolf everything.

"Look. Jack. Your mom and I ..."

Jack held up a hand. "Don't worry. I know. You guys both love me." He slapped Wolf's hood and walked back toward the front door.

"I love you," Wolf called after him. "Have a good weekend. Give me a call and tell me how the camp went. Or give me a call during."

Jack waved over his head without turning and disappeared inside. Wolf stared at the closing door, then flipped on his headlights and backed away.

CHAPTER 8

"OH! That's what I'm talking about!" Wolf watched the ex-sheriff of Sluice County, Harold Burton, lean back on his bar stool and pour a brown shot of liquid down his throat, slam the glass on the bar counter, and wipe his mouth. His hand shot up in a fist and his eyes clinched shut. "Ahhh, I'll take another beer, please, sire."

Jerry Blackman, owner of Beer Goggles Bar and Grill, stood behind the counter. "How many is that you've had?"

"I've got a cab on retainer."

Wolf came up next to Burton and leaned his elbows on the bar. "Yeah, I bet you do."

"Oh!" Bob Fitzgerald, one of Hal Burton's drinking buddies, pointed at Wolf and covered his mouth. "Busted!"

Burton swiveled and burst out laughing. He gripped Wolf in a vicious headlock and started scrubbing his hair. "This guy is my boy! Get him one, too!"

Wolf escaped Burton's painful embrace and smoothed his hair.

Looking resigned and exhausted, Jerry raised his eyebrows at Wolf.

Wolf nodded. "I'll take a Newcastle."

"That's what I'm talkin' 'bout!" Burton repeated, slapping the counter.

"Wow, I didn't expect to see you drinking with such aggression. What happened? Cheryl leave you?"

Burton's smile faded as he reached for the next draft beer that sloshed in front of him. His face was red and puffy, like he'd just been upside down for an hour, and his walrus mustache was wet. "Nah. She's outta town. She gets home Tuesday. She'll be none the wiser."

Wolf smiled to himself. After leaving Sarah's, he'd called Burton on his cell phone, and when he hadn't gotten an answer he'd called Burton's wife, Cheryl. She'd pointed him straight here. She may have been out of the state visiting her sister, but she was as aware of her husband's predictable movements as if he wore an ankle monitor.

Jerry pushed a dripping bottle in front of Wolf and waved him away when Wolf pulled out his wallet.

Wolf watched Jerry leave down the back of the bar, swerving in between another bartender frantically stacking glasses and the shelves.

The overhead speakers blared jam-band music Wolf had never heard—two electric guitars, bass, drums, and keyboards. It was ten o'clock, and the weekend crowd was swollen and alive, like the Chautauqua River flowing outside the windows.

He put a five on the counter and took a sip of the beer. It was ice cold, and with the mood he was in, tasted like he could sit and drink six of them.

"What's goin' on?" Burton looked at his watch, did some drunken mathematics in his head and looked back up at Wolf. "I thought you were with Sarah tonight. It's early, ain't it?"

"No, not tonight," Wolf lied, taking another sip. "Listen, I have to talk to you."

"Shoot." Burton swilled his beer.

Wolf stared expectantly.

"Oh, like in private?" Burton turned to the back of the room. "There's a booth ... you wanna go there?"

Wolf sat across from Burton in a rear booth by the windows. The pleather cushion squeaked as he looked out the window at the river below. The light of a full moon reflected off the shifting rapids of the raging water, which was running high now that it was the peak of melt-season. A few warm days in a row and this building might be swept down the river.

"Runnin' high." Burton read his thoughts.

"We found Nick Pollard today."

Burton lifted his drink, took a sip, and then clacked it down hard, beer splattering onto the table and into Wolf's lap.

"Shit, I'm sorry!" Burton raked the spilled beer back towards him with his hairy arm, squeegeeing it onto the booth seat next to him.

Wolf looked closer at Burton, into the glossy, half-closed eyes, and saw there was little consciousness left in the man. Burton in a bar was like a dog locked in a room with a fifty-pound bag of food; he was going to get all he could until he could ingest no more.

"You found him?" Burton rubbed a hand over his silver buzz-cut hair. "Where?"

Wolf wiped the table with some napkins. "In the lake."

"In the lake!"

A table of men and women stared at them, laughing.

"What the hell you lookin' at, scrubs?" Burton's voice was like a train horn.

Their faces dropped and they looked at their table.

Wolf raised his eyebrows. "You done?"

"With what?" Burton grabbed his own handful of napkins

and helped wipe the mess, leaving wet beads on the tabletop. "In the lake. God damn, your dad was right."

"About what?"

"Your dad scuba dove down there, oh ... must have been five times. Never found anything. It was too deep. Couldn't get to where he wanted to go."

"He did? How did he know where to dive?"

"The moon guy." Burton looked down into his beer and burped, then took another swig.

"The moon guy? What are you talking about?"

"Vietnam vet, lives up on the lake, on top of that cliff. Used to draw the moon. Had a telescope."

Burton put the glass to his lips again and a stream of beer flowed down his chin.

"Can you start from the beginning?" Wolf asked. "I wanna know what you guys knew back then. Tell me about Nick Pollard. The whole thing."

"The whole file's in records."

"Yeah, I know. But I wanna hear it from you."

"Well, I'm gonna need another beer for that. This one's empty."

Wolf slid his bottle in front of him.

Burton smiled and settled into his seat. "Let's see. It was the fifth of July when Nick Pollard's mom called us. Afternoon. Said her son never came home the night before. We said, *So what?* The kid was a misfit. One of those kids always runnin' with the wrong crowd. Druggie. Weed, probably coke, meth."

"Probably?"

Burton shrugged. "Ran with the crowd. Like I said." He sipped his beer and then gazed out the window for a few seconds. When he looked at Wolf again he broke into a big smile. "It's good to see you."

"Nick Pollard's mother called you. Said her son was missing. You guys checked on it, I'm assuming."

"Yeah. Yeah. We did. She said Nick went up to Cold Lake because he was dating a girl who lived up there. Went up to watch the fireworks show with her. And then he never came back."

"Who was the girl?"

"Kimber. Kimber Grey, with an 'e'. We went up and talked to her and her family that afternoon. I me-member they were pretty standoffed. Standoffish. Said they ne'er saw him that night. Said he musta been lyin' to his mother." Burton took another swill and put the bottle down on a wet napkin so it teetered at an angle.

Wolf stabilized it.

"And then what?"

"I'm gonna be hurtin' tomorrow. I'm freakin' hammered. Every time—"

"And then what?"

Burton looked at him, twisting his face with ridiculous effort. "Where was I?"

Wolf leaned back. "Nick Pollard's mother says Nick went up to visit Kimber Grey at her cabin on the lake. The Greys said they never saw him. What did you think about that?"

"But they were fuckin' lyin'!" Burton's train-horn voice triggered sideways glances, and as the speakers played the opening bars of a familiar bluegrass tune, Wolf's knuckles played tabletop percussion. His abrupt palm slap shook Burton back to the conversation.

"Who was lying?"

Burton looked over at a different table of people across the room and his eyes went mean.

"All right. I'm taking you home."

"I've got a cab on retainer."

"Let's go."

Wolf mimed to Jerry that he was taking Burton home. Jerry nodded, held up Burton's credit card and put it in a drawer. Wolf gave him the thumbs up.

The screen door squeaked and slapped shut behind them, and Burton stumbled over a knot of grass and landed on his knees on the gravel lot.

"Shit!" He got up, pushing Wolf's hand aside, and stumbled forward, barely putting his arms down in time to break his fall.

By the time he'd got into Wolf's truck, the old man's bloodied, pasty forearms looked like candy canes.

"You going to be all right?" Wolf eyed the pile of flesh and bones in his passenger seat.

"Yeah. We worked that case." Burton lifted an index finger.

As Wolf reversed out of his spot, Burton folded his arms and burrowed himself against the dangling, unused seatbelt. Within moments, Wolf heard the old man snoring.

CHAPTER 9

WOLF PULLED through the arch to his ranch at 11:18 p.m. to a familiar sight. The one-story L-shaped house and barn off to the side—built by his father a lifetime ago and completely rebuilt after an explosion three years prior—stood lonely in the moonlight with black holes for windows. He was used to it—coming home after dark to a dark house. He liked solitude, but loneliness was niggling at him tonight.

But there was something different after all. He leaned forward and squinted when he saw the shiny paint of Sarah's black Toyota 4Runner in the circle drive. His longing for company turned to anticipation. Looking inside the cab of her vehicle as he slowed to a stop, Wolf saw it was empty.

Pulling forward, he parked in the carport and got out.

He stood and stared at Sarah's SUV through the fog of his breath, listening to the sounds of the forest to the rear of the house. A symphony of crickets chirped and he heard an owl somewhere in the distance.

The hinges complained as he pushed open the kitchen door and stepped inside, and he thought it was warmer than he was used to. The thermostat had definitely been raised. The kitchen and the entire house beyond were dark. Curtains were drawn in the living room, blocking out the glint of the full moon.

A faint parallelogram of light showed his bedroom door as open, moonlight illuminating the interior.

"Sarah?"

No answer.

"Sarah! You there?"

Something felt wrong. He walked fast to the rear of the house, his pulse quickening with each step.

He pulled the chain to the ceiling fan hanging in his family room as he walked under it, and had to squint in the sudden brightness. When he got to his room he reached around the corner and flipped the light switch, like he was a cat pouncing to catch his prey.

The light went on and he saw what awaited him.

Sarah sat on his bed, the sheets pulled up to her armpits. She dug her fists into her eyes and bared her teeth.

"Ah, turn that off."

"What are you doing?"

She made a visor with her hands. "I wanted to see you. To say I'm sorry. Can you please turn that off?"

Wolf flipped the switch and the room went dark again.

The sheets rustled, and then Sarah was in front of him, wrapping her naked body around him, locking her wet lips over his, plunging her soft tongue into his mouth.

She pulled back and pushed him. "Ah! You're freezing!"

Through the swimming circles of light in Wolf's vision, he watched her stark-naked figure jump back onto the bed, lie down, and pull the sheets over her head.

He smiled, pulled his clothes off and climbed in after her.

CHAPTER 10

WOLF WOKE up from a dreamless sleep, and found himself alone in bed. The clock said 7:14 a.m. He rolled to his side and rubbed his eyes, wondering for a second whether he'd imagined the night before; then he caught sight of Sarah's jeans, T-shirt, sweater and underwear neatly folded on the chair in the corner, and he smiled, remembering pulse-quickening images and sensations from the night before.

He got up and pulled on his boxer shorts, then walked toward the noise in the kitchen.

Sarah paced by the opening of the kitchen straight ahead and then poked her head back into view. She was wearing a red-and-black flannel shirt of his with nothing on underneath.

"I'm making French toast," she said with a smile.

He pulled her into his arms and kissed her, and after a few moments, she dropped the spatula and they made their way back into the bedroom.

They made love for ten minutes until the alarm squealed because of the smoke billowing from the black flaming square of egg-covered toast in the pan.

Wolf ran into the kitchen, dumped the toast in the sink, and ran back to the bedroom. They made love for another ten minutes, with such hunger and passion that Wolf found it impossible to contain the noises coming out of his mouth.

Sarah didn't seem to have a sound filter working in her brain either.

It was like they were animals, making up for lost time, letting out years of pent-up tension in a few short, unimaginably hot minutes.

An hour later, Wolf drove down the dirt road to town, not once seeing the road in front of him, registering nothing in the outside world. Instead, his SUV passed through vivid memories of Sarah's naked body, the smell of her neck behind her ear, and the sound of her panting.

When he reached the stop sign at Highway 734 running into town, with supreme reluctance, like a crack addict saying no to a hit off the pipe, he shifted his thoughts from Sarah to the seven severed heads in plastic bags they'd pulled out of the lake. And then to the Pollards, who had been waiting twenty-two years to learn the fate of their missing son.

He turned down the radio. The engine idled with a soft purr. He looked left and right, considering heading south toward the ski resort and Hal Burton's house.

The man would still be in bed—fully clothed, just the way Wolf had left him last night. Angry. Worthless until he'd slept off the booze.

He twisted the wheel right and headed into town.

CHAPTER 11

Private investigator William Van Wyke was used to pushback, so he sat back in the chair and waited patiently for his chance to parry.

"Whatever you think you're doing, it won't work with me." The slick-dressed man looked at his gold Rolex and stood up from behind his desk. "It's clear you're blowing smoke up my ass. Now get up, and get the hell out of my office. And let me tell you something else. You listen real, real good. If you want to do contract work for any law firms in Boise any longer, or any other firm in the state of Idaho ... scratch that ..." He leaned forward and hissed, "If you want to live—"

Van Wyke slapped the manila folder on the mahogany desk and sat back with a frown. "Please. Continue. If I want to *live?* Were you just going to threaten my life?"

The city council chairman and president shut his mouth, staring at the manila folder. He glanced at Van Wyke and then raked it across the desk.

Van Wyke watched the chairman's eyes as he twisted and opened it, and it was even better than Van Wyke had imagined it would be.

The chairman's mouth gaped open as he took in the photos, one by one. "How the hell did you ...?" The color drained from the chairman's face. He wiped his forehead and crumpled back into his leather desk chair.

"Did you see that last one? You're a swallower. Interesting. Shit doesn't just spew out of your mouth, it goes the other way, too." Van Wyke bent over, picked up his shoulder bag and stood.

"What do you want? Are you working for Smith?"

"No." Van Wyke slung the strap over his head and took a step closer to the desk. His voice dropped and he lowered his chin. "But your opponent in the race for Senate may get a folder exactly like this in his mailbox. Now how's that going to look? A man like you, with your firm anti-gay message as the backbone of your campaign in the reddest state in the west, found to be sucking cock in a back alley at four in the morning? You piece of shit hypocrite. No, I don't work for Smith. I work for me. I'll be in touch with my demands, and I suggest you act swiftly." He leaned onto the desk and bent closer. "And let me tell you, I've operated in a lot seedier alleys than that one where you liaise with your diseased fun-boy, and I know a lot of men who would slit your throat and drop you in the center of Payette Lake in a second if I told them to. Not if I asked, if I *told* them. Got it?"

The chairman swallowed. "How much we talking here?"

Van Wyke paused at the door. His plan had been to make the man wait, to let him shake overnight in his oversized bed while his ugly wife slept next to him, text him in the morning while he was at church, pretending to be a good Christian. That would have been perfect, but Van Wyke was also on a tight deadline.

"One."

"One? Hundred thousand?"

"Million."

He scoffed. "I don't have a million dollars."

"By Thursday."

"My God. I don't have that kind of cash just lying around. I'd need to sell my house to get that kind of money. I have two children in Ivy League schools. I—"

"Thursday." Van Wyke turned back to the door.

"Okay, okay. Wait. Wait. I can give you two hundred thousand. I can get that. I can get that Monday. I just can't do a *million*. I just can't."

"That's a shame." Van Wyke twisted the knob. "Good luck in the race."

"Wait, wait." Boise City Council Chairman Phillip Chatham all but crawled around his desk. "Please. I can get you more. It's just not going to be now. You have to wait until I'm inside. Then I'll be slicing the pie. Then I can get more." He held out both hands. "Please. Don't do anything rash. Be reasonable about this."

Van Wyke stood silent and waited for five ticks on the grandfather clock that stood against the wall.

"Two hundred. Monday," he said. "I'll contact you from the same number. You'd better answer."

Van Wyke walked out of the building into a sunny Saturday morning. The air was damp, heavy with moisture sliding in from Washington and Oregon, but not nearly as heavy as his thoughts. He opened the door to his black Mercedes Benz M-Class SUV and sat on the soft, warm leather. He pulled out his phone and dialed.

"Yeah."

"Hey. It's me."

"Who?"

"Van Wyke."

"Who?"

Van Wyke chittered a nervous laugh and rubbed his eyes.

"What do you want?" The voice was evil-sounding. With every passing day, the man's malice deepened.

"I'd like to discuss a proposal."

Silence.

"I can get you two hundred thousand by Tuesday. Then I would like to discuss a future agreement for the remainder, plus interest."

There was no answer. Then came a static tick, followed by a dial tone.

He threw the phone onto the passenger floor. His breath wheezed. His throat constricted. His heart hammered out of his shirt.

For five minutes, he sat with eyes closed, trying to calm down enough so he could drive home. *If only things had turned out differently.* There were so many instances in his life where he'd dealt with the wrong people, taken the wrong turn, but he'd always found his way back out of trouble. How the hell had he got himself into this? How had he managed to get on the wrong side of such dangerous men in Boise, Idaho? Idaho? There were more animals than people here, damn it. He was the man who dug up the dirt on other people, not shoveled himself under it.

He clenched his teeth. It was that *bitch*, with her perfect body, and her perfect face. And her perfect lies. The rage inside made him shake like a boiling pot.

There were no other opportunities. This city councilman had been his last hope, and now that hope was gone.

He jumped in his seat as someone knocked on the glass next to his head. He relaxed when he saw the black man's face outside his window.

"Hey. What's up?" Darnell's voice was muffled.

Regaining his composure, Van Wyke lowered the glass.

"You all right?"

"What do you want?"

"Mind if I come in?" Darnell said in that eager tone of voice he used when he had something for Van Wyke.

"I'm not in the mood right now for work. Can't this wait until Monday?"

Darnell laughed and then scrunched his face in confusion. Van Wyke had always told his apprentice that a PI worth the fees he charged worked seven days a week.

"A PI worth the fees you charge—"

"Yeah, yeah. Get in."

Darnell walked around the front of the SUV, and Van Wyke took the opportunity to pluck his phone from the floor mat.

Van Wyke's protégé got into the passenger seat in a fluid, athletic movement.

At five foot ten and two hundred pounds of pure muscle, the high-school dropout from Chicago could have played division-two basketball or football had he wanted to, had he continued with high school and gone to college, but the young man sitting in the passenger seat had not had the same opportunities as Van Wyke growing up.

While Van Wyke had grown up playing junior golf, studying, and fishing on the Snake River, rowing himself out into the water when he needed to escape from his alcoholic father, Darnell had sold crack cocaine on the street corners of the Cabrini Green projects, dodging bullets daily. His escape: hiding inside the Lincoln Park High School library.

Van Wyke had been born into opportunity, and Darnell had made his own, starting with finally getting "out." "Out" being Boise, Idaho, because it had been *the whitest place he could think of* to start over when his mother had died of cancer. Darnell had never known his father.

Coming to Idaho, Darnell had found it difficult to find a job. He was black, and everyone else was not. He was alone, and everyone else had families. He was homeless, and everyone else had warm homes to go to. But somehow he'd managed to defy astronomical odds by talking his way into becoming a caddy at the Sandy Ranch Resort in Coeur d'Alene. Apparently when he'd gotten the idea he wanted to make big bucks at the golf course, he'd sat himself in the Boise Library for days on end, watching YouTube videos on the public computers and reading books, and then created a history for himself as an accomplished golfer and caddy.

The first golfer Darnell caddied for had been William Van Wyke, who had been on a three-day outing with a junior partner in a law firm he did investigative work for.

Van Wyke had smoked Darnell out as a fraud on the first hole, but he'd been intrigued more than angry, and by the end of the trip, and four rounds of golf later, he knew Darnell's entire story, and found that he'd connected with the troubled, extremely determined young man.

"I could use an assistant like you," he'd told Darnell back then. So, Darnell had come south with Van Wyke, and that was the beginning of his now three-year-long apprenticeship to become a qualified private investigator offering services to some of the most prestigious law firms in Boise, Washington, Oregon, and Montana.

"Everything cool?" Darnell asked.

"Yeah." All that opportunity, and Van Wyke had pissed it away. He looked away from Darnell, hoping the sudden envy of his apprentice was invisible.

"The Chatham thing work out?"

"Yeah. Your pics were persuasive."

"But? He doesn't have the cash."

Van Wyke leaned his head back. "You're a smart man."

"Well, I've got something very interesting for you to check out."

Van Wyke remained unmoved, physically or mentally, leaning back on his headrest with closed eyes. He heard Darnell unzip his bag and the brush of him pulling out his laptop, and then a tiny beep as it powered on.

"Shit. You have to move closer to the building. No Wi-Fi signal here."

Van Wyke shook his head. "Hey, listen. I can't check out YouTube videos right now with you. I've got a lot of stuff to figure out."

Darnell stared at him in silence until Van Wyke turned to meet his gaze.

Darnell's brown eyes were dead serious. "You need to see *this* YouTube video."

Van Wyke did as he was told, driving over and parking near the entrance to the building.

Council Chairman Chatham was walking out of the building, and flinched at the sight of them in the Mercedes before shuffling into the parking lot.

"He don't look happy." Darnell chuckled and clicked open a browser window.

After a quick Google search, a news website called Channel 8 Rocky Mountain Action News materialized and Darnell clicked a button.

"What's this?"

Darnell looked at him. "I remember a story you told me once about a guy who you helped liquidate all his assets in one day. Do you remember that?"

"Yes."

"And then you said he burned his house down and skipped town before paying you?"

"No. His house *was* the payment. He signed the deed over to me and then burned it down, and then skipped town. Get to the point."

"Here you go." Darnell pecked the laptop and twisted the screen towards him.

"... *here at Cold Lake, twenty-seven miles northwest of Rocky Points, Colorado, where Sluice County law enforcement and rescue-team divers have been working through the afternoon yesterday, and then all through the night, and are now resuming their work this morning, searching the bottom of the lake for what we are being told are multiple dead bodies. Now, I'd like to stress to our viewers that I will be describing in detail the condition of these bodies, which may not be suitable for children viewers ...*"

Van Wyke's curiosity was piqued. His pulse raced.

"... *severed heads, and torsos that have been sliced open. According to our sources, the eyes of the heads have been removed. All in all, a grim find by a local fisherman. And the question is now, could this be the break local law enforcement has needed to crack a cold case that has stumped them for decades?*"

The camera panned out, revealing a tall man with a hunter-orange hat standing next to the reporter. "*I have with me here the man who was fishing and actually snagged one of the severed heads with his fishing hook, and then brought it back into his boat. Mr. Oliver Chevalier. Sir, can you—*"

Darnell stopped the video and looked at Van Wyke.

Van Wyke was staring out the window in deep thought. "Kipling. My God, you found him." He felt energized, and then he snapped his head toward Darnell. "Has the Boise Sheriff's Department gotten hold of this?"

Darnell shrugged. "I don't know. How'm I supposed to check without tipping them off? They would swarm down there."

Van Wyke rubbed his face. "How quick can we get to Colorado?"

"Flying?"

"Driving."

Darnell went to an internet map and plotted out the course. "Boise ... to ... Rocky Points, Colorado ... Eleven hours, nineteen minutes, according to this."

Van Wyke checked his watch and smiled with renewed hope that he might live through the week. "That means ten and a half the way I drive. That puts us there before sundown tonight. You ready for a road trip to Colorado?"

Darnell pulled his seatbelt across his chest. "Do I have a choice?"

"No." Van Wyke reversed out of the spot and in front of a Jaguar F-Type sports car. He smiled when he saw in his rearview that it was Phillip Chatham stewing behind the wheel.

Van Wyke stopped, reached over and checked the glove box. The Kimber Ultra Carry II .45 caliber sat where he knew it would, the clip fully loaded, and he had a box of rounds in the spare-wheel compartment. He pushed the glove box closed and looked at Darnell.

"You packing?"

Darnell blew air between his lips and gazed out his window. Of course he was. You couldn't take the projects of Chicago out of Darnell.

With a push of the accelerator, they screeched out of the lot and were on their way to the Colorado Rocky Mountains.

CHAPTER 12

"Whoa." Rachette leaned forward in the passenger seat and spat into an empty Coke can. "Now that's a shithole."

Wolf turned off the SUV's engine in front of Wendy Pollard's residence, silently agreeing with Rachette's assessment of the property.

They got out under a stone-gray sky. A horizontal sliver of white cloud hung motionless against the pine-covered mountains, the tops of which were obscured by cloud. A light, almost invisible mist swirled in the air, moistening Wolf's face.

"Let me do the talking if it comes up about the press."

Rachette spat into the weeds. "You got it."

Mrs. Pollard's husband had left her three decades ago, leaving his wife and two boys to grow up in a singlewide trailer in a rental park next to the river. Of course, Nick had been missing for years, and according to Deputy Wilson, who knew the Pollards' history as if it were common-sense knowledge, Mrs. Pollard's eldest son, Ken, had left well before Nick had gone missing. Ken hadn't gone far, though, moving into a small rental apartment in downtown Rocky Points and taking a job at one of the two garages in town as a mechanic.

The off-white paint of the place was cracked and flaking, what was left of it clinging like tissue paper, the exposed surface underneath brown and running streaks down the sides. In the small yard in front stood knee-high grass, weeds, and wild-flowers that looked to have never been cut by a mower. Wolf could only imagine what the inside looked like. Unfortunately, the weather was conniving to make sure they would see first-hand.

Wolf and Rachette stepped to the metal door and knocked.

A rustle came from inside and Wendy Pollard cracked the door, the scent of vodka following her head out the opening. She squinted as if it were sunny. Her hair was messy and matted on one side, and she was tightly wrapped in a torn lime-green robe.

"Hello Mrs. Pollard," Wolf said.

"Yes. Hi Sheriff Wolf."

"This is Deputy Rachette. May we come in to speak with you?"

"Yes. Please, come in. I'm sorry for the mess." She opened the door wider. "My son, Ken, is coming over. I called him after you guys called. He should have been here by now." She shook her head and bit a fingernail.

Wolf stepped up the stair and Rachette followed him in. Inside was black shag carpet, crusted with dried mud at the entrance and littered with tiny particles of trash throughout. In the kitchen, which comprised a counter, sink, and cabinets on the far wall, was a pile of dirty dishes on the verge of crashing to the floor, and vodka bottles lined the floor against the near wall.

"Please, take a seat if you like." She gestured to a brown loveseat that sagged in the middle.

"No thanks," Wolf said.

"I saw the news. Did you find him up there?" She stood looking up at Wolf with desperately wide eyes.

Wolf nodded. "I'm afraid so. We've confirmed dental records with Dr. Unruh in town."

"Can I see him?"

Wolf looked down at his hands. "Ma'am, I'm not sure that's a good idea. We really don't need identification from you. It's been a long—"

"Because his head was ... I saw the news. I saw. I ..." Wendy's eyes dripped. Then she opened her mouth in a silent scream and buried her clenched fists in her eyes.

The first sound was a long moan. Body-wrenching sobs followed.

Wolf wanted to kill the person who had leaked the story, voiding any attempt to tactfully contact surviving family and friends. Instead, Mrs. Pollard's twenty-two-year nightmare had emerged from hibernation and struck without warning on a television screen. Was one of the mutilated bodies her baby, Nick? Had she been so near him all these years? Unanswered questions and unresolved emotions undoubtedly choked her.

Wolf placed a hand on her shoulder as he made silent promises of retribution to God, the universe, and himself.

A car roared into the yard, and the driver braked hard. A car door slammed. Hurried footfalls approached and the front door flew open. An overweight man in his forties with long hair and a beard, Wolf recognized the man barging inside as Ken Pollard.

"Mom," he said.

"Ken Pollard?" Rachette asked.

Ken Pollard ignored Wolf and Rachette and walked to his mother, wrapping his arms around her.

Rachette looked up at Wolf and Wolf nodded to him. They both stepped back to a respectable distance and waited.

Wolf watched Ken cry just as hard as his mother, and he felt a wash of emotion pass through him. These people had been waiting for this moment for twenty-two years, and now it was here.

Ken finished his embrace with his mother and glared at Wolf, and then at Rachette.

"What the hell kind of operation you guys running, Dave? When were you going to tell us? It's all over the news. I haven't checked the mail. Maybe you sent us a postcard. Shit."

Rachette sniffed. "Mr. Pollard, we were going to—"

Wolf put a hand on Rachette's shoulder. "I apologize to you, Ken, and to you, too, Wendy. We wanted to confirm facts first and notify you second. The medical examiner made the positive ID late last night. It was my call to wait until this morning to notify you."

Ken shook his head and gave his mother a quick embrace, then stomped to the door and flung it open. "Get out. Please."

"Ken, in order to find out who did this I need to speak to you guys. Ask you a few questions."

"Your dad already did that a long time ago! Why don't you go read his interview notes or whatever?" He shook his head. "My mom was horrified to hear about this on the news. So was I. Do you know how long last night was for us?"

Wolf wrung his ball cap in his hands and looked over at Rachette. "Let's go."

CHAPTER 13

"Sheriff, it's been twenty-five minutes." Rachette looked at his watch and then shoved his hand back in his jacket pocket and shivered. "Should we maybe, possibly, go review your father's report in the warmth of the station?"

Wolf stared at the front door of the Pollard's trailer, the drizzle beading and dripping off the front of his ball cap, and ignored Rachette for the fifth time.

Rachette hunkered under his coat collar. "Okay. Okay."

The aluminum knob rattled and the door squeaked open. Ken Pollard stood with a resigned look, an unlit cigarette dangling from his mouth. He opened an umbrella and gave it to his mother, who materialized in the doorway next to him with her own cigarette.

Silently they stepped down to the front lawn.

"I thought he left us at first." Ken Pollard flicked open a well-used Zippo lighter and lit his mother's cigarette, then his own. He snapped the Zippo shut and took a deep drag. "Like, ran away. When they couldn't find his truck, it was like he'd just ditched out on us." Ken looked into the distance. "At least I was hopin' that's what happened. I was hopin' this whole time he was sittin' pretty in California somewhere. I was hopin' that blood on the payphone was a red herring, or whatever you call it."

Wendy Pollard exhaled her own drag and chewed her thumbnail in silence.

The light drizzle swept past them.

"Can you describe exactly what happened that last night you saw Nick, Mrs. Pollard?" Wolf asked.

"It's just like I told your father—it was Parker Grey, that girl's father. He did it. The crazy asshole." She took a drag with a shaking hand.

"What did Nick say he was going to do that night?" Wolf asked.

"He said he was going up to Cold Lake to meet Kimber. He'd been talking about her all week—Kimber this, Kimber that. I told him to bring her over, said I wanted to meet her. He said he was going to and to get off his back." She fought off another wave of emotion with a drag of her cigarette. "Then he got all dolled up, put on some cologne, took his truck and left. That was the last I saw of him."

"You said he was going to *meet* her?" Rachette asked. "So, he was meeting her in town? And then they were going up to the lake?"

She frowned. "No ... I don't know. I don't remember. I think he was just going up to her place. Her house. To watch the fireworks they have up at the marina every year. He said they had a boat they were going on."

"What about his friends?" Wolf asked. "Did he say he was going to be with them?"

Ken grunted. "His friends. Remember those pieces of work? I went and talked to them when they couldn't find him. They said they weren't with Nick, and they all heard the same thing from him—that he was going up to Cold Lake to see Kimber Grey."

"Who were his friends you talked to?" Wolf asked.

"Luke Hannigan. Brad Skelty. Called him Skelter back then. Real pieces of shit. Druggies. I checked in on their stories. Made sure they didn't just sell off my bro's truck and buy drugs with the money or something."

Wolf jotted the names on his notepad. He vaguely remembered the two kids as boys, but knew them well enough now that they were men. They hadn't cleaned up at all since. Brad Skelty had two DUIs, and when the pot laws of Colorado had taken effect, Hannigan was one of the first to get a grow license in town. His sudden, instant, and large, supply of product was a point of contention with the Sheriff's Department, but they had no usable evidence to move on him yet.

"And you believed they were telling you the truth?" Wolf asked Ken.

Ken clenched his fists. "Yeah. They were telling the truth."

"You roughed 'em up pretty good, huh?" Rachette said.

Ken stared at Rachette, his nostrils flared. "Yeah. That's right, I did. It was my bro."

"And why do you think it was Kimber's father, Mrs. Pollard?" Wolf asked.

"Because it was," she scoffed. "Your father figured out the guy was crazy. Schizo. Took meds and everything. Parker Grey did it. He was up at the marina that night with his family, and then he left, went and killed my boy, and then went back. Left his family right there at the marina and took off. To go kill my son. And *then* he disappears the day after your dad goes to talk to him? Up and walks away from his family? *Then* the mother disappears on top of that?" She took a drag, locking eyes with Wolf. "Oh, it was him. And now the way you found Nick? And where? That's just off shore from the Greys' cabin, for Chrissakes."

Wolf asked, "Ken, did you talk to the Greys?"

Ken peeled his eyes from Rachette and looked at Wolf. "Yeah. I talked to them. Your dad had his dick in his hand, so I had to."

"Hey, why don't you watch your mouth and have a little respect there, Ken?" Rachette puffed his chest and took a step forward.

"Both of you calm down. Ken," Wolf softened his voice, "we're trying to figure all this out once and for all."

Ken relaxed and sucked his cigarette. "They said he never showed up that night. Kimber said she never even had a date with him lined up. They were all lying. Every one of 'em."

"You gonna find my baby's killer?" Mrs. Pollard asked.

Wolf took a breath filled with second-hand smoke and looked up at the clouds gliding past, so pregnant and low they looked like he could reach up and touch them.

Rachette cleared his throat. "Of course we'll find him, ma'am."

Wolf blinked and looked at Rachette, then back to Mrs. Pollard. "I'm sorry for your loss, ma'am. If you can think of anything else, please give us a call."

She bit her thumbnail and turned away.

CHAPTER 14

WOLF PULLED the dusty CD-ROM case out of the cardboard box. It read:

Katherine Grey Interview (Wolf, Burton)

Kimber Grey Interview (Wolf, Burton)

With a small jolt, he paused and stared at his father's handwriting. He stopped himself short of touching the ink and handed the case to Patterson.

She inserted the CD into her computer tower and they waited while it clicked and whirred.

"Coffee." Rachette got up and walked to the back hallway. "Anyone else?" He emerged with the pot, filling his chipped blue-and-orange Denver Broncos mug.

"Yep." Patterson said.

"Sure." Wolf said.

Rachette filled Wolf's mug. "Black."

"Thanks."

Rachette leaned over and poured coffee into Patterson's mug. "And a double non-fat skinny mocha frap, with two pumps of vanilla and heated to one hundred twenty-seven degrees."

"Good one." Patterson grabbed the mouse. "Saying frap

implies it's frozen ... and yet you heated it to one hundred and twenty-seven degrees."

"You're welcome."

She brought up a media-player window showing Katherine Grey sitting at a wooden table.

As Patterson maximized the video and pressed play, Wolf recognized the gouge in the side of the table on screen, and knew the interview had taken place in interrogation room B. The realization hit him—he was using all the same desks, tables, chairs, walking on the same carpet that his father had all those many years ago. For an instant, he felt like he was with his father, but the warm feeling vanished as quickly as it had come.

Rachette returned and sat down.

The video was a less-than-HD recording. Katherine Grey, the mother of Kimber Grey and wife of supposed crazy-man Parker Grey, shifted uncomfortably in her chair, her image blurring and then sharpening as she moved.

Katherine was an attractive woman in her mid-thirties, her brown eyes wide and attentive, slightly upturned at the edges. Her skin was pale, or perhaps it was the harsh light of the overhead lamp, and she had a small mole on her cheek, like a beauty mark, a genetic anomaly that her daughter, Kimber, shared with her.

She wore a tank-top blouse and had thin, wiry arms, the muscles rippling beneath her skin with the slightest of movements. Her jawline was razor-sharp. With zero fat on her body, she possessed the common physique of someone who lived ruggedly in the mountains.

"Can you please state your name?"

An electric shock zipped through Wolf's body as he heard his father's voice.

"Oh, he sounds just like you," Patterson whispered in awe.

Wolf heard the smack of Rachette back-handing her shoulder.

"... Grey," Katherine Grey said.

"And can you tell me where you live?"

"I live up on the western shore of Cold Lake, in Cold Lake, Colorado."

"And your address?"

Wolf could see that Katherine Grey's hands were motionless in her lap as she spoke.

"... tell me what you were doing on the night of the Fourth of July?" Wolf's father asked.

"My husband, daughter, and I went over to the marina for the Fourth of July party and the fireworks display."

"And"—a pause, a shuffling of paper—"what time was that at?"

"They had a barbecue cook out ... let's see, we left at seven by boat, got there like seven-fifteen."

"Can you tell me when the fireworks were?"

"They were supposed to start at 9:30 pm. Whether or not they started on time, I couldn't say. I didn't keep track of time."

"And your husband, Parker Grey, he was with you?"

"Yes."

"And did he ever leave that night?"

"Yes."

"Can you please explain?"

"He got a phone call. Maureen McKenzie came out and told us, told him, that he had a phone call. He left, and then came back."

"He left to go where?"

"Oh, sorry. He went to the bar, the Tackle Box, right there on the marina."

"So, someone called the bar for your husband?"

"Yes."

A pause. "Who called?"

"I don't know."

Another pause. "Was this during the fireworks display?"

"Yes."

"Can you estimate how long after the beginning of the fireworks show Maureen came out and told him he had a call?"

"Uh ... I don't know, ten minutes?"

"Okay. Please continue."

"So he left for the phone call, and then he came back, probably just a couple minutes later. He was upset, clearly upset about something. I asked him what was wrong, and he kind of just avoided."

"Avoided the question?"

"Well, yeah. He just said, *Nothing. Nothing's wrong.* But I could see something was wrong, and then he said he was leaving, and he'd be back. I was confused, because I figured we'd be leaving with him, since we'd all come together and it was so late. But he just said he'd be back, and if he wasn't back by midnight to get a ride back over with someone else. Then he got in the boat and drove away."

"Did you ask who called him?"

"Yes. He wouldn't say."

There was the sound of a door opening and closing, and then a cough. "Would you like a cup of coffee, ma'am?"

It was Burton, with a lot less gravel in his voice than he had now.

She nodded, and a remarkably thin arm of Burton's reached in and placed a cup of coffee in front of her.

After a brief pause, Wolf's father cleared his throat. "And then what happened?"

"Well," she took a sip of coffee with steady hands, "we watched the fireworks, and then hung out for another couple of hours. By that time it was past midnight, and people were already pretty much streamed out of the place. I went into the bar and called our house. My daughter and I were just about to try and hitch a ride when my husband came back."

"In the boat?"

"Yes. In the boat."

"Okay, then what?"

She looked up at the ceiling and shook her head. "It was just so weird when he finally showed up. He was wearing a different outfit. Different shirt, different jeans. I asked him about it, and he just ignored me. He was upset, so I dropped the line of questioning. He was so serious the whole ride back. Never looked at Kimber or me."

"And then what happened? When you got home?"

Katherine's lip quivered. "We got home, and he went crazy. He was yelling at Kimber, and I was scared for her. I was so scared." She closed her eyes and a tear slid down her cheek. When she opened them, her face was a mask of horror. "I went outside to have a cigarette. To get out of the house. I couldn't take listening to it. And that's when I saw a plastic bag on the ground next to the house. It was strange because we never put trash alongside the house. You know you can't do that with the wildlife up here. So I approached it and ... then I saw it."

"Saw what?"

"The blood. The bloody clothes."

Taking a deep breath, she closed her eyes and steeled herself.

"What bloody clothes?" Burton asked a little too forcefully.

She opened her eyes. "The clothes he'd been wearing before, earlier in the night, were in the bag. I opened it and looked inside. They were soaked in blood. It was so much. I freaked out and ran back inside. I thought he might be killing my daughter."

A scraping noise on the video pulled Katherine Grey's gaze upward.

Burton's crotch came into view as he leaned against the wall behind her. "You told us yesterday that your family, husband and all, stayed at the fireworks show all night. You never mentioned anyone leaving. You never mentioned that phone call your husband got."

"I know. I know. I saw the blood, and you have no clue how scared we were."

"We have no clue? Okay. So why don't you clue us in, sweetheart?" Burton said.

Katherine Grey turned toward him, and turned back with the remnants of a glower.

"Damn," Rachette chimed in, "look at Burton go."

"Shut up and listen," Patterson said.

"Mrs. Grey, may I call you Katherine?" Wolf's father asked.

Katherine nodded.

"Katherine, what time did you guys get home from the boat ride back? From the fireworks show?"

"It was twelve-thirty, no probably one a.m. by that time."

Burton bent down and got in her face. His mustache was the same minus the gray and his face was bone thin. "Which one was it? Twelve-thirty or one?"

"I don't know." Katherine leaned away from him. "I didn't have a watch on. I just remember, yes, it was twelve-thirty when he came back and picked us up."

"Because you were in the bar and you looked at the clock," Burton sneered.

She looked at him and nodded.

"Words." He walked out of view of the video shot. "We need words for the recording."

"Yes." She glared at him.

"Sergeant Burton," Wolf's father said, "could you go get us another cup of coffee? Maybe a bottle of water for Katherine?"

There was a long pause. "Yeah, sure thing."

The door squeaked open and clicked shut.

"Please, Katherine. When you went back inside, after seeing the clothing, then what happened?"

"I went inside and he was still going crazy. He took Kimber and locked her in the room, and then started yelling at me. Telling me I was raising a slut, and how she was going to turn out being a hooker, and ... he just lost it."

"You say, *the room*. Can you please tell me what you mean by that?" Wolf's father asked.

Katherine took a sip of coffee again.

A tell, Wolf thought. What exactly it was telling about her, he didn't know yet.

She set it back down and smoothed her shirt. "For the last few years, my husband has been exhibiting symptoms."

"Symptoms?"

"Yeah. First he was hearing things. He'd come up to me and ask, 'Did you hear that?' and I'd have no clue what he was talking about. One day I listened to him when he was in an empty room, answering questions that nobody asked. I put two and two together, and figured out he was hearing voices.

"Then I could tell he was seeing things. Horrific things, I think, because he would go rigid. Sometimes he would sit there frozen and stare at the wall as if he was looking at a tarantula or something. Only nothing would be there."

Katherine took another sip of coffee, then closed her eyes. Her lip quivered and she took a shaky inhalation.

"What is it?" Wolf's father asked.

She opened her eyes. "We have rodent traps around the house. Have to for the garden we plant every year. One day I saw a dead squirrel out the back of our house. But it was," she brushed her hair behind her ear, "decapitated. The body was sitting next to the head, and it was slit from top to bottom on the underside."

Katherine took another sip of coffee.

"I knew that Parker had done it. And then later I saw his fishing knife, down in the shed by the lake. It was covered in blood, but not fish blood. There was fur on it."

Another sip.

"Did you speak to your husband about it?" Wolf's father asked.

She nodded. "I did."

"And what did he say?"

"First, he said he was cleaning it for meat, and forgot about it, which spooked me to hell, to say the least. After a while I pressed him and he admitted that's not what happened. Turns out he had just killed it, and did what he did to it, because he had to. He said that. He *had* to. Which spooked me even more.

"But then he came out with it all, telling me everything about the voices, the hallucinations, the way he was becoming paranoid, afraid of social situations. He said it had been going on for years. And I started thinking about our situation, and of course it all made sense to me at that point. We'd moved from Tennessee to the lake, from a commune with over two thousand people up to a lake in the middle of nowhere, Colorado. The new life had always been his idea. It was my husband's idea to homeschool Kimber. And when I disagreed, he insisted. It was his idea to live this life. He was secluding us, cutting us off from society, because he desperately needed to deal with his own sickness."

She stared into nothing.

"And after he told you about everything? About his sickness? What happened?"

She nodded. "When he killed the squirrel, I'd never been so

scared in my life. I'd never felt something like that before. The fear was so paralyzing. So I put the twenty-two pistol we have in my pants and went and talked to him. Told him how scared I was. Told him that I wanted him to get help. He was good about it. He went to a doctor, and got some medicine, and started taking it."

"And did the medicine help?"

"Yes. Yes, it did. I never caught him hearing voices again. Never saw him looking at things, and I didn't find anything else, you know, dead."

"Do you know who his doctor was? The name? Where?" Wolf's father asked.

"I know he went to Grand Junction. The first time. For a psychiatrist. But he didn't tell me who when I asked. And that's what was strange. The paranoia seemed to *still* be there ... it was better, he was better, he acted so nice and normal after that, but the paranoia was still there. And it was like that, the way he evaded the question of exactly *who* the doctor was in Grand Junction. Little things that really didn't matter to me. But he wouldn't tell."

Katherine Grey picked up her coffee cup and tilted it all the way back. It was empty.

Wolf's father cleared his throat. "I'm sure Sergeant Burton will be back soon with more coffee."

Burton came in on cue and set another cup down. He picked up the empty cup and left the room.

"Look at these two work," Rachette whispered. "It's like a ... a—"

"A good time to still be quiet," Patterson said.

"We were talking about the room," Wolf's father said.

"Oh, yeah. Sorry. The room. Like I said, the medicine worked, but it was patchy. I mean, it worked most of the time, but he would still have psychotic episodes. And they seemed to get worse and worse with time. One of these episodes happened a couple of years ago after my daughter had gone out with the car. She wasn't sixteen years old yet, and she was just taking a joy ride, you know? Like teens do. Especially extremely lonely teens like her.

"Anyway, Parker and I went into town in his truck, and as soon as we left she took my truck and drove it around the lake to the marina. She knew a girl who worked at the marina, and wanted to go see her.

"Parker had to turn around because he forgot his wallet, and we ended up going back home and we caught her. Saw she was gone and so was my truck. So Parker flipped out. We sat there and waited until she got back.

"The whole thing triggered this long episode in him. We had an extra bedroom in the house, so he fixed the mattress up with Kimber's sheets, put rebar over the window outside, painted it to match her room, and put a lock on the door. Then he put her inside it and"—she twisted her wrist—"locked her away for the entire night and the next day."

Katherine Grey looked down at her hands and a tear rolled down her cheek.

"That day the fear came back for me. And ever since that day, I've been trying to work up the courage to carry out a plan to escape with Kimber. But I've just been too scared. Despite all the psychotic crazy symptoms that make my husband weak, Parker is still one of the smartest, most resourceful men I've ever known. I always knew he would catch us if we left him. And he's told me before, if we leave he'd come find us, and 'do just like the squirrel' is what he said once."

"Excuse me." Wolf's father's face appeared in front of the camera, as if he was checking that the record light was on, and then disappeared.

The unexpected sighting of his father in real life, his

eyebrows furrowing, his light-brown eyes squinting, his mouth twisting, sent another jolt through Wolf's body. He ignored Patterson and Rachette glancing his way and steadied his breath.

"Sorry about that. The night of the Fourth of July, into the morning of the fifth, your husband locked your daughter in *the room* he'd built for her."

"Yes."

"And that night, what was he saying?"

"He was yelling at her, telling her she was a whore, and she needed to learn how to respect her father, and all sorts of other stuff."

"Did he ever mention Nick Pollard specifically?"

"No. He didn't. But he was saying that Kimber was a whore, going out with boys in town. But no, he never did mention his name."

A pause. "So now we get to the question of what brought you here now." Wolf's father shuffled a paper. "It's now the sixth of July. Where is your husband, Parker Grey?"

"He's gone."

"Gone where?"

"I don't know. He took his truck and left."

"And why are you here now?"

"Because as soon as I saw he was gone, I didn't want to wait around for him to come back. Now was our chance. Because when you guys came to the door yesterday, I knew that my husband had killed that boy. I saw the clothes. And he knew I knew."

CHAPTER 15

"DO YOU STILL HAVE THAT CLOTHING?" Wolf's father's voice came out of the computer speakers.

On screen, Katherine Grey shook her head. "He took it. Parker took the bag."

"We'd like to come up and check the house. Gather forensic evidence."

Katherine nodded. "Of course."

The video went black and Patterson's speakers went silent.

"Whoa, whoa," Rachette said.

"What's going on?" Wolf asked.

"I don't know." Patterson clicked the play button again. The video started from the beginning. She clicked the scrubber on the bottom and pulled it to the right and released it. It snapped back to the beginning.

"What the hell?" Rachette stood up.

Patterson ejected the CD and looked at the bottom of it. "Ah crap."

It was cracked like a dried-up lakebed, chunks of the reflective surface completely missing.

Rachette snorted. "Frickin' CDs."

Wolf stood up and stretched. "Can you fix it? Somehow salvage the data?"

Patterson looked up. "I don't know. I think if it's flaked off, it's gone. I'll check into it."

Her phone vibrated on her desk and she picked it up. "It's Lorber," she said, hitting the answer button.

"Okay." She looked up at Wolf and then at her watch. "Okay. Okay."

Wolf looked at his own wrist and saw that it was just after three in the afternoon. Patterson tapped the screen on her phone and looked up.

"What?" Rachette asked.

"Lorber still hasn't identified any of the other seven bodies yet. Wants us to come in to see what he has and pick up the files."

Wolf nodded.

"I ... uh." Patterson shifted uncomfortably and looked again at her watch. "I would go, of course, if you need me to, but I kind of had plans tonight."

"She's meeting Scott's parents." Rachette walked around to the front of her desk and sat on the edge. "Oh man. Good luck with that."

Wolf raised an eyebrow. "Is that right?"

Patterson's facial color was answer enough.

"Yep," Rachette answered for her, "gettin' serious." He picked up a pen from Patterson's desk, twirled it, and it clattered out of his hand and underneath her keyboard.

"All right," Wolf said. "Rachette, you and I go to Lorber."

"Let's do it," Rachette said.

"And let's take separate vehicles," Wolf said.

"Why? Oh, I get it, you're going on a date, too. Big Saturday night with Sarah?" Rachette studied his fingernails.

"Aww, poor guy," Patterson sang, fishing out the pen and

putting it in a drawer. "You're gonna find someone. One of these days one of these waitresses is gonna crack under your misty gaze."

Rachette leaned forward and his face shook with exertion.

"What are you doing? Are you trying to fart?" Patterson stood up and walked to Wilson's desk.

Rachette relaxed. "Do or do not. There is no try."

Wolf held his breath and headed past Rachette. "See you there. Have a good night with Scott's parents. And not that my love life is either of your business but, no, I'm not going on a date. I'm going to head up to the lake afterward to talk to Kimber Grey. Her mother's gone, her father's gone, and now her interview is gone. We need to talk to her."

Rachette frowned. "I figured we'd tag team it like Burton and your dad. What am I gonna do?"

"You're going to come back here with Lorber's files and start looking through the missing-persons databases."

Rachette smacked his lips and nodded. "Ah. That should be pleasant. Seven decayed heads, fifty states' worth of mispers, twenty-two years' worth of them."

"So you're not going on a date," Patterson said to Wolf, "but you admit there *is* a love life." She appraised Wolf with a nod. "I suspected so. You and Sarah are so obvious. That's what happens when you're in love."

Wolf turned and walked away.

"Wait a minute," Rachette said quickly.

He stopped reluctantly and turned.

"You know, I need to tell you guys. I dated this girl once."

Patterson scrunched her face. "What? Kimber Grey?"

"Yeah."

"Really," Wolf said.

"Really," Rachette said.

Silence took over.

"I'm serious. I did."

"Okay." Wolf nodded. "So ... did you discuss the case with her?"

"Well, we didn't really ever talk. I mean, I guess we didn't really date. Per se."

"Oh." Patterson pointed at him. "Okay. I get it."

"If I may continue? Anyway. I kind of, you know, made out with her one night. And she's crazy." He picked up another pen from Patterson's desk.

"Sorry, how is that different from any other girl, according to you, that you ever dated?" Patterson asked.

Rachette looked to Wolf for back-up and received none. "I'm just saying. I thought she was acting crazy back then, and now that I know her father was crazy, well, her behavior is now explained."

"And what behavior was that?" Wolf asked.

"She was all over me one night. Groping me, kissing my neck at the bar. I was pretty excited, you know? Older woman?" He bounced his eyebrows. "She said let's go outside, so we went out to the car, and then she just shut down. Completely stopped kissing me, got out of the car, and wouldn't talk to me. Just walked right back into the bar as if I was a ghost." He held up a finger. "And then, three days later, I saw her, and she pretended she didn't even know me. And then, shut up Patterson, and then, a few days later, she came up to me on the street and started talking to me, like we were long-lost friends again." Rachette shrugged.

Wolf turned around and walked to the vehicle-pool garage door.

"Thanks for making me dumber with that story," Patterson said.

"Yeah, shut up."

"You sure you don't need my help?" Patterson asked.

Rachette jogged up behind Wolf and past him out the door.

"No. Go ahead. I'll see what Kimber says tonight, and we'll reconvene tomorrow. Good luck with the parents."

CHAPTER 16

WOLF AND RACHETTE walked into the examination room, where seven heads were laid out on two gurneys, lit hard with the bright lights above—all with different colored wisps of hair of varying thickness, all slight variations on the shade of pale-bluish death, all misshapen by varying degrees. Near them were eight more gurneys parked in two lines of four, each with a body laid out on its back, each body in a differing state of deformity and corrosion, each stirring equal amounts revulsion within Wolf.

"God damn," Rachette said, "Lorber, you're crazy to have this job. Sick. And crazy."

Lorber loped to a counter and put on some latex gloves. "Deputy Rachette. Great to see you as always. Patterson couldn't make it?"

"Meeting the parents," Rachette said, oblivious to Lorber's disapproving glance.

Lorber pushed his glasses up his beak nose and narrowed his eyes. "Aha. Well, that's a shame."

Rachette gave him a suspicious look.

"As you can see, gentlemen, seven heads, seven decapitated bodies. One complete corpse. I've got each head and body numbered in order of how they match."

"Patterson said you ID'd Nick Pollard and no one else," Wolf said.

"Correct. Nick Pollard is numbered one. The rest are going to take some time."

"What have you found out?" Wolf asked.

Lorber set down his clipboard and took off his glasses. He walked to the heads and swept his arm wide, as if he was Vanna White.

"You can see the waxy look of all the faces. That's saponification, as Patterson mentioned earlier. It's preserved the flesh, but completely screwed up time of death. It's basically impossible for me to discern. Even with Nick Pollard's body. It's impossible to tell if he died at the same time he disappeared."

"Can't you assume Nick Pollard died that night, the Fourth of July, and use it as a sort of baseline?" Rachette asked. "And then determine if the other bodies were older or more recent than that?"

Lorber looked at him with surprise. "Astute question. But no. There are simply too many variables to account for. Some of the bodies had torn plastic. Other wrappings were completely intact. The different materials the victims were wearing, natural versus synthetic, would have changed the rate of decay and saponification." He walked in between the two rows of four gurneys. "Each of the bodies had stab wounds on the torsos. Five of them, as you can see here, were slit from just above the genitals to the ribs. The exposure of the intestines to varying degrees would have changed the rate of decomp, and the extreme cold at those depths, in that lake, slowed the rate of autolysis and putrefaction."

"All right. So you have no time of death," Wolf said. "What else? Fingerprints?"

"No usable fingerprints. Completely decayed."

"Wallets? What about the clothing? Labels tell you anything? Receipts?"

Lorber made two fists and opened his hands. "Nothing. Not a thing. No wallets. Receipts. No tell-tale signs of anything. I was just in the process of looking up the design models of the shoes of each of the victims. I've taken DNA samples. The process will take my assistants a while, at least a week, and then we'll check them with CODIS."

Wolf walked to the heads. Each head was frozen in an unnatural expression, looking waxy and flattened to one side or the other, slightly elongated or puffed.

"These seem like clean cuts," Wolf said, pointing to the necks.

Lorber nodded. "I agree. Looks to be a long sword of some kind that did the deed, or a machete. Most of them look like a one-blow severing of the head." He stepped toward one of the heads in the center. "This one, however, was chopped a few times. That's how I initially matched it with the body."

Wolf blinked the image of a killer doing the deed out of his mind. "All male?"

Lorber nodded.

The bodies were nude and each was more or less clearly male. Wolf, however, had learned long ago to confirm the obvious with Lorber rather than assume. Lorber, having a highly analytical, scientific mind, often neglected to mention some of his more developed theories, assuming other people saw them as he did.

"From radiocarbon dating of the tooth enamel, I've deter-mined seven of them being anywhere from late teens to early twenties, though this one here, number eight, doesn't fit the mold. He's older. Looks to be forty, plus or minus three years. Obviously his head is still attached."

Wolf looked at number eight. The face was bearded, the mouth gaping open, revealing a swollen black tongue and brown teeth. On the forehead was a gaping exit wound. The one eye-socket was devoid of an eyeball, but there were no cut marks.

Lorber walked near. "Number eight, shot in the back of the head from point-blank range. If you look in his mouth, our number eight has some pretty extensive dental work. I'm checking with Dr. Unruh and the offices in Ashland. I'm doing the same with the other heads. The seven heads are all missing their eyes, as you can see." Lorber walked away and shoved a gloved finger inside a skull as if testing the finger size of a bowling ball. "Clearly these are ritualistic killings. Perhaps the killer believed the eyes were the window to the soul, and wanted to ... I don't know, I'm not a profiler." Lorber twisted his finger in the socket and removed it with a faint sucking sound.

"Easy doc," Rachette said.

"Ritualistic, or the opposite," Wolf said. "They're gutted like fish or rodents. Chop off the head, slit the underside to remove the insides."

Lorber pulled the corners of his mouth down and looked at the bodies as if for the first time. "I guess. Only the insides are all there." He shook his head. "The eyes. The barbarism of cutting off the heads."

"Yeah." Rachette swallowed. "Pretty damn sick."

Wolf bent over a head and looked into a slice mark through an eyelid. "In the early nineties there was a guy in Texas who removed his victims' eyes. Kept them for souvenirs."

"I think it's safe to say that whatever the reason was, it was messed up." Rachette was looking pale, talking rapidly. "Where're the files, doc?"

"Over there on the counter."

Rachette walked over and opened the thick file folder. "So basically you're saying you have nothing. And it's up to me to find out who these guys are?"

Wolf ignored their banter and walked to a numbered row of bricks on a metal table. "These are what the killer used to weigh down the bodies?"

Lorber nodded. "Burnt clay brick, made by a Denver company called Tracer Building Supplies."

Wolf frowned. "How did you figure that out?"

"Says on the side of three of them."

Wolf leaned down and saw the logo pressed into the side of one.

"I'm out."

Wolf turned just in time to see Rachette disappear through the door.

Lorber smiled. "Patterson's meeting the parents, huh?"

"Keep me posted on anything else you find," Wolf said.

"You got it." Lorber pulled his gloves off and walked Wolf to the door.

Wolf shook his long, sweaty hand and left.

Rachette was outside, standing with his head tilted to the clouded sky, welcoming the mist beading on his skin.

"You okay?"

"Ah," he said, sucking in a breath through his nose.

"That good, huh?"

"Sorry. Something just came over me. It was all those heads. I can see why they used to put heads on stakes back in history, to scare the crap out of people, make them subservient or whatever. That shit is not right. I'm not gonna sleep tonight. I know it."

Wolf tilted his back, too, feeling the cool mist on his cheeks. It was disturbing. And that it'd happened so close to home made his hair stand on end.

The vibration of his phone snapped him out of his thoughts and he pulled it out of his pocket. It was Patterson.

"Hey."

"Sir, I talked to Wilson. He agrees—there's nothing we can do about the CD. It had to have been that damn storage room. Twenty-two years of extreme temperature and humidity fluctuations is not good for evidence, apparently."

"Okay, thanks."

"You sure it's okay for me to go out to dinner tonight? I can cancel."

"No. Have fun. See you tomorrow." He ended the call.

"What's up?" Rachette asked.

"Patterson says the rest of the Katherine Grey and Kimber Grey interview is damaged beyond repair."

Rachette nodded in resignation.

"Get back to the station and get after those files." He started walking.

"Will do." Rachette stepped next to him toward the parking lot. "Not sure how it's going to go."

"I know it's going to take a while, but it's all we have to go on. Do what you can until the end of your shift and then hand them off to Wilson tonight. Tell him it's top priority. And then both of you get back on it tomorrow."

Rachette nodded. "So your dad thought it was Parker Grey who did this?"

Wolf nodded. "Far as I can tell from his notes, it looked that way to him."

"None of those bodies were female in there."

Wolf shook his head.

"But Katherine disappeared, too," Rachette said. "The day after the interview we just watched."

Wolf nodded.

"Why?" Rachette asked. "Did she leave to go find Parker? Or was she killed, too?"

"All good questions." Rain drops slapped the ground and they jogged to their vehicles. "I'll let you know how it goes."

CHAPTER 17

WOLF TURNED up the windshield wipers to a steady beat and flipped on his headlights as the SUV rolled down the muddy road.

Just like the foggy view outside, he was going into this interview almost blind. Instead of watching Kimber Grey's reactions to his father's questions on video, Wolf was going to be talking to a woman he'd never met, listening to her relaying her side of things, and over two decades later. That would have been fine had he known the interview video was waiting for him when he got back.

Beyond the droplet-covered windshield, the surrounding forest was socked in with fog, cutting visibility to fifty yards or less. Somewhere to his left, past the trees and thick weather, sat Cold Lake, which he could smell through the vents.

Crawling down a steep grade at ten miles per hour, Wolf feathered the brakes as a couple of craters in the road came into view. Flanked by car-sized rocks on either side, the bottleneck forced him to almost stop and enter the dip straight on. The rear bumper scraped as he dropped in, and then he lifted in his seat and the rock and dirt beneath the tires smoothed out.

Just before he let off the brake and coasted, he jammed to a stop, sure he'd seen something on a tree next to the rocks. Hoping his parking brake would hold on the steep grade, he stepped out. The rocky wet earth gave way underneath his work boots as he stepped back toward the massive potholes.

Sure enough, he'd seen something on the tree—a camouflage-painted rectangular game camera with a shiny black lens in the center, more or less pointed straight at him. A four-inch-long antenna jutted out from the side of the device. He'd seen these newer-model cameras before, and knew them capable of transmitting pictures and video feeds via Wi-Fi.

Raindrops slapped on his coat, coaxing him back into the idling SUV.

After a short coast down the road he stopped and studied a perpendicular road jutting to the left. The fog had lifted just enough to see that the road veered up before disappearing around a bend and into the pines. He pushed the button on his phone screen to check the map, but there was no service. He checked the Wi-Fi settings and found one secure network requiring a password called "XXXXX."

He continued straight, using his memory of the map that he'd studied before leaving the County Hospital parking lot.

Two gentle turns and a brief straightaway later, he reached his destination.

Someone was out front of the cabin, wielding an axe, chopping down on a vertical piece of firewood with a fierce blow that sent two chunks flying to the ground.

The person turned, and as his wipers swished he saw a pretty face buried inside a blue parka hood.

Kimber Grey, Wolf recognized, though much older than the photos he'd seen in the file sitting on the passenger seat.

Not that she looked old. She appeared young, and her jeans

were snug, showing she was fit. She gave another piece of wood a savage blow, revealing her strength.

She had been seventeen when Nick Pollard went missing. And within days, her father, her father's truck, and her mother were gone too. That was twenty-two years ago. Wolf had done the math: she was thirty-nine, just a year younger than Wolf, and had lived at this location her entire life since that fateful summer. And yet he could not remember ever seeing this woman in person other than at this moment.

"Kimber Grey?" Wolf got out and zipped up his parka. The air was thick with the scent of fresh-cut lumber.

"Yep." She kept her back to him, raising the axe behind her and swinging down with precision. The wood clanked to each side and she bent over, picked up another piece, and placed it on her stump.

The wood-frame construction cabin stood two stories, with the entrance on the upper level. The lower floor was halfway sunk into the ground. Wooden steps climbed up to the entrance, which was a shiny wood-slab door. A covered deck wrapped around to the right and presumably to the back of the property. A large bay window revealed open curtains and a spinning ceiling fan inside.

"I'm Sheriff David Wolf of the Sluice County Sheriff's Department. I'd like to talk to you for a bit."

"Okay." She chopped another piece.

Wolf heard a faint motor to his left and turned, noticing the land ended abruptly fifty yards away. He figured that was the cliff-line, and on a cloudless day, the view would have been of Cold Lake's shimmering waters.

"Can you please stop with the axe?"

She jammed the axe into the stump, pulled down her hood and turned around. "Sorry, I'm low on firewood. Need to get some stocked up. Still gets plenty cold up here in the summer, you know?"

She flashed a smile, and Wolf saw the mole above her lip, like her mother's. She pulled off her leather glove and pointed to the beauty mark, then pointed at Wolf's face.

"We both have these damn things," she said.

Wolf smiled and shook her hand, which was hot and sweaty, slender, fitting easily inside his. When she took it back it was like pulling sandpaper from his grip.

"Kimber Grey," she said.

"Nice to meet you. I'd like to talk to you about the"—he gestured to the lake—"recent activity on the lake. I take it you've heard?"

She put her hands on her hips and stretched her back. "Yeah. I've heard. I've been watching it."

"Do you think we could go inside for a chat?" Wolf asked.

"Follow me. You drink coffee?"

CHAPTER 18

WOLF SAT at a small eating table and watched Kimber work in the kitchen.

She made coffee with elegant movements: lifting a back leg as she bent into a cupboard and pulled out a French press, jumping just the right height to grab a bag of coffee grounds stored on top of the cupboards. There was no wasted action. She knew every centimeter of the kitchen, and she was well practiced with what she was doing. Apparently she liked her caffeine.

By the time she was depressing the plunger the clouds outside had slid to the east, revealing the silver lake below. He wondered how much the property had cost when they had moved here all those years ago. Now it would be worth a pretty penny.

"How many acres you have here, if you don't mind me asking?"

She poured the coffee and set it down in front of Wolf. "Sixty-three. It's mostly that way, up towards Olin Heeter's place." She faced the lake and then pointed left.

Wolf remembered his father's notes, and Olin Heeter's

mention of seeing something being dropped in the lake on the night of July 6th.

He sipped the strong coffee and then stood up and bent over the counter to get a better look out onto the land below the house. The cliff line below ran parallel the side of the house. Grassy land ran up to the precipice off to the left, and to the right scrub oak obscured the edge. A wood staircase with a hearty handrail disappeared over the edge. There was no fence. He considered it a small miracle Kimber Grey had survived her childhood in this place.

"That's quite a ways down."

"Oh yeah." She leaned over next to him and pointed towards the scrub oak. "If you don't want to go down the stairs, you can always rappel down my rope."

A turquoise-and-pink climbing rope was attached to a sophisticated top-rope anchor system that hooked to two tree trunks, dangling over the edge and out of sight. He whistled softly and walked back to the table. Sitting down, he noticed she looked satisfied she had impressed him.

"You climb up that?" Wolf asked, remembering her callused hand.

"Yep."

"And who's belaying you from below?"

"I self-belay."

Wolf nodded.

"You rock climb?" Kimber's amber-brown eyes locked on his as she took a slow, careful sip of her coffee. Then she set her cup on the counter and leaned back on her hands, back arched, presenting her smallish breasts and erect nipples through the thin fabric of her long-sleeved shirt.

"No. Not unless I have to."

"So you found Nick Pollard."

"What makes you say that?"

"So you did?"

"We did. Why did you suspect that?" Wolf asked.

"I thought it would have been obvious to you. You watched the interview tapes of me and my mom that your father made, right?"

"Actually I haven't watched your interview yet. I wanted to get your version of events from you first."

She reached for her coffee cup and twisted to look out the windows. With slow deliberation, she caressed her jeans, and then slid her fingers inside her rear pocket.

"Okay. So what do you want to know?"

"Everything. I'd like to start with that week of the Fourth of July. Tell me about you and Nick, and about that night."

She turned and walked over, then sat down across the table. With an exhale she closed her eyes and her brown eyelashes swung to the top of her cheeks like Chinese fans. Her chestnut hair was pulled back in a ponytail that couldn't tame the wavy thickness of it. Frizzy strands popped up everywhere and she tucked one long one behind her ear.

She smelled like flowery scented deodorant and sweat.

"It's been so long," she said.

"Take your time."

She looked at Wolf and smiled without teeth, as if he was being the kindest person in the world to her. At that moment, Wolf admitted to himself that she was an attractive woman. Had he been a single man, he'd have declared her beyond attractive.

"Let's see. I started seeing Nick two weeks before that."

"How did you two meet?"

She smiled. "I went to a party some guy was having out in the woods one Saturday night. I remember I heard some other kids talking about it over at the marina, and I just showed up. By myself."

Wolf nodded.

"Anyways, I didn't get out much with my parents, being how they were. I wasn't invited, and I didn't know anyone. I was seventeen, and just wanted to see what all the fuss was about. The whole high-school scene. The whole being-social scene. So I walked up to the keg, and I remember everyone was staring at me like I was a bear or something coming out of the woods, and he came up and started talking to me. Wouldn't leave me alone, actually. After a while I guess I started to like him. He was, after all, a boy talking to me."

She shrugged and sipped her coffee.

Wolf saw her mother's spitting image in her actions.

"So you two dated a few times leading up to the fourth?"

She nodded. "Yeah. We went out twice. Went and saw a movie down in Ashland once. And I went to his house for dinner."

Wolf took a sip of coffee, thinking about how Nick Pollard's mother had said she'd badgered Nick into bringing Kimber over, but that Nick hadn't. So that was a lie. But was it Kimber Grey's or Wendy Pollard's?

"The place the Pollards have on the hill?" Wolf asked.

Kimber looked at him. "No. The one by the river. Mrs. Pollard has another place? Didn't think they had that much money."

Wolf sipped his coffee. "And how about the Fourth of July? Were you two planning to meet that night?"

"No. I'm not sure why Nick's mother said that. Maybe Nick was lying to her, I don't know. But we never had any plans for meeting that night."

"Tell me about that night."

"My mom and dad and I went in the boat to the marina to watch the fireworks. When we were there, my dad got a call and he left in a hurry. Then he came back later and picked us up."

She took a sip of her coffee and seemed to steel her thoughts. "I remember he was so sullen on the trip back. And then when we got in the house, he went crazy."

"Meaning?" Wolf asked.

"He was screaming and throwing things. Calling me a whore. Yelling at me about how I was disgracing the family." She shrugged. "I don't know."

"Did he hurt you?"

She shook her head.

"And then what did he do?"

"He locked me in the room. That was it. I went to sleep." She shrugged again.

"The next day my father came to visit you, asking about Nick Pollard's disappearance."

She nodded. "Yeah. He was a nice guy, your dad. He was concerned for us."

"But that day, the fifth of July, you guys didn't mention your father had left the fireworks show the night before."

She shook her head. "I didn't tell your father anything. I didn't speak that day when your father came over. I talked to your father the *next* day, after my dad had left. When we went into the station and did the interviews."

"Okay." Wolf nodded. "Were you concerned for your safety when my father came asking about Nick Pollard that next day? On the evening of the fifth?"

"Yes," she said without hesitation. "Because my father had a bag of bloody clothes lying next to the house. I saw it the next day. Then I thought about how my father had yelled all those things the night before, and ... I put two and two together."

"So you saw the bag of bloody clothes, too?"

Kimber nodded.

Wolf frowned. "So, he left it outside all night? The bag of clothing?"

"Yes. It was up against the house."

"So it was there when my father was there talking to you about Nick."

"Yes."

"Why didn't you tell my father about the bag? About your suspicions?"

"I hadn't seen what was in the bag yet. I checked it later. After your father left."

Wolf leaned back and took a breath. "My father came the next evening. The evening of the fifth. So you saw the bag of clothes the next evening."

She shook her head impatiently. "Why are you asking the same questions over and over?"

"You said you saw the bag of clothes the next day. Now you're saying you actually saw it the next evening."

She snorted a laugh. "I saw it the next day, then I looked in it the next evening."

"What exactly was your father yelling at you about? Do you remember what made you think he'd done it?"

She looked annoyed at his change in tack. "I don't know. The whore thing, I guess. He kept telling me I was a whore. Like, because I'd gone out with Nick, I'd been going out on the town and screwing every guy or something." She looked at Wolf. "Then the cops show up because he was missing? And he left the fireworks show? And then the clothing with blood on it? Didn't take much to put two and two together."

Wolf nodded and sipped his coffee. "Do you have those bloody clothes?"

She snorted again. "No. Like we told your father, my dad left with those clothes. Your father never found any blood traces. They scoured the place." She looked into her cup. "What? Are you testing me or something?"

Wolf sipped his coffee. "Like I said, I haven't watched your interview yet. Do you know who called your father that night? At the marina?"

"No. They say it was a woman. I still don't know who it could have been."

"It was the number to a gas station down the valley, right at the junction of Highway 734," Wolf said. "That didn't ring any bells with you back then?"

She shook her head.

"And it still doesn't after all these years?"

She shook her head.

"And did you or your mother suspect he was seeing someone else? Cheating on her?"

She frowned and then shook her head.

He stood up and walked to the kitchen doorway. So far he'd seen the entryway to the house, which was a cramped T-Junction that went left and right. They'd gone left into the kitchen.

"Could I see this *room* I keep hearing about?"

She stood up. "Yeah, sure. It's not the same, though. I've made sure of that."

She led the way through the kitchen doorway, past the front door and into the living room, which was a good-sized rectangular space with creaky wood floors and the bay window. A wood-fired stove stood against the interior wall on a brick hearth, which extended in a semicircle a few feet in front of it. The stack of wood on the hearth was reduced to slivers.

Wolf bent down and ran his hand over a logo on one of the bricks. *Tracer Building Supplies.*

"What?" Kimber asked.

Wolf stood up. "Who made this hearth?"

"I don't know. It was here when my father bought the place. Must have been Mr. Heeter, I guess."

"Mr. Heeter?" Wolf asked.

She pointed out the window toward a house on the hill a

quarter mile down the shoreline. It was a two-story structure with a deck off the back, higher than the Greys' cabin, and clearly visible above the tops of the pines.

"Mr. Heeter. My parents bought the place from him."

Wolf nodded and looked past her into the hallway. "The room?"

She turned and flipped a light switch and a coverless light bulb lit up the corridor. There were three doors, one on the near left and two on either side of the hallway at the end.

She stopped at the first door. "This is it."

She twisted the knob and pushed the door open. It creaked on its hinges and cool, stagnant air that smelled like fabric hit Wolf's nose. An uncovered square window straight ahead illuminated the space in soft natural light. There was a crisply made single bed against the left wall, a dresser, and a nightstand.

Wolf ran a hand over the door jamb.

"I removed the lock, and the bars on the window," she said, following his eyes.

"May I?" Wolf asked, stepping into the room.

"Be my guest."

The boards underneath him squeaked as he walked to the picture window. Looking out the glass, he noted the grooves cut into the wood on the outside frame—three on each side and two on top and bottom.

"That's where the bars were. My dad cut those grooves and put rebar in there. I cut them out when he left."

Wolf shifted his gaze to the woods beyond. Old-growth trees butted up against the back yard of the property, the darkness within deepening with each passing minute. He put his face to the window and saw the lake through the trees off to the left.

He turned around when a series of digital *ding* sounds came from the living room, like a car door left ajar, only much louder.

Kimber glanced quickly toward the noise and then seemed to dismiss it.

"Is that the doorbell?"

Kimber hesitated, then shook her head. "No."

"What was it?"

She walked out into the living room and Wolf followed. She pulled a phone out of her pocket, focused intently on the screen, then tapped and pocketed it.

"I have an array of motion-activated cameras and perimeter alarms set up around the property." She pointed up at a tiny speaker mounted in the corner. "When they're tripped, they trigger the alarm."

Wolf walked to the window and looked outside. "So did you know I was coming?"

"Yes. I have it set to notify my phone, and I knew that someone had driven in, but I didn't know it was you."

"That was your camera on the tree, by the two boulders."

She nodded.

"So you can watch who comes in and out."

"I have to get on my computer and sit and stare if I want to do that. But that's definitely not my style. I would guess that was Mr. Heeter leaving. Or a deer. Or a bear." She shrugged. "Who knows?"

"So a motion sensor being tripped out in the woods or a person leaving on the road is the same sound?"

She nodded. "Yep. Not exactly top-of-the-line, but good enough for the job."

"And what exactly is the job your system is performing?"

"I'd like some more coffee." She disappeared back into the kitchen.

Wolf stepped to the window and looked out. He looked down at his truck, noting that the beads of water had almost dried on the paint. Despite the lifting clouds, it was dark, and getting darker, and he saw little past fifty yards into the trees. The west windows of Mr. Heeter's structure were glowing pink now, reflecting the sunset.

He walked into the kitchen and saw Kimber standing by the sink, stirring her coffee.

"So ... tell me about it," Wolf said, leaning against the counter. "Why all this security?"

"My father left us on the sixth. The day after your father came to talk to us about Nick. My dad knew the cops were onto him. He knew my mother and I knew about him. About what he'd done. And then, a couple of days later, my mother left. I'd heard him threaten my mother numerous times. *If you two leave me, I'll hunt you down*, stuff like that." She stared into her swirling coffee. "She left a note. And she just left."

The file on Wolf's passenger seat contained a copy of the note. "What did the note say?"

"It said she was going into town, and she'd be right back. Into Rocky Points. Then she ... just never came home."

"She took her truck?"

"Yes."

"And your father took his truck the day before?"

She nodded.

"So you were stranded up here."

Kimber's eyes swam with tears, glittering in the vague light of the kitchen. "She called me the next day from some payphone from somewhere. She said she was going back home. Back to Tennessee. She apologized, and said she had to follow her heart and *go back home*. She left the truck down in Rocky Points, in the grocery store parking lot with the keys in it. I had Mr. Heeter take me down."

Though he knew the incredulous story already, he felt a mild shock as he watched her tell it.

She wiped her eyes and smiled defiantly. "Sorry. Old habit. Playing the victim."

She walked to the wall and flipped on the light switch. The kitchen filled with yellow light, washing out the majestic views outside with hard interior reflections.

"I have to say, I don't blame you for being upset. Your parents both abandoned you. But that doesn't explain the security measures. Do you think your father took your mother? Is that why you've rigged the place like an army base? Because you think he'll come back for you, too?"

She shrugged. "I don't know. Maybe my father came back, and then made my mother write the note. Then took her or something. And then there's always been Mr. Heeter. Not exactly the most normal of men."

"You think Mr. Heeter is dangerous?"

"No," she said with a chuckle. "He's sweet. But maybe creepy? Like a dirty old man? I mean, I live below him, and he lives up the hill. He has a big telescope, and who knows where he's pointing that thing at all times. He's always been socially awkward, too, and now that his wife is dead he's worse. His wife was definitely his better half. He's a Vietnam vet, and I think whatever happened to him over there screwed with him. Dangerous, though? I don't think so."

She rinsed her coffee cup and put it on a drying rack.

"And what about your father?" Wolf asked. "You think he's coming back for you?"

She shrugged. "Your father and his department looked into my mother. They never found her in Tennessee. Or any trace of her making the trip there. Your father figured she hitchhiked out of town, because buses didn't run back then from Rocky Points to Vail, which was the nearest place you can pick up a bus. But the bus company in Vail didn't remember her either. No credit-card receipts. Not that there would have been any. Our family always used cash.

"After all that investigation into my mother and father and not getting anywhere, believe it or not, it was *your* father's idea all those years ago to put motion sensors out there. He came out and helped me rig up the system. I've updated it a bit here and there over the years, adding the Wi-Fi camera on the road. But, basically, it's all your dad's fault I live like I'm on an army base." She smiled and sniffed.

Wolf returned her smile, feeling pride in his father.

"So you've been living here by yourself for the last twenty-two years?"

She nodded with her chin up.

"And how have you kept the place up? How are you making a living?"

"Don't worry, Sheriff. I pay my taxes like the next person."

Wolf shook his head. "No, I mean it must be tough. You hunt for food? Fish?"

"Yeah, I do that. But I have money. My father came into money back in Tennessee. An inheritance. That was the reason we came out here and how we could afford this place. But when they left, my father and then my mother, they never touched the money. They just left it here for me."

Wolf stared at her.

There was a muffled caw of a crow outside. He looked out the window, focusing through the reflections. The western sky glowed orange, but over the lake the sky was black.

"And you haven't had *any* contact with your father since that day he left?"

She shook her head.

"Do you suspect he's ever come back?"

She shook her head.

"What about that alarm just now? That doesn't even bother you?"

She shrugged. "I've been living alone for so long, I've gotten used to it. I was freaked out at the beginning, but I have multiple guns within arm's reach, I can see three hundred and sixty degrees from inside the house, and I just go on living my life. I figure that if my father is out there and wants me dead, he'd have done it a long time ago."

He looked at his watch—8:32 p.m.

"Listen, as you've probably heard, we found more than just Nick Pollard out there. My father came here with the notion that your father may have killed that boy. Now, we've brought up a total of eight bodies."

She closed her eyes. "I know. I saw the news."

"I've gotta get back to the station." He pulled out his card and gave it to her. "I'll be back in touch, all right?"

"Oh, wait. Look." She pointed next to the phone on the wall.

Wolf saw a business card that said *Daniel Wolf, Sluice County Sheriff*.

"Your father pinned his card right here twenty-two years ago. Told me to use it if I needed it. I'll just pin yours right under it."

Wolf nodded, still staring at the plain white card with a raised SCSD logo and glossy black ink reading: *Sheriff Daniel Wolf*.

"Ma'am, I want to be clear. I'd like to be back in touch with you soon, so if you'd please stay available, I'd appreciate it."

"Yeah, of course. So don't go driving off and disappearing?"

"Exactly."

"I'll look forward to it." She made no effort to hide the suggestiveness in her voice.

Kimber saw him out the door and closed it behind him. He

walked down the steps into the darkness, and when he looked back up saw her drawing the bay window drapes, looking out into the night beyond him.

Outside the night air was damp and chilled to the bone, as if the cold air pooling on the lake had billowed over the lip of the cliff and was now lapping against him. Faint laughing and chattering voices came from the water, and when he looked, he could see a tiny cluster of lights all the way across the lake. He realized the noise was coming from the marina bar on the opposite shoreline. It looked to be miles away across the water.

He sat in the SUV and looked up at the cabin windows. The slit between the drapes fell closed, fingers pulling out of sight.

With a deep breath he fired up the SUV and backed away.

CHAPTER 19

WOLF'S ENGINE whined hard and the headlight beams bounced against the pines as he left up the dirt road from Kimber Grey's.

He stopped for a moment at the road that came in from the right—the road to Mr. Olin Heeter's place—and got out.

Wolf's feet crunched on the wet dirt road as he walked into the spray of light from his SUV and studied the ground. There were no tire marks on the road other than Wolf's incoming tracks. None came or went in the soft earth from Mr. Heeter's home.

Again, Wolf wondered about the alarm Kimber Grey had heard.

He did a slow circle, studying the dark forest around him, and saw nothing. His SUV hummed softly, and billowing exhaust floated through his headlight beams.

He got in and turned up the road toward Olin Heeter's.

A quarter mile up the road, the trees opened and a cabin loomed, dark and deserted-looking.

He parked in front and the headlights raked the house, illuminating windows covered with pulled curtains.

He shut off the lights and engine and got out.

Wind rushed through the pines surrounding the hilltop house, sounding like a distant waterfall that rose and fell in strength. The lake shimmered in the moonlight below, and in the distance a light from Kimber Grey's cabin gleamed through the trees.

The front yard was overgrown with weeds and wildflowers and no lights were on. Add the covered windows, and the place had all the signs of being deserted. But Kimber seemed to speak about the man like he was a fixture in her life.

He stepped to the front, climbed onto the squeaking wood porch and pushed a glowing doorbell button.

A classic ding-dong chime sounded within.

There was no answer, though Wolf could have sworn he heard a thump and then the creak of a floorboard.

He knocked and waited for more noise from within, but none came.

He turned and looked into the forest behind his SUV. The moon passed beneath a cloud, lighting it up around the edges, dropping the ambient light.

He flicked on his flashlight and swept the beam over the forest's edge, seeing nothing beyond the first tree trunks. He turned and shone it into the nearest window, illuminating fabric drapes pulled tight.

He stepped off the porch and kicked something. When he swung the light down into the grass he saw a geode, cracked in half, with exposed purple crystals on the inside. He set it back down on the porch next to the support beam of the deck and walked along the front of the property to his right, bobbing and swiping the light beam ahead of him and against covered windows as he went. The land inclined down as he walked around the side of the house, revealing a lower level with walkout sliding glass doors in the rear. They were covered with drapes on the inside as well.

As he looked down the rear wall of the house, a low whoosh of wind came from his left, where a row of rocks had been stacked in a three-foot-high straight line, like a rear perimeter fence one might see in the rural Irish countryside. Beyond it was nothing but the mercury-pool lake far below and the pinprick lights of the marina in the distance.

The howling of the wind grew louder as he stepped nearer the precipice.

Reaching the wall, he leaned forward and shone the flashlight downward. Moths flitted through his beam, riding on a steady wind that climbed up the cliff.

Craning his hand out, he pointed the beam down and failed to see the shore below. He remembered seeing this cliff from the boats on the lake, and knew the drop was straight down and higher than the house was tall, which made the drop at least thirty feet in his estimation.

Upon closer examination, he saw a dock jutting out into the water with a bobbing fishing boat moored to it, which looked like a miniature bath toy from this height.

With a start that raised his pulse, he sensed someone behind him and twisted around. Sweeping the flashlight back and forth, he saw nothing but the vacant rear lawn of the house.

"Shit," he said.

His history with cliffs was clearly playing with his mind.

Another look at his cell phone confirmed that there was still no reception. The screen showed 9:09 p.m., and he was now longing for home. Sarah had said this morning that she would come to stay at his house again tonight, and he had the sudden itch to get the heck off this lake and back down to Rocky Points.

He looked down at Kimber Grey's home, still lit brightly but obscured somewhat by the trees from his angle, and then he headed back across the lawn.

In the corner of his eye he thought he saw movement towards the house. He jabbed the flashlight beam toward the spot, and could have sworn he saw the corner of a drape shift in one of the windows.

"Hello? Anyone in there?"

His heart pounded a steady clip in his ears.

He took a deep breath and marched toward the back of the house, flashlight beam locked on the spot, but the fabric in the window remained unmoved.

"I'm with the Sheriff's Department! Mr. Heeter?"

He let his eyes wander across the other windows, thinking that if the person inside suspected they'd been spotted they might go look from another vantage.

"Hello? Sluice County Sheriff! Mr. Heeter? I'm here to talk to you!"

Wolf flicked the beam to the next window, careful to aim it in the small crack between the two drapes.

Nothing.

He stood stock-still, quietly mouth breathing.

There was no movement or sound.

He flicked off the flashlight and stood silent for three full minutes, listening to the pulsing whoosh of fish-scented air cresting the cliff behind him. Between gusts he heard crickets chirping in the surrounding woods and nothing else.

If there was someone inside, they were determined to stonewall him, and he had no business making them do otherwise. Defeated by either the person inside or his own imagination, he walked around the house and back up to his awaiting SUV.

He got in and started the engine. Flicking on his headlights revealed drapes still drawn and a door still closed.

Wondering if his imagination was running wild, he reversed out and started forward. Then he slammed on the brakes, because the geode rock he'd placed back on the front porch wasn't there.

With his pulse skyrocketing, he shut off the engine and jumped out. Keeping his hand on his pistol, he pulled his flashlight and pointed it forward, carefully walking to the front porch again.

Inside the long grass near the wood deck entrance, violet crystals reflected his flashlight beam back at him.

He bent down and picked up the geode, studying the ground around it. Numerous blades of grass were flattened and bent. Someone moving toward his SUV? Or were they his own footsteps from earlier? He swept the beam back and forth and decided, no. He'd gone to the left, to the side of the house. These depressions led to the road. And besides, he wasn't going mad. He'd put the rock down before leaving.

He followed the trail of disturbances to the gravel drive. The earlier rains made it easy to spot a few rocks and pebbles kicked out of place. He also spotted a single footprint, though only a partial, so he was unable to gauge its size.

He shone the light into the forest and listened, feeling ridiculously exposed.

"Is anyone there?" he asked, not expecting an answer and not receiving one.

He turned full circle, pulled his pistol and shone the light through each of his windows into his vehicle.

Heart still walloping, he got inside and drove back down the hill, crawling at under ten miles per hour and keeping a close eye on the forest. The trees were too dense to see anything, however, and he would have to stay curious for the time being. He wasn't about to go traipsing through the woods after an unknown person who could or could not have been armed.

At the base of the hill he looked left at the T-Junction. His dash clock said 9:15. He sighed and took a left back towards Kimber Grey's.

When he went down the road and pulled in front of her house, he was surprised to see her squinting against his head-lights, standing halfway up her porch steps as if expecting his return. He made a wide loop and pulled up with his driver's-side window down.

"You okay?" he asked.

She nodded once with an expressionless gaze.

"I was just up at your neighbor's, and thought I saw someone up there. I think there was definitely someone up there. They went off into the woods."

She lifted her chin and looked into the trees.

He waited for her to say something, but she remained silent.

"You ... get any alarms on your motion sensors?"

"If I do, I have a pistol and a rifle. Don't worry about me, Sheriff."

He studied her calm expression and then nodded. "Yeah. Okay." He shifted into drive. "Well ... be careful."

As he drove away up the steep incline, he studied his rearview mirror, and saw Kimber Grey keep a motionless vigil on her steps until she disappeared out of sight behind the trees.

Who was this woman?

Kimber Grey was a woman who'd survived for twenty-two years on her own, he reminded himself, and she'd survive another night with or without him. He hoped.

The dash clock read 9:20.

He flicked on his high beams and kept his speed just south of unsafe through the woods, thoroughly ready to get off this lake, back to the Chautauqua Valley, and into his warm bed, preferably coiled with Sarah's warm body.

When he finally got to the County 74 junction, his phone still had no reception.

The dash clock read 9:31.

Damn it. As he drove along the northern edge of the lake east, he knew now was the best time to stop at the marina bar to ask questions. Its parking lot was packed and it looked hopping judging by the people milling on the deck. The crowd meant it would be a bad time get answers, but tomorrow morning—Sunday morning—would be worse.

They would have a landline at the bar, the same one that had transmitted the mystery call to Kimber's father all those years ago, and he could call Sarah from there. Hopefully she was still at his house.

He pressed the gas, taking the gravel turns with a little more slide.

CHAPTER 20

PATTERSON IGNORED the hand caressing the inside of her knee under the table and answered the question. "I went to the University of Colorado. In Boulder."

"Oh, you're kidding! I went to grad school in Boulder." Scott Reed's father smiled. "That's where I got my Master's in Aerospace Engineering. Scott threatened to go there back in the day, but as you know he ended up at Metro State."

Scott's caress abruptly stopped. "And my father hasn't let me hear the end of it since."

His father shrugged and took a sip of his wine. "Nothing's wrong with Metro, son. It's not CU, but ... nothing's wrong with Metro." His tone said otherwise.

Patterson and Scott sat across the table from his parents at the Red Ruby Café, which was a jeans and T-shirt kind of place off Main with some of the best American cuisine that money could buy.

Scott had chosen the venue, but his father had chosen the seating arrangements, making sure, quote, "I have a view of the televisions."

"So, how's work going with you, Scott? The, uh, snow cat

running well?" his father asked, his eyes rising to the TV screens again.

Scott's breath looked to be quickening, and his face was turning red behind the water glass pressed against his lips.

Patterson figured it was her turn to reach over and place a hand on his leg, so she did.

Scott looked into her eyes and his face relaxed.

"You two are so good together," his mother said, beaming at them.

Patterson smiled. "Yeah. We are."

The waiter came over, providing a welcome distraction. "Here are your appetizers."

"The wings here are the best in Colorado," Patterson said, feeling her face go red as she remembered she'd already said as much when they'd ordered the food. Damn, she was nervous, and Scott's father wasn't helping the situation one bit. The man seemed to feed and grow stronger on discomfort, and every word out of his pompous mouth made sure there was plenty of discomfort to feed his cruel spirit. It was amazing that Scott was related to this man at all.

If it had been her father across the table, she'd have stood up and shook a fist in his face right now, told him to be nice or go home. Underhanded, passive-aggressive behavior wasn't tolerated in her family. Her and her three brothers had grown up using far less subtle tactics to communicate. In fact, she'd once thrown a beer in her brother's face at a restaurant much like this one.

Smiling to herself at the sudden memory, she picked at her food.

When the awkward silence became too much to bear, she cleared her throat. "You know, Scott has written a novel and he's working on a second."

"Oh my goodness." His mother set her beer down. "Are you serious?"

Scott gave Patterson a rueful glance and nodded. "Yeah. I am ... I have."

"Oh really?" his father said. "What's it about?"

Scott wiped his fingers with a napkin. "It's a mystery about a man who's an avid outdoorsman. He comes across a murder victim in the woods and ..."

Scott let his sentence die, because his father set down his drink and straightened, looking past them as if he'd just seen something terrible.

"God damn it! Another strike out. They paid way too much for that asshole. I'm sorry, son. What's it about?"

Scott picked up a chicken wing. "Forget it."

"No, I want to know. Have you found a publisher yet?"

Scott ignored him.

"John," his mother said in a whisper.

"What? I'm asking about his book."

Scott threw his napkin on the table and scooted his chair back. "We're going to take off. It was good seeing you, Mom."

Patterson looked up in shock at Scott as he left, then across the table. His mother was slack-jawed and his father was concentrating on a hot wing with indifference.

"Oh no, Scott," his mother said. "John, tell him not to go."

Scott was already gone, swerving his way around tables in the bar and heading to the door.

Patterson wiped her hands and stood up. "Ummm, I guess we're going."

"It was nice to meet you," Scott's father said with a quick smile that didn't reach his eyes.

His mother's lower lip quivered and her eyes welled up. "I'm sorry."

Patterson had no response for that, so she scooped up her

rain parka and purse from the back of the chair and nodded. "It was nice to meet you." She stepped quickly through tables toward the front door. "Asshole," she said under her breath.

Scott was outside the front windows waiting with his back turned.

Making the final push to the door, she stopped dead in her tracks when she realized she'd seen and caught eye-contact with Sarah Muller, Wolf's ex-wife.

Sarah was one of those women that always demanded a second look. She was stunning, with electric-blue eyes, thick true-blonde hair, and a figure that made men stop and stare every time. But that wasn't what had halted her. It had been the large man next to Sarah stroking her leg under the table, an action clearly visible to Patterson since the bar table was so tall and Patterson was so short.

Wasn't she dating Wolf again? she thought.

Sarah's eyes widened with recognition and her leg whipped to the side, and then the man's hand grabbed air under the table. The man followed Sarah's eyes to her.

Sarah looked like a frightened animal, but the man was cool and confident.

Patterson's blood was already boiling with the botched dinner and the father from hell, and before she could think about it she was right next to them, thrusting out her hand.

"Hi Sarah," she said.

Sarah reached out a timid claw and gripped her fingers.

Patterson shot her glare at the other man, thrusting her hand toward him. "And you are?"

He smiled and swallowed her grip with his. He squeezed with increasing pressure and Patterson met every foot-pound of force.

"I'm Carter."

"Carter who? Don't think I've seen you before."

He let go and his smile vanished. "Carter Willis. I didn't get your name."

He was a good-looking man, but if he got up from his chair, Patterson was sure there would have been slime on it. He was dressed impeccably, polished platinum jewelry on his wrists peeking out beneath a crisp expensive shirt and blazer. A politician or important businessman, if Patterson had to guess. Perhaps too muscular for something as simple as that, though. The man was dangerous-looking, she decided.

"Your name?" he persisted.

Patterson ignored him and eyed Sarah, who was stirring her drink with a plastic straw.

"See you later." She turned without waiting for a response from Sarah and marched out the door.

"Who was that guy with Sarah?" Scott said in greeting as she got outside.

It was cold on the sidewalk, a steady pin-pricking drizzle blowing in from the north, so she burrowed against Scott and wrapped an arm around him.

"I don't know. Some asshole." They turned their backs to the blast of weather and walked to her car.

She looked up at Scott and her heart broke for him. His eyes were vacant, his face expressionless and sagging, his walk slow.

"I want to go back to my place," she said, determined she was going to make this man feel good the rest of the night.

He nodded.

She burrowed deeper against him as they walked, shaking the image of Carter Willis's groping hands out of her mind.

CHAPTER 21

Bass pumped out of the brightly lit Tackle Box Bar and Grill.

Wolf walked across the parking lot and a couple of young men stared at him from a darkened nook near the trees, clearly hiding something in their hands behind their backs.

Wolf sniffed the air. "Marijuana is legal now. As long as you're not driving, I don't care." He continued past them and down a wooden plank entryway, which hovered a few feet above the shimmering water.

Boats creaked on small waves generated by the cold, crisp wind that had replaced the rain and clouds.

The door wrenched open before Wolf could reach for it, and loud music and a couple dressed in weathered denim poured out. Walking arm in arm with unlit cigarettes dangling from their mouths, the couple stopped short. The man stepped to the side and held the door for Wolf.

"Sheriff," the man said.

"Thank you." Wolf stepped into the humid room. It smelled of fried bar food and beer, stale cigarette smoke, and yet more marijuana. The jukebox in the corner played an eighties hair-metal song and two women who were probably roadies back then danced in front of it while their boyfriends played pool.

Hair, leather, and chains were the overriding theme of the twenty-plus patrons inside the bar.

He walked to the counter and a younger man with a pony-tail and hemp necklace greeted him with a raised chin. "Sheriff?"

"Hello. I'm looking for someone named Maureen McKenzie. Worked here twenty-two years ago. Do you know her?"

The man nodded. "Yeah. She owns the place. She's in back." He thumbed towards a doorway behind him.

Wolf nodded and then reached down to pat his pocket when his phone began vibrating. It was going nuts.

He pulled it out and looked at it, seeing that he'd been granted a tiny sliver of cell reception, and now two voice messages and a text message were coming in.

Wolf looked at the text message. It was from Rachette.

Call me immediately. Found Parker Grey!

Wolf's pulse jumped. Looking at the voicemails and seeing they were both from Rachette, he skipped listening to them and called instead.

As the phone purred in his ear, he turned and studied the inside of the bar. A few people averted their eyes. At the sight of his badge and gun, the mood had shifted to somber impatience. People wanted to get back to using the F-word loudly, drinking their fourth or fifth or tenth beer before they got back in their cars and drove on the dirt roads to their houses.

"Hello, I'm Maureen," a husky voice came from behind him.

"Hey!" Rachette's voice exploded in his ear. "I've been trying to get hold of you!"

Wolf turned around and held up a finger to the heavy-set red-headed woman. She frowned, shook her head, and walked away.

"What's going on?" Wolf asked.

"We found Parker Grey. I'm on my way up to you right now. Where are you? I thought there wasn't any cell reception at her house."

"You found him? Where is he?"

Rachette's voice broke up.

Wolf walked away from the bar and retreated to a quiet corner without speakers. "Where is Parker Grey?"

"I didn't catch that. Where are you?"

Wolf sighed. "I'm at the marina. The Tackle Box Bar and Grill."

"I just left County now. I'm about twenty minutes away."

Wolf frowned. "Why are you still at the hospital? I thought you went back to the station."

"I did. Then I came back."

"Why?"

"I started my missing persons search with the Colorado database and got an immediate hit on one of our vics. A kid named James Trujillo. Seventeen years old. Most likely a runaway. Last seen hitchhiking north out of Alamosa six years ago."

Wolf pulled his eyebrows together. "Six years ago?"

"Six years ago."

"So Parker Grey stayed close and kept killing. You said you found him. Where is he?"

"Parker Grey is lying on a gurney in Lorber's exam room with a bullet hole in his head."

CHAPTER 22

WOLF HIT the end-call button and walked slowly to the bar, his thoughts wading through the revelation.

Maureen McKenzie stood with both hands on the bar, an expectant look in her bloodshot eyes.

Extending his hand, he gripped and shook hers, thinking of a dead trout as he did so.

"So? What can I do for you?" She coughed, and it was like a blast of radio static.

"I need to talk to you about this man." Wolf produced the photo of Parker Grey and held it out.

His thoughts wandered again to the alarm at Kimber Grey's house, and to the strange encounter at Olin Heeter's, from which the adrenaline had yet to wear off. It had been a *person*. He was sure of it. And by the looks of it, the person had been hiding inside Olin Heeter's place. If it had been Olin Heeter himself, he would have kept himself holed up inside. Only someone who was breaking and entering would have had reason to flee. And who was it? Definitely not Parker Grey.

"You listening to me, Sheriff?"

Wolf snapped out of his thoughts.

Maureen now wore red-framed glasses and stared expectantly. She took them off and dropped the photo on the bar. "What do you need?"

"Sorry ... I need to talk to you about this man."

She shrugged. "Sure. Parker Grey. Yeah, I recognize him. Like I said, go ahead and talk."

"Do you remember the night of the Fourth of July, twenty-two years ago, when Parker was here with his family watching the fireworks? He received a phone call here, at the bar.."

She nodded. "Hell yes, I do. That was the last time I saw or spoke to him." She grabbed a glass and put it under a tap, filled it halfway with beer and took a sip. "Used to be a regular here. Would come across the lake in his boat every Friday and Saturday night. You want one?" She held up her now empty glass.

"No, thanks. Can you tell me a little about that phone call he got?"

She nodded, the red skin under her chin wobbling. "Yeah. Why don't we step outside?"

He followed her out the back door to a wooden deck over the water. The weathered slats squealed under her weight with each step.

She pulled out a crinkling pack of cigarettes and lit one, and then held the pack to him.

"No thanks."

Maureen took a greedy pull and blew it out. "It was during the fireworks. I remember I was right here, watchin' 'em over the lake, right there." She tilted her head and pointed toward the moon. "And then my bartender came out and said there was someone on the phone lookin' for Parker Grey. I remember being like, 'We ain't running a secretary service,' and then Gabe —that was my bartender—said she was saying it was an emergency. So I stormed in and got on the phone, and this girl demanded to talk to Parker Grey. And I said, 'Listen, honey. He's not here in my bar, so you're out of luck.' And she started getting hysterical, like crying and stuff, and then I was kinda creeped out. I didn't want to be the one not telling him about an emergency. So I told her to hold on, and I went out to the lawn, over there by the parking lot where everyone was set up, and started looking for him."

She sucked another drag, ignoring the ash as it broke off and tumbled onto her arm.

"Can you describe the voice?" he asked. "Was it an older woman? A younger woman?"

"Younger," she said without hesitation. "Early twenties or something."

"Okay."

"Or could have been a boy, I guess."

He blinked. "If you had to bet, which one would you say it was?"

"I don't gamble. But if I had to, I'd say it was a woman. I guess she sounded too mature to be a little boy."

"So, you got the call, and then you went and found Parker?"

"Yeah. I found him pretty quick and told him he had a phone call and it sounded like an emergency. So he got up from his blanket and came in with me and talked. I didn't hear what was said. But—"

"Sorry to interrupt, but when you came out to tell him, was he with his wife and daughter, Kimber?"

She nodded. "Yeah. They were sitting on the same blanket. I remember whispering in Parker's ear, 'cause I didn't want to freak out his wife and kid about the whole thing."

"Okay, thanks. Continue please."

"Yeah. So, he came in, and I watched him on the phone for the conversation. He was talking all intense into it, ducking down and covering his mouth when he spoke and stuff. And then he just hung up all of a sudden and stormed out."

"Upset-looking?"

"Yep. Real upset looking."

"And then what?"

"I went back out here to the rear deck, and everybody watched him get in his boat and tear outta here. A couple of the guys were calling after him, asking if everything was okay. When he didn't answer, they was givin' him shit."

"So he left, without his wife and daughter?"

She nodded. "Yep."

"And did you see him come back later?"

"Yep. I was out here again. Saw him drive up in his boat. I remember we were all yelling at him again. I remember he was ignoring everyone, just like when he left. Then he came in and got his wife and daughter, and they left."

"He came in here?"

"Yeah. His wife was in here with her kid talking to people, looking to get a ride back home. But then he showed up."

"Do you remember when that was?"

"Shoot. I have no idea. Midnight?"

Wolf put his hands on the wobbly wooden railing and looked across the water. He counted seven lit cabins on the western shore, a constellation on the dark mountain on the other side of the lake. The sky was clear and speckled with stars. A full moon hung overhead, its stripe reflection slicing the lake in two.

"Thanks for your time."

"Yep."

He walked back into the bar and then out the front, hearing raucous laughter as the door shut behind him.

He reached his SUV in the parking lot and stood patiently

waiting for Rachette. A vehicle approached, but it was a black Mercedes Benz SUV with Idaho plates.

His cell phone indicated no missed calls, which was disappointing. He pushed Sarah's number and listened to it go to voicemail after two rings.

With growing impatience, he gazed across the lake again. They'd pulled up those bodies, and now he couldn't shake the feeling that things were happening over there. Right now.

"Shit," he said under his breath and got in his SUV. Firing it up, he backed out and began the journey back to Kimber Grey's cabin.

CHAPTER 23

VAN WYKE's ass was killing him as he pulled into the parking lot for the Cold Lake marina.

"Says the lake is named for a temperature inversion at fifty feet under the surface. Every twenty or so years the water will flip ..." Darnell was droning on, looking at a Cold Lake brochure complete with a miniature map they'd picked up at the gas station outside of Rocky Points.

"Hello," Van Wyke murmured, slowing to a crawl as his headlights passed over the reflective paint of a Sluice County Sheriff's Department SUV.

Darnell snapped the brochure down and slipped it in the side pocket of the door.

"The guy's outside his truck. I guess we should have expected this," Darnell whispered, as if the cop could hear them. "They did just pull up eight dead bodies."

Van Wyke kept quiet as they passed. The cop watched them approach and then became preoccupied by his cell phone.

They silently parked and got out of the car. Van Wyke stretched his arms and legs. It had been a grueling drive from Boise.

He sucked in a breath, smelling the fishy scent of lake water mixed with marijuana smoke.

"Damn," Darnell said, meeting him at the back of the SUV. "Buncha hippies up here. You smell that? And with that cop right there?"

Van Wyke watched the Sheriff's Department vehicle back up and peel out of the lot, the engine revving high before shifting to the next gear. The roof lights turned on and twinkled into the distance, following the dirt road along the edge of the lake.

"Let's go." He walked toward the bumping bar.

"Yeah. Black man, middle of Hicksville, biker bar ... what could go wrong?"

Van Wyke ignored him and they went in.

Heads turned, but the patrons left them alone as they walked up to the bar. A young man with long hair and a hippy necklace put his hands on the counter.

"What can I do you guys for?"

Van Wyke leaned conspiratorially on his elbow and pulled out his PI license, which looked vaguely like a driver's license and demanded zero respect, but more often than not, he found, did the job of loosening lips.

"I'm a private investigator, looking for a sheriff's deputy. You happen to see one in here?"

The guy nodded eagerly. "Yeah. He just left."

"Do you know where he went?"

The man frowned. "No clue. Hey, Maureen. Do you know where the sheriff just went? These men were supposed to meet him."

The sheriff.

"I don't know. Who are you guys?"

Van Wyke flashed a winning smile and then his PI license again. "Private investigators working with the local Sheriff's

Department. I was supposed to meet the sheriff here." He snorted. "Typical. We don't wear an official badge, so they don't give us the time of day."

She nodded with commiseration.

"I thought I saw him leaving. Do you know where he was going? Looked like he was hauling ass along the lake."

"Oh, well then he was probably going up to Parker Grey's. He was just asking about him."

Parker Grey?

Van Wyke popped his eyes with eagerness. "You know exactly where Parker Grey lives? We'd love to catch him."

"Yeah, just follow the lake around on County 74, then turn left on County 16. Follow it down to the south a mile or so. Can't miss his place. The road dead-ends right on it. Only Parker Grey don't live there no more. Just his daughter."

Van Wyke nodded. "Really?"

"Hey, here he is. I think the sheriff just pulled up." She pointed lazily out the window toward the parking lot, and sure enough a Sluice County Sheriff's Department SUV was pulling in. "You can ask him yourself."

Van Wyke nodded, his pulse ramping up. "Thanks."

He stepped quickly for the door with Darnell following close. They marched to the parking lot, passing a different uniformed man who jogged past. It definitely wasn't the sheriff they'd just seen. This deputy was much shorter and younger.

"Hey," Van Wyke called to him. "You lookin' for the sheriff?"

The uniformed man frowned and stopped. "Yeah. Why?"

"He just peeled outta here, went up the road along the lake." Van Wyke pointed in the distance and thankfully saw the faint strobe of blue and red.

The deputy squinted and started walking back towards the lot. "Shit," he muttered, and then started running.

"Damn," Darnell said under his breath. "That was close. We were about blown. Where you goin'?"

Van Wyke hurried to the SUV. "We're following them."

CHAPTER 24

KIMBER GREY'S EYELID TWITCHED. She stepped out onto the wooden deck and all but collapsed into the railing. "Are you certain?"

"It's been confirmed by our medical examiner at the hospital. It's definitely your father's body."

She clamped her eyes shut. "I don't get it."

"Listen, I think you might be in danger," Wolf said.

She looked at him and moved her lips, but made no sound. Her eyes looked fixed in some other time, confused as her mind tried reordering her past.

"My mother?" she whispered, asking herself the question.

Wolf cleared his throat. "What about your mother?"

"I'm just trying to figure out who did this."

"There's more to it. One of the bodies was a missing person from six years ago."

Kimber's face dropped and she looked at Wolf.

They turned at the sound of crackling tires and saw the bouncing headlights coming through the trees. A few seconds later, Rachette drove down from the woods and parked in front of the cabin.

He got out quickly and came to the base of the stairs. "Everything all right?"

Wolf nodded.

Kimber said nothing.

Wolf turned to her. "Kimber, I'd like you to come into town. You may be in more danger than you think. The discovery of these bodies, it may have triggered some sort of action with this killer."

"Yeah, okay. You don't have to convince me." She walked to her doorway. "Just give me a second to get my things."

He watched her march into the house. Then he stepped down the stairs and stood next to Rachette.

"What do you think?" Rachette hitched up his duty belt and looked out toward the water.

"I think we need to come back tomorrow, scour these woods, and get back up to Olin Heeter's place and check it out."

"Olin Heeter?"

Wolf nodded. "The place on the hill up there. I was just up there and had an encounter with someone."

Rachette looked at him. "An encounter? What do you mean?"

"The house was dark, but somebody was inside. They ran out the front door and into the woods while I was around back of the place."

"Jesus."

They stood listening to the silent forest for a few minutes, hearing thumps and creaking from inside the cabin.

Rachette looked up the stairs to the cracked open door. "Where's she going to stay?"

"The Edelweiss, or some other hotel in town." Wolf cracked a smile at Rachette's disappointed face. "Did you think I was going to say 'with you?'"

"Pfft, what?" Rachette shrugged. "Yes. Yes I did."

CHAPTER 25

"THERE IT IS." Van Wyke shut off his headlights, his brakes screeching softly as he stopped on the dirt road. The dark and deserted-looking cabin loomed at the end of the road a hundred or so yards in the distance.

"What the hell were the cops doing here?" Darnell leaned forward and squinted. "And who's Blazer was that?"

Van Wyke ignored the question and the SUV rocked as he shifted into park. "And Parker Grey doesn't live here but his daughter does? How does that make any sense? His *daughter*? I don't think we're in the right spot."

Van Wyke gazed out the windshield, surveying the dark forest uphill from the cabin. "There's only one way to find out."

He grabbed his pistol and stepped out into the cool night air.

Darnell stepped out, went to the back seat, dug into his laptop bag and pulled out his own pistol. With crunching footsteps, he walked around the back of the truck and joined Van Wyke.

A howling coyote sent Van Wyke's pulse spiking, and Darnell shook his head. The forest surrounding them was pitch black and dense, and every little noise put Van Wyke on edge.

He'd come so far, thinking about this moment for over ten and a half hours, thinking about how he would get what he was right-fully owed back from the man who betrayed him.

Parker Grey. It either was him or it was not. There was only one way to find out. And if it wasn't? They were going to have a long night ahead of them, and a long day ahead tomorrow, and that was with cops everywhere. They would have to canvass door-to-door and confirm residents' IDs until they found their man.

Van Wyke clenched his teeth as he gazed down at the dark-ened cabin. If Parker Grey was their man, and this was the cabin they were looking for, there was a good chance a million in cash was inside. Van Wyke knew this because Van Wyke had watched the man take three million in cash, stacked neatly in a briefcase, twenty-five years ago.

And Van Wyke's payment for hooking the man up with people who could buy seven million dollars' worth of boats and real estate for cash, no questions asked? A signed quitclaim deed and the keys to a two-million-dollar house in the resort town of McCall, Idaho.

Van Wyke clenched his teeth, thinking of the trip up to McCall he'd made that fateful day, only to see a pile of charred ashes for a house, straight down to the charcoal foundation, surrounded by a flock of cops. That had been his payment.

Dustin Kipling, or Parker Grey, or whatever he wanted to call himself now, would regret doing that to him. He had made Van Wyke bend over backwards, calling in all sorts of favors with all sorts of unsavory people, for free. Van Wyke never worked for free.

"Looks like nobody's home," Darnell said.

"Mmm," Van Wyke said. "You have a flashlight?"

Darnell looked at him and shook his head. "Damn. Nice preparation."

Van Wyke pulled out his cell phone and looked at it. "This thing has a flashlight setting."

"Oh yeah, me too."

"Let's not use them until we get inside. Until then, let's keep out of sight. We're gonna have to stick to the trees."

He turned back toward the cabin and squinted. There was a gap in the trees to the left of the cabin, and it looked like the land just ended abruptly. There was a smooth horizontal silhouette cut against the shimmering lake. The top of a rise, he thought, or a cliff.

Van Wyke flinched at a bright flash to his right, and a slapping noise behind him at almost the same instant. Just as his mind registered the sharp crack noise that had come from the same spot, something hit Van Wyke in the face, and he watched in stunned confusion as the illuminated screen of a cell phone twirled off his jawbone to the ground in front of him. When he heard a loud bonk against the car behind him, he twisted just in time to see Darnell's head bounce off the rear door as he collapsed into a heap.

"Darnell? Darn—"

An angry zip of air next to his cheek froze him in place, and a spark on the dirt followed by a loud whining ricochet sent him diving to the ground for cover. A split second later he felt a stinging punch in his side, then his shoulder. And then his chest exploded in unimaginable pain.

He opened his eyes, and his vision swirled like he was a teenager who'd drunk too much wine. Blinking, he saw a figure out of a science-fiction movie coming at him from the trees. A dark apparition with a protruding single lens for a face, an eerie red glow within.

No. It was a person with a silenced rifle and a night-vision scope on their head, he told himself. He blinked again and tried to raise his gun, but to his surprise there was no feeling in his arms. He swallowed and gagged on coppery blood. Gasping, he grunted, trying to ask who was there.

Another punch of pain in his chest, and he lay still this time. He knew the life was ebbing from his body, and it was a sensation like falling from a great height, only there was a sickening dread. An unimaginable sense of regret.

He saw two legs step near and then the person rolled Darnell over. Digging in his jacket. Pulling out his wallet. The legs stepped toward him, and then he felt himself shift this way and that, never seeing who was doing it, because his vision had gone out.

The dread lifted.

The regret disappeared, along with everything else.

CHAPTER 26

RUNNING on fumes from five hours sleep the night before, Wolf took a sip of coffee and a bite of his chocolate-glazed donut, hoping the two would react inside his body to give him some energy. With heavy eyelids, he looked up at the clock on his office wall—8 a.m.

He looked at his cell phone for the third time in as many minutes, and there was still no missed call or text message from Sarah. It was ... what was it? It was disconcerting, he thought. She hadn't answered his late call last night, nor responded this morning. He wanted to think she was sleeping in, but she never did that.

Had he stood her up? Had she been there at his house, waiting for him all night and then left after he didn't show up? If that was the case, then why not leave a note for him?

There was a double tap on his office door.

"Come in."

Patterson poked her head in. "Still no answer at Heeter's place at Cold Lake, or his place in Ashland."

"All right." He stood up and his knee cracked, sounding like a dry stick snapping in two.

"Sir," Patterson said. She scratched the back of her neck, avoiding eye contact with him. "I need to talk to you. About last night."

His phone vibrated in his pocket and he pulled it out with a little too much enthusiasm. It was not Sarah. It was Margaret Hitchens.

"It's your aunt," Wolf said. "I can talk to her later."

"No, no ... please. Take it. We'll talk later. It's nothing."

He narrowed his eyes, sensing it was clearly not nothing. The phone wriggled again and stopped. "Tell me. What is it?"

She rolled her eyes. "I ... last night I was out with Sarah ... I mean, I was out with Scott. And his parents."

He crossed his arms.

"Anyways, long story short, it sucked, but that's not the point. On the way out, I saw Sarah." She closed her eyes. "Shit, I shouldn't be shoving my nose in other people's business."

"You saw Sarah." Wolf waited for the small jolt in his body to dissipate. "So what?"

"She was with a guy. Some big dude with fancy clothes on. Name was Carter Willis. I went up and introduced myself."

Wolf nodded, controlling his breath. "Yeah?"

"And ... I don't know. Aren't you two dating?"

He stared at her, considering the implications of the question. Were Sarah and Carter acting more than friendly with one another?

"Not really," he said.

"Oh. I thought you guys were. I guess ... I don't know. Never mind." Patterson shook her head and walked out his door.

"Hey," Wolf called.

She turned.

"Thanks."

"Of course."

Who was this guy? One thing he knew: If Carter Willis was a gay former colleague of hers, then Wolf was a billionaire.

He sighed and looked at his phone again. Against his better judgment he called back Margaret Hitchens.

"Hey, how's it going, Sheriff?"

"Hi, Margaret. Fine. What's happening?"

"Are you around?"

Wolf leaned to the side and peeked through the open blinds of his window, then ducked back when he saw Margaret's face pressed against the window of her real-estate storefront office across the street.

"No." Wolf pulled his chair over and sat down out of sight.

"Oh, I thought you were there."

"What's going on?"

"Oh, I wish you were there. I have great news." There was a rattling in the background, and then the sound of a door slamming shut.

"Well I'm not, so what is it?"

"Geez, you wake up on the wrong side? Never mind, let me help your mood. Because of your ineptitude with a lasso, you've helped your campaign." She was breathing hard.

"Oh. Good."

"Oh good? That's all you have to say?" There was the sound of a door opening and closing in the background, and hurried footsteps.

Wolf took the phone away from his ear and hung up.

Margaret burst into his office with phone in hand.

"Good morning, Margaret. I'm glad Tammy is just letting you in whenever you want now."

She stopped and put her hands on her hips. "She knows how to treat your campaign manager. Maybe you could learn a thing or two. You know, the employees in this building are counting on us, too. No one wants to work for that asshole, MacLean."

"Really? I hadn't thought of that. Sit."

"No thanks. Move." She came around the desk and grabbed his computer mouse. "Have you seen this?"

Wolf marveled at this sixty-year-old woman's vivacious hunger for winning; and watching her in action, he was suddenly more grateful than ever that he'd employed Margaret Hitchens for his campaign manager.

Employed wasn't the right word, Wolf thought. He hadn't *employed* Margaret Hitchens, because he wasn't paying her a dime, and he had had nothing to do with her working for him in the first place. It was more like she'd stepped forward and recruited him. She had demanded she run his campaign, and had vowed—with a look in her eye that had made Wolf swallow —that he would win no matter what.

She clicked the mouse and stood back. "There."

Wolf leaned forward and watched a shaky video of him failing at lassoing a calf, and then failing again. The video cut, and then he was failing again.

"Yeah. I've seen this first hand." Wolf snatched up his empty coffee cup and walked to his door.

"You're missing the best part."

Wolf paused and looked back.

A deep male voice bellowed over the speakers. "David Wolf for sheriff. He never gives up in a fight. Never fails to finish what he's started. Never ..."

Wolf shook his head and walked into the hallway, poured himself a cup of coffee, and walked back into his office.

Margaret was standing now, arms folded with a disappointed look. "David, I turned this into a commercial, put it up on Channel 17, and then up on the local for Ashland, and now all the news channels are showing it this morning. Look at the number of views on this YouTube video. That's like two views per capita of Byron and Sluice counties combined!

"It's perfect. MacLean comes barging in with his photographers, and ends up making you the star." She shook her head in astonishment. "Oh, the irony. I wish I could have seen his face when that commercial came on. I bet he laughed. Thought we were kicking ourselves. And I bet he's shitting his pants now. It's perfect footage, showing exactly the type of man you are. And *right* before the debate."

Wolf took a sip, feeling a fish wriggle in his gut at the thought of speaking in front of a large, sweaty audience with cameras pointed at his face, being broadcast to thousands of homes.

"Are you done? I kind of have a lot of work to do today, with eight dead bodies showing up at the lake and all."

She frowned. "You have eight bodies, but you have a debate that can make or break your future tomorrow night. Don't you forget that."

"Yeah." He set his cup on the desk. "How could I forget?"

She softened her look and walked to him, placing her wiry hands on his shoulders.

"I know you're nervous. But the more you know that packet I gave you front and back, the more relaxed you're going to be. The more confident in front of the cameras you'll be."

Wolf tightened his lips into a line and nodded.

"Pop quiz. What are you going to say about the pension issue?" she asked.

Wolf eased past her to his seat and pulled himself on the wheels to his desk. "That I like pensions."

She rolled her eyes. "Okay. Okay. I'll let you get to work. Just study that damn packet." She looked around the room. "Where is it?"

Wolf pulled his desk drawer open, took out the packet of papers, showed it to her, and dropped it back in.

She pointed at him. "Study it, David. Two days, today and tomorrow. You have two days to study."

He nodded. "Yep."

"So are you ready for the good news now?" She clenched her fists and her face shook with a wide smile.

"There's more?" Wolf looked at his watch and stood. "Look, I've got a situation meeting in five minutes."

"Senator Chama wants to talk to you. Tonight."

"I thought he was all for MacLean."

"He was. Until this." She pointed at the computer. "I'm telling you, this video is spreading like wildfire through beetle-kill trees. He called me this morning after they aired it on *Denver News*."

"And he wants to meet me tonight? On a Sunday night?"

She shrugged with a chipper face that made Wolf want to bend over the trashcan.

His phone rang and he looked at her with raised eyebrows.

"Yeah. All right. I'm outta here. Chama's coming here tonight at six p.m. So be here, or I'll murder *you* and throw you in the lake."

Wolf picked up the phone. "Sheriff Wolf ... Hi, Mr. Frehauf. I was hoping you could meet me today to talk for a bit..."

Margaret waited with folded arms until Wolf finished. He hung up and walked past her. "I've got a meeting, Margaret. I'll see you later."

"Six o'clock." She followed him down the hall. "Don't forget!"

CHAPTER 27

WOLF STOOD at the front of the situation room with a pen in hand, waiting for his five on-duty deputies to take their seats around the large rectangular table.

As they sat, slits of morning sun came in through the blinds and lit up swirls of steam rising from their coffees. Along with caffeine, each deputy had a stapled packet of paper with them— the photocopied report Burton and Wolf's father had compiled on the case twenty-two summers ago.

"All right," Wolf said. "Let's go over what we've got."

"We've got a sick bastard killing people," Baine said with a humorless chuckle.

"Let's talk about the father." Wolf wrote Parker Grey's name on the board.

"He's dead," Rachette said.

"I still want to talk about him."

"He fits the bill as the killer," Wilson said. "We've got Katherine Grey's testimony on video that he came back with blood on his clothing. And then," Wilson pointed at Wolf with a pen, "your father and Burton tracked down that psychiatrist in Grand Junction, and confirmed his diagnosis. Schizophrenic, with psychotic tendencies. The doctor said he told Parker Grey that he could legally put him in the loony bin, because of the murdered-squirrel story he admitted to. The doctor said Parker Grey was potentially a danger to himself or others. Prescribed him anti-psychotics."

"Where's that psychiatrist now?" Wolf asked.

"Dead." Wilson said. "Natural causes."

"Yeah, there's just that one big problem," Rachette said. "We found the father's body with the other victims. So that means it wasn't him."

"Just because we found the father's body doesn't mean he's exonerated," Patterson said.

"Agreed," Lorber's voice barked out of the laptop in the center of the table. "Thanks to the cold water of the lake, it's impossible to know when Parker Grey died exactly. He could have disappeared on the fifth of July, gone into hiding and gone on killing, and then he was killed himself."

"By someone else, years down the road." Patterson finished his thought.

"With a bullet to the head, mind you, not the same MO as the other kills. Maybe his kills were the decapitations, and someone killed him with the gun." On the computer screen, Lorber bit a donut.

"And dumped him in the same place as the other victims?" Wilson's face was skeptical.

Wolf scribbled on the pen board. "Timeline," he said. "Let's go over what we absolutely know, and when."

Patterson raised her pen. "Nick Pollard goes missing twenty-two years ago."

Wolf wrote that.

Rachette cleared his throat. "And we've got the phone call coming from the Pumapetrol gas station down the road the night of the fourth. Call went out at 9:39 p.m. according to the phone company records from twenty-two years ago. Burton and your father found Nick Pollard's blood on the receiver of that phone. So I think that we can definitely say Nick Pollard died that night, sometime before 9:39 p.m."

"Not necessarily," Patterson said. "He went missing that night. His blood was put on the phone at 9:39. But died? He could have been wounded, and some girl was helping him. She gets his blood on her hand, calls Parker Grey from that payphone at the gas station ... and then Parker Grey comes and picks her up."

The room went silent.

Baine scrunched his face. "Why?"

"I'm just saying. We don't know what happened. All we know is, there's Nick Pollard's blood on the phone, and when the phone call went out."

Wolf sipped his coffee and turned back to the board. "All right. We've got Nick Pollard: missing twenty-two years ago. Parker Grey: missing two days later, on the sixth of July. Katherine Grey: she bolts a day after that, on the seventh of July, supposedly goes back home to Tennessee, which no one has been able to confirm. James Trujillo's body is in with the others—he went missing six years ago, last seen in Alamosa, Colorado. What else do we have on him?"

Baine held up a finger. "I talked to the Alamosa PD. James Trujillo's grandmother reported him missing six years ago. She's since deceased, and there are no other next of kin. They stopped looking for him before they started, because the grandmother was apparently on all sorts of medication, and they thought he just left on his own accord."

Lorber's voice croaked through the speakers. "But we now know he was stabbed fifteen times, slit from the stomach to the neck, decapitated, and then thrown into Cold Lake in a plastic bag."

The room went silent.

"Thanks, Doc," Rachette said. "Maybe you could sing it next time?"

"The point is," Wolf said, "we know that whoever is responsible for these grisly killings has been doing it at least up until six years ago." He turned to Wilson and then Rachette. "How we doing on those missing-persons database searches."

Wilson held up a hand. "Real slow. I've got no other confirmed IDs."

"None of the DNA samples are done," Lorber said. "But I do want to say, the timeline of Nick Pollard's death is looking to be a lot earlier than six years ago. The decomposition has been stalled, but his body is nowhere near as pristine as James Trujillo's. And neither is Parker Grey's. I'm going to start testing, using Trujillo's body decomposition at six years, and I'll be able to extrapolate when the others were killed give or take a few years. But nothing definitive."

Wolf paced in front of the room. "Okay. Thanks, Doc. The fingerprints on the phone? We've triple-checked those, right?"

"Still no match in any database," Patterson said.

"And," Baine chimed in, "where the hell is Pollard's truck? That thing just vanished off the face of the earth back then. It's gotta be in the lake."

Wilson shook his head. "They ran sonar around the entire perimeter of the lake back in the day. Never found anything."

"Then they didn't look deep enough," Baine said.

"And how is someone going to dump a truck *deeper* into the lake?" Rachette scoffed. "You can only get it out so far, and they checked already."

"I don't know, jump it off one of those cliffs?"

"Pfft, those cliffs aren't over the water. They're over land."

"So someone took the plates off, scrapped it, sold it, painted it, whatever."

"Then I guess you have your answer," Rachette said.

Baine sank back in his seat, glaring daggers at Rachette.

"Pollard's yellow Toyota pickup truck." Wolf wrote it. "Good question. And here's another. What if Parker Grey was killed on the sixth? Where's *his* truck?"

Wolf scribbled that question on the board.

Patterson cleared her throat. "Like Rachette said, they scoured the edges of that lake. It doesn't look like Parker Grey's truck or Nick Pollard's pickup are in there. But we could get the sonar guys to do another lap."

Wolf nodded. "It's probably a good idea. Let's talk about the neighbor, Olin Heeter."

Patterson raised a hand. "I checked property records this morning. Olin Heeter was the original owner of the land and structure the Greys bought. Olin Heeter quitclaimed it to Parker Grey twenty-five years ago. There's a cash transfer on record of one hundred thousand dollars. I'm not an IRS agent, but that sounds fishy to me. There's over sixty acres and a house on the land. Seems worth more than that, even twenty-five years ago. But I could be wrong. Otherwise, Olin Heeter also has a primary residence down south, in Ashland.

"His phone number was listed so I called it. No one answered there, either. The guy is seventy-one years old. Vietnam veteran. Wife is deceased, died of a heart attack three years ago." She upturned hands. "I can't find him."

"And no sightings up at his place in Cold Lake?" Wolf asked.

Yates cleared his throat. "I'm headed back up after this meeting. I'll ask around and report back ASAP."

"Good." Wolf nodded. "All right. Let's talk about Kimber Grey."

"I think she's fishy," Baine said.

"More like bat-shit crazy," Rachette said.

Patterson fluttered her lips.

"What?" Rachette asked. "Looks to me like she's the only one left standing. Dad's dead. Mom's gone. She's sittin' pretty."

"We have no evidence." Patterson shrugged. "And I know what I just argued before, but if Nick Pollard was killed the night of the fourth, before that payphone call was made, we have plenty of witnesses that put Kimber at the marina all night. And it's not her fingerprints in Nick Pollard's blood on the phone. The rest of her story, being locked up in a room all night, I could take with a grain of salt, but facts are facts. If Nick Pollard died that night, she didn't do it."

Rachette picked up his packet. "Says here that Olin Heeter told Burton and Wolf's father that he was"—Rachette flipped a page— "quote: 'Painting the moon on the sixth of July and saw Parker Grey out in his boat dumping something in the water. I saw it clear as day, because it was right in the reflection.' End quote. Parker Grey, according to Kimber and her mother, was supposedly gone on the sixth. The same day."

Wolf folded his arms. "Olin Heeter might have assumed it was Parker Grey just because it was his boat. If Kimber and her mom were telling the truth about Parker leaving, on that same day, then that means they could have been the ones out there dumping something."

"Yeah, and now we're pulling up bodies," Baine said.

The room went silent again.

"So what does all this mean?" Yates asked.

"It's what I like to call a whole lot of nothing," Lorber said through the tinny laptop speaker.

Wolf put the pen down and looked at the dejected faces. "We're not going to solve the case in here. We've gotta get out there and work it. It's been sitting dormant for twenty-two years, and it's cold."

Baine shrugged. "And what do we do? Just go through the

same leads your dad and Burton did? They were pretty good cops, and they never found anything."

"But we have something they didn't. Like you said, we have bodies. In the end, my father and Burton were stumped. A crew of rescue divers couldn't find anything. The sonar wasn't as advanced back then, the bodies were down deep, and apparently my father was diving in the wrong spot. In the end, they had to assume Nick's blood was on that phone because," Wolf shrugged, "because who knew why. But we have Nick Pollard's body.

"But, like we said, we have no time of death for any of these bodies."

"I'll keep working on it," Lorber said through the speakers.

Wolf rolled his neck, stretching a kink that tightened by the second. "I'm meeting Chad Frehauf, the Pumapetrol gas station clerk who worked the night the phone call was made. Yates, make your way back up there to Heeter's place on the lake. Wilson, you're going up with him. If there's no answer, I want you to check the surrounding woods, check out his boat."

Wolf forked his fingers. "Patterson and Rachette, you'll go to Heeter's other place in Ashland."

"Does that mean we have to work with Byron SD?" Rachette asked.

Wolf nodded.

"Oh. Great."

"I'll call MacLean and tell him you're on your way. Let's move, people."

"What about me?" Baine sat up straight.

"You stay in town and keep an eye on Kimber Grey."

Baine raised his eyebrows and nodded.

"An eye." Rachette got up and the room burst into motion. "And that's it."

CHAPTER 28

WOLF PULLED into the parking lot of Pumapetrol Gas and got out.

Rachette honked twice as he and Patterson coasted by toward Ashland.

He waved without looking and shut his door. Twisting on his heels, he felt the warmth of the morning sun on his back. Maybe June would finally make an appearance today. He stood tall and stretched his arms overhead, and then reached into his cab and picked up the Nick Pollard file folder from his passenger seat.

Slamming his door, he turned and stared at the skeleton of a payphone mounted on the cinderblock south wall of the gas station. The phone book had been ripped off, the handset had been severed and taken by SCSD twenty-two years ago, and the body of the phone looked like it had been beaten to death with something blunt. The file in Wolf's hand reported that the last person to use this phone in working condition had Nick Pollard's blood on their hands. Twenty-two years ago, they failed to identify a person to the fingerprints, and even with the exponential growth of the databases since, the prints yielded no further explanation now.

What did that mean?

The person, a woman, killed Nick Pollard and then came and used the phone to call Parker Grey? Or the woman—or teenager, or young woman, or boy—injured Nick Pollard, used the phone to call Parker Grey, and then Parker came to pick said person up and finished Nick off with a mutilation ritual killing? Then brought his body up to the lake and dumped it in? Or perhaps the person had gotten blood on their hands trying to help Nick Pollard.

A rumbling engine came up from the south and pulled Wolf from his thoughts. A beat-up mid-eighties full-sized Chevy pickup lumbered in and rocked to a stop next to his SUV.

The door squeaked open and slammed shut, sounding like a muffled gong. A man walked up with a dirty trucker hat twisted sideways, covering a head of long, greasy hair, his thumbs tucked into grease-stained and ripped jeans. The rest of him was covered in denim that looked like it had never touched a bit of soap.

"Mr. Frehauf?" Wolf asked.

Frehauf reached in his jacket pocket and pulled out a crumpled pack of Marlboros. In a practiced move, he tipped one into his mouth and lit it, took a deep drag, and kept it dangling from his lips.

Wolf held out a hand, and shook Frehauf's thin and sweaty grip.

"You remember the Fourth of July, twenty-two years ago?" Wolf asked with a wry smile.

Frehauf exhaled and pinched an eye shut against the rising smoke. "Nope."

His chest rattled rhythmically, like rocks in a coffee can, and Wolf took this to be a laugh. "Just kiddin'. I do remember. Cause

I remember that deputy comin' and talkin' to me about that night. I'm not sure how helpful I was. Or how helpful I can be now, though."

"Says here you talked to a Deputy Burton from our department."

"Yeah, I guess. What do you need to know that I ain't already told that deputy?"

Wolf shifted, turning his back to the sun, eying the crossroads a couple of hundred yards to the north. A car came into view down County 74 from the direction of Cold Lake and slowed to a stop at the junction before turning away north on 734 towards the forested Williams Pass and Rocky Points beyond.

"My report says you stated someone in a black Chevy Blazer drove down County 74, from Cold Lake, and into the gas-station parking lot that night."

Frehauf pursed his lips and jetted a plume. "Yeah. Pulled in right here."

Wolf consulted the report. "Says here it was about 10:30 p.m. Probably kind of difficult to remember that with all the people coming in and out of the station that night. After all, it was the Fourth of July ... wasn't it busy?"

Frehauf shrugged. "Half and half. Half the night it was dead. Busy before the fireworks show though. A whole mess of people came in from both directions, buyin' beer, snacks, stuff like that, before they made their way up to the lake. A lot of young folks. Then it was dead for a spell, up until about midnight when they started comin' back down.

"That's how I remembered the Blazer, because it came down early, before the rest of the crowd. It was the only truck I seen for an hour, right in the middle of the dead spell. It pulled in all slow, and parked on the side of the building. Right here where we're standing, I guess. Only nobody got out and came inside. He just drove into the lot. I remembered seein' the headlights flashin' around. Course I couldn't see him from where I was inside"—he sucked another drag— "and then that same Blazer just went past the windows and headed up 734. That way." Frehauf pointed north towards Williams Pass.

"You don't remember seeing anyone inside the vehicle?"

"Nope."

"I notice you keep using the word *him*."

"Yeah, I don't know. I guess it was kind of a manly vehicle. And it was drivin' around like a man. I don't know. Guess it could have been a woman. Shit."

"You're sure it was a Blazer?"

"Yeah. A Blazer. You know, all boxy and big. Chevy."

"And what about outside before the Blazer came in? Did you see anyone in the parking lot hanging around? A girl or a woman?"

Frehauf shook his head. "Like I told that deputy back then, I didn't see anyone hangin' around. I woulda' been spooked and remembered that. I was working alone on my second night on the job. Middle of nowhere. Middle of the night, know what I'm sayin'? Spooky. Specially for a rookie."

Wolf pulled out a picture of Nick Pollard's beat-up yellow Toyota pickup. "How about this truck?"

"I'm tellin' ya, it's like I said back then, I don't remember anything but that Blazer comin' down. I remember it because it was during the dead time. Anything before that or after, when it was hoppin' with kids buying beer and hotdogs, I was like a chicken with my head cut off. Tryin' to learn the register, tryin' to bag hotdogs and taquitos. Them kids were rippin' me off, a whole mess of 'em in here." Frehauf shook his head and chuckled. "But I do remember that Blazer."

Frehauf took a deep drag down to the filter and dropped the

cigarette on the ground. "That all? I gotta do some grocery shoppin'."

Wolf nodded. "Yeah, go ahead. And thanks for your time."

Frehauf pointed at Wolf and clicked his tongue, then walked around the front of the store and went inside.

Wolf twisted his heel on the smoldering filter, burying it deep into the dirt. He walked to the payphone. Then he walked along the edge of the building toward the front. Countless cigarette butts, pop-tops, cellophane pull strips from cigarette packs, and other crap was strewn on the ground—decades of convenience-store litter blown into a drift against the wall.

He rounded the corner and peeked in the windows, which made up the entire front of the building.

The cash register was right on the other side of the glass. Frehauf would not have been able to see someone hanging out by the payphone, Wolf deduced, because his back would have been up against the interior of the concrete wall. The man behind the register looked over his shoulder at Wolf and widened his eyes. With a sheepish grin he saluted Wolf, and Wolf returned the gesture.

Inside, Chad Frehauf was bringing a case of beer to the register and he set it down, nodding at Wolf through the window.

Wolf backtracked and went to his SUV, opened the passenger door and set the report on the seat.

Frehauf came around the corner, lighting another cigarette, juggling the case of beer as he did so.

Wolf picked up the report, closed his door, and walked to the edge of the road and studied the stop sign terminating County 74, and then up Highway 734 until it bent out of sight.

"Mr. Frehauf. It says here in this report that you told the deputy you saw the Chevy Blazer drive away up County 74."

Frehauf blew out a puff and frowned. He shook his head,

then pushed out his lips again. "What? No, I said he went up 734." He twisted and pointed straight up the highway towards the north, like he had done minutes earlier, not up the road to the west towards Cold Lake.

"You're sure?"

"Yeah. I mean ... I remember he didn't go back up the road the way he came down. Went up 734 towards Williams Pass."

Wolf looked at the report again.

Burton's handwriting said, *Mr. Frehauf pointed in the direction of the junction of County 74 and Highway 734 and told me "I saw the Blazer (vehicle in question) take off up County 74."*

"Mr. Frehauf. You said it was your second day on the job that night?"

"Yep. I was fresh into town from Mississippi. My sister lived in Ashland down the road. Got me this job. Her friend used to own this joint. Mississippi was gettin' to me, know what I'm sayin'? Hot as shit down there."

Wolf nodded patiently. "Do you think that you may have said the wrong road all those years ago? I mean, County 74 and Highway 734 ... kind of sound the same, don't they? Maybe you accidently said 74 instead of 734."

Frehauf narrowed one eye and then looked at the ground, trying to access a memory. With a start, he pointed a finger at Wolf and then bounced it up and down. "You know, my sister ... oh man." Frehauf took a drag. "I remember my sister and I got into it once back then, because I gave her directions to a ... shit, I'm just gonna tell you, seein' it's legal and all now ... a *weed* hook-up."

Wolf nodded.

"I told her directions off of 74, but I meant 734. Got her all sorts of lost. She was pee-issed. So yeah, I guess I could have done that same thing."

CHAPTER 29

PATTERSON WATCHED Rachette squirm in his seat to get a better look in the side-view mirror.

She unbuckled her seat belt. "Here goes nothing."

"Do you think it's him? I hate that we have to work with him."

"I guess we'll find out."

Patterson stepped out onto the dirt road and shielded the sun with her hand. She watched the Byron County Sheriff's Department SUV blow past them, turn into Olin Heeter's driveway, and park.

As the vehicle passed she caught a glimpse inside the windows and confirmed it was MacLean, along with that creepy undersheriff who was latched to him all the time.

She closed the door and looked around the rural country on the outskirts of Ashland. Ashland and Rocky Points, and it's surrounding terrain, were as different as cross-country and alpine skiing. The town of Ashland was bigger and more popu-lated but, to Patterson's taste, infinitely less appealing with its vast expanse of flat land in between the north–south oriented mountain-range strips that ran the length to Williams Pass in the north and out of sight into a haze to the south. Rocky Points was quainter among trees. Here there were none; only low sage brush and other fragrant foliage that made her nose itch.

A university town, Ashland had a thriving population of young people who tended to inhale as much marijuana smoke as oxygen on any given day. It was a short distance from Rocky Points Ski Resort over the pass to the north, so students with a hunger for mountain living flocked here from every corner of the country. Liquor stores and take-out restaurants thrived, and houses were generally drab and utilitarian, owned by out-of-towners who rented to the students. Properties with any money dumped into them were few and far between. And looking at Olin Heeter's place, he'd dumped his money into his lake house, not here.

"Nice abode," Rachette said, hitching his duty belt up and smoothing out his shirt. His eyes were anywhere but on Olin Heeter's place.

"Deputies." MacLean stood by his passenger door, appraising them. "Sheriff Wolf couldn't make it?"

"No, sir." Rachette stepped in front of Patterson with an outstretched hand. "Deputy Rachette, sir."

Patterson moved in next, wondering why they were introducing themselves by name. MacLean had already called them by name at the lake, but she did it anyway. "Sir, Deputy Patterson."

MacLean smiled and looked between the two of them. Nodding in silence for a few moments, he seemed to reach a conclusion.

Patterson gestured to the one-story ranch house, ignoring the tall man staring at them on the other side of the vehicle. "Thanks for meeting us here, gentlemen. We'd just like to speak to Mr. Heeter. Ask him a few questions."

MacLean turned toward the house. "This isn't our best area of Ashland."

She decided to not respond to that and focused on the house. The front porch was cracked concrete, sinking on one side. The siding was cream-colored, warping and deteriorating, and the roof fit the same bill—canoeing big time in the middle. A single-car garage in front of MacLean's vehicle was covered by an off-kilter roll door.

"Okay. Let's do it. I'll let you two do the talking." MacLean walked quickly to the front door.

"Sounds good," Rachette said, walking on his heels.

"You two ever met my undersheriff?" MacLean asked, not breaking stride. "A good man to get to know. He'll be my right-hand man moving forward."

Patterson suppressed her revulsion as she noticed that the undersheriff was staring at her.

Rachette paused and looked up at the man. "Hi. Undersheriff Lancaster, right?"

Lancaster looked at Rachette like he was an annoying dog and shook his hand. His gaze slid off Rachette and slathered up and down Patterson.

She narrowed her eyes and shook his hand, keeping contact with the man's ape-like grip to a minimum.

They walked to the porch and MacLean rapped on the door. "Sheriff's Department!"

They waited for several moments with no response.

Rachette eased his way next to MacLean.

"What are we doing here, Deputies?" MacLean asked without eye contact to either of them.

Rachette cleared his throat. "We pulled those bodies out of the lake, sir. Twenty-two years ago, Mr. Heeter said he saw someone dump something in the lake. We need to clear that up."

MacLean eyed Rachette. "Is Olin Heeter a suspect?"

Rachette shrugged.

"No, sir," Patterson said. "But definitely a person of interest."

MacLean nodded and reached for the doorknob. He twisted and pushed, but it was locked. "Do you have any suspects?"

Patterson frowned. "Sir, we don't have probable cause to enter the premises."

MacLean looked over his shoulder at his undersheriff. "You smell that?" He sniffed, pushing his mustache up against his nostrils. "Smells like rotting flesh to me."

Lancaster remained motionless and mute.

MacLean stepped off the porch and walked to the single-car garage. "Open this up."

Patterson and Rachette exchanged a glance and Rachette followed after him.

"Deputy Rachette, Lancaster, I want you two to search the property. I want to know if this man is here. Deputy Patterson, come over here and speak with me, please."

Patterson's face flushed. "Sir?"

Without responding, MacLean walked to his rear door and opened it. After a second of fishing inside he stood up with a manila envelope.

Patterson stood dumbfounded until MacLean craned a finger in her direction. She looked over at Rachette; he was eyeing them with trepidation as Lancaster yanked the garage door up from the bottom.

"No car."

Lancaster's voice was deep, and Patterson realized she'd never heard the man speak until now.

"Go around back and check it out."

Lancaster nodded and walked around the house.

Rachette stood unsurely, looking at MacLean, the envelope in his hand, and then at Patterson.

"Around back." MacLean pointed.

"Yes, sir." Rachette walked after Lancaster.

MacLean smiled. "Okay. Now that we're alone, I have a few things for you."

"Things for me?"

MacLean went to the back of his SUV and opened the hatch. He beckoned her there and held out the envelope. "Open it. You can use the back here as a desk if you'd like."

"What is this?" She joined him and grabbed for the envelope, but he pulled it back out of her reach.

"It's bad news for you and your partner, I'm afraid." He dropped the envelope inside the rear of the vehicle. "Go ahead."

Patterson's face went hot at this man playing games with her, and she nearly told him to shove the envelope up his ass. But instead, she picked it up.

With shaky fingers, she bent the metal prongs, opened the flap, and saw a thick stack of glossy photographs inside. She took them out and frowned at the top photo.

It was a close-up shot from a distance of Rachette with a girl. The girl was bent over, digging inside the trunk of a beat-up blue Subaru. Rachette stood next to her in plain clothes, jeans, and a green T-shirt, hands on hips, looking over his shoulder.

She eyed MacLean.

His eyes glittered with amusement. "Go on."

She flipped to the next photo and put the first one face down on the rubber mat in the vehicle's rear.

The girl had stood up now, holding a red backpack by one strap. Rachette was now looking at the backpack, otherwise unmoved.

The next photo was the girl closing the trunk, Rachette staring at her ass.

The woman faced the camera in the next photo, her eyes closed as she brushed long blonde hair behind her ear. Rachette stared at her, looking mesmerized by her movements.

Patterson flipped to the next photo.

"Ah, here it is." MacLean tapped the glossy picture.

Patterson finally comprehended what she was looking at.

The next image had been taken a moment later, and the woman was handing the backpack to Rachette. He was taking it with a dumb-looking smile.

Patterson flipped faster now, the anger rising—at Rachette, and at this cologne-drenched asshole standing next to her, who in a month was going to be her new boss.

Next photo: Rachette with the backpack slung on his shoulder, embracing the woman in a close hug. The woman's back was arched a little, her hips pressing into his.

Next photo: The woman walking to her driver's-side door, Rachette adjusting his crotch.

Next photo: Rachette at the open rear door of his own beat-up Volkswagen. The backpack being tossed into the back seat. Rachette looking longingly over his shoulder at the woman driving away.

Patterson's stomach dropped with the next photo. It was a mugshot of the woman taken at the Byron county jail, time-stamped two months ago with a booking number rather than a name. The girl was beautiful, no older than her early twenties. Her brown eyes were vacant of emotion, her face slack. Patterson was used to seeing pockmarks, scabs, bruises, unkempt hair, bloodshot eyes, and other unattractive qualities in mugshot photos. Not this woman, though. She was clean-looking. Her skin was smooth and flawless.

Behind the mugshot was a two-page stapled copy of a Byron County police report dated the same as the mugshot.

There was movement around the left side of the house.

"No way in, sir," Rachette said.

Patterson looked up from the paper in her hand and instinctively leaned forward to hide it in the SUV's rear, though Rachette wouldn't have been able to see a thing from such a distance.

"Go ahead, keep reading," MacLean said under his breath as he walked away. "Okay, I'll head back with you two. Did you check the windows?"

Patterson watched the three men round the side of the house and out of sight, Rachette in the rear like an excited dog.

She read the report. Byron County Sheriff's Department had stopped the woman, Gail Olson, for speeding on 734. A search of her car produced twenty-two pounds of pot and one hundred thousand dollars in cash.

Patterson whistled. Twenty-two pounds of pot was far beyond the legal possession limit of one ounce, especially since the woman did not have a distributor's or grower's license, or any documentation connecting her to a legitimate business in Colorado.

Under questioning, the woman admitted to acting as a runner for an illegal grow op. Though she stated she was unaware of the details of the operation, Patterson knew it was probably a group of shady individuals exporting illegally out of the state and/or the country. And if she'd read the previous photos of this woman and Rachette correctly, Rachette was her latest recruit.

"Oh yeah, that's what I said." Rachette laughed with the sheriff as they came around the side of the house again.

MacLean looked genuinely interested in Rachette's story. Lancaster followed silently, walking like Lurch.

She put on a poker face and tucked everything back into the manila envelope, then stepped away from the vehicle.

Rachette's expression went flat when he eyed Patterson and

the envelope she carried, but rebounded brighter than ever when MacLean smacked his back.

"All right. Tell your sheriff you didn't see a car. Did you find a car up at the lake?"

"We haven't checked his place up there, yet," Rachette said. "Sheriff Wolf knocked on his door last night. No answer. He never said anything about a vehicle."

MacLean nodded. "Well, better check back up there."

Patterson flicked a nod to the open garage door. "As long as you're bent on going inside, there's a door to the house in the garage."

MacLean looked and Rachette and Lancaster followed his gaze.

"Yeah. So there is," MacLean said. "Rachette, go check it out."

Rachette walked into the garage, sidestepping wood debris on the floor.

MacLean stepped over to Patterson. "Show those to Sheriff Wolf by tonight, please." His voice was low and malicious. "Tell him I'll be in touch."

"Locked!" Rachette yelled from the garage.

"All right," MacLean said with finality. "I think we're done here. We'll follow up for you later, see if he comes home. Close up the garage."

MacLean went around the back of the SUV and closed the hatch door. He locked eyes with Patterson, and his expression said, *By tonight, or else.*

CHAPTER 30

WOLF'S TIRES scraped and he cranked the wheel hard to the right to compensate. The final descent of the dirt road to the tailing pond was steep and he'd taken it at a little too much speed.

Bouncing in his seat, he decided to let off the brake and let it ride to the bottom, rather than risk sliding sideways. Bouncing wildly, the SUV rolled for a few more yards until it flattened out, and with a sigh of relief he slowed to a stop next to the water.

He turned off the engine and got out.

Closing his door, he walked to the rear of the SUV and twisted full circle. Across the water, a hole in the mountain, once an entrance to a mine, gaped halfway up the slope. Underneath it a color-streaked plume of rock ran down to the orange-red pond Wolf stood next to now.

The engine ticked rapidly and the scent of burning brake pads wafted across his nose. Wolf looked at the ground under his feet and back up the road he'd come in on. The land around the pond was relatively flat, but it was going to take some serious clawing in four-wheel drive to get back out. All in all, the place was relatively inaccessible.

The pond was about as big as half a football field, tinted Denver Bronco orange by what he assumed to be acid mine drainage.

He pulled out his phone and looked at it, surprised that, even in the crater-like depression, he still had a sliver of cell reception.

With a tap of his finger he pulled up the map function again and stared at it.

One point four miles of road, most of it dirt, connected Wolf's location to the Pumapetrol gas station.

He cocked an ear and heard the sound of a trickling stream along the far edge of the pond.

He walked the shoreline, studying the surface carefully. When a tiny eddy swirled, he kept his eyes glued to the spot, picked up a rock and threw it.

The water splooshed within a yard of where Wolf had aimed, and a fish flopped, splashing water before disappearing.

With a resigned sigh, he stripped off his clothes to his boxer shorts, and after a few seconds of rapid breathing to psych himself up, he stepped into the water.

He clenched his teeth, feeling the biting cold and occasional jagged rock beneath his feet as he waded in. Soon he was waist deep, and then, with a gasp, his crotch submerged. A few more yards out, his teeth chattered as the water reached to his shoulders. Then he lifted his feet and kicked, swimming a slow breaststroke toward the center of the pond.

Only a moment later, he was pulling his thighs toward his body when they collided with a line of jagged metal.

CHAPTER 31

"I'm telling you, you need to learn how to be more person-able with these guys."

Patterson stared out her window at the passing sagebrush, opting to remain silent through Rachette's rambling.

"I saw the way you looked at Lancaster. He's not such a bad guy, you know. Cracked a few good jokes when we were around the back of the house. I think he's just quiet when he's around MacLean."

Patterson looked at Rachette with half-closed eyes. "Really? A good guy, huh?"

Rachette rolled his eyes. "And the way you acted with MacLean." They rode in silence as he swung his gaze between her and the road. "You gonna tell me what's in that envelope, or what?"

Her pulse quickened again at the prospect of talking to Rachette about the bombshell that lay across her lap. For now, she just turned back to her window and looked outside.

"Seriously, what the hell is that?"

She closed her eyes. "All right, listen—"

Her cellphone trilled, and with a silent scream of thanks she looked at the screen. "It's Wolf. Hello? ... Yeah?" She looked over at Rachette with raised eyebrows and then leaned toward the windshield. "Yeah, we just passed the gas station now ... what?"

She leaned to look in the side-view mirror and turned to Rachette. "Turn around!"

Rachette slammed on the brakes. "What?"

She hung up and pocketed the phone, letting the packet of pictures fall to the floorboard by her feet. "Wolf found Nick Pollard's pickup truck."

CHAPTER 32

WOLF WATCHED as Rachette's SUV slowed and parked behind Baine's truck. Behind Rachette and Patterson, a shiny white government-issued ended the train of vehicles. When it parked, Lorber stepped out with Dr. Blank.

The four of them convened and scuttled their way down the final incline.

Wolf walked to meet them at the bottom of the road.

Lorber looked past him at a Toyota pickup matching Nick Pollard's make and model, though rust color rather than yellow, now dripping on the pond shore. "You found it. How the hell did you find it?"

Wolf retold the story about the Pumapetrol gas-station clerk's mix-up between Highway 734 and County 74.

"So Parker Grey came and picked up someone, and went up 734." Lorber put his hands on his hips. "So how did you get to this spot?"

Wolf walked to the pickup with them in tow. With each step, the skin on his thighs screamed as it rubbed against his jeans. Wolf's legs had collided with the rusted tailgate, slicing his skin in multiple spots. Now his thighs felt like they were being prodded with soldering irons.

"I studied my cell phone map, focusing on the area north of the gas station. My dad and the department all those years ago had been fixated on highway 74 and Cold Lake, but Parker Grey had driven north instead. And why was Parker at the gas station? To pick up whoever made the phone call to him. A woman, or a boy ... somebody with Nick Pollard's blood on their hands.

"So I wondered why they were shooting off north, past the Cold Lake turnoff, and got to thinking they might have been rushing to Nick."

"So she walked her way to the gas station," Patterson said.

"Why didn't she drive Nick's truck?" Rachette asked.

Wolf shrugged. "Maybe she didn't know how to drive a stick. It's a steep climb up that road. I don't know."

"Was it sticking out of the water?" Lorber asked.

"No."

"So you"—Lorber tilted his head—"*sensed* the truck was in the pond? Probed it with a stick?" He looked around.

"I had a hunch it might be, since this is the only place within ten square miles along 734 where one could hide a truck for twenty-two years."

"How did you find it?" Lorber asked. "You're killing me, here."

"I swam. Ran into the tailgate with my legs."

Lorber scoffed. "Jesus Christ, you swam in that?"

Wolf nodded.

"You—" Lorber grabbed Wolf's arm and ran a finger over his skin. "Do you know the toxic ores found in dark-red water like this? The PH level? You're lucky you didn't dissolve. It's like swimming in battery acid. Worse! I mean, my God ..."

"There's fish in the pond. There's water running into the pond from the north and out to the south." Wolf resisted the urge to scratch his skin and turned to the truck. "I want you to scour this truck, inside and out."

Lorber laughed. "Sure. There's not going to be any organic material, that's for sure. Fish in there ..." He squinted and bent toward Wolf's bare arm again. "You'd better take a shower as soon as possible."

Wolf turned to Rachette and Patterson. "What happened at Heeter's place?"

"Heeter wasn't there," Rachette said. "And no sign of his car."

"And how was MacLean?"

Patterson remained silent, looking into the distance.

"He was all right." Rachette glanced at his partner.

"Is something wrong?"

Patterson shrugged. "No."

"Okay. Any word from Yates and Wilson at the lake?"

They shook their heads.

Wolf hoped the two deputies were all right. He wondered if he'd encountered Olin Heeter last night. "I'd sure like to know if Heeter's car is up there. You have a make and model on it?"

"No," Rachette said, looking at his partner again.

Patterson seemed to be avoiding any and all eye contact.

"Rachette," Wolf said, "why don't you call Tammy and get on that."

"You got it."

They watched Rachette ascend the road, and then Patterson sprinted away after him.

"What's their problem?" Lorber asked.

Wolf watched her dash up the hill, up the road past Rachette to the SUV, and open the passenger door. A second later, she closed it and walked past a confused-looking Rachette, and back down the hill to a just-as-confused-feeling Wolf.

She thrust a manila envelope in his hands. "Here."

CHAPTER 33

PATTERSON WATCHED with growing unease as Wolf flipped through the pictures. Her boss seemed unmoved, silently studying each photo with calculating eyes before moving onto the next. When he'd finished studying the stack, along with the police report on Gail Olson, he looked at Patterson.

"What did Rachette say?"

"I haven't had a chance to talk to him about it, sir. I didn't—"

Panic shot through her when he looked up and yelled at the top of his lungs. "Rachette!"

"Sir," she whispered, "I didn't know if I should talk to you first, or ... or ..." she let the sentence die in her throat, and her heart sank when Wolf offered her no condolences.

Rachette trotted down. "Yeah?"

Wolf slapped the stack of photos into his chest. "What's this all about?"

Rachette fumbled the pictures and then studied them. He flipped from one to the next, and with each photo his face deepened another shade of red. When he reached the final pages, and then the Ashland PD police report, his eyes narrowed and he looked up at Wolf.

"Sir. This is me and this girl I've been kinda seeing. But"—he pointed at the police report—"that's not her name. She told me her name was Jessica."

Wolf blinked.

Rachette turned to Patterson and squinted. "What the hell, Patterson? That's what was in the envelope and you didn't tell me?"

Patterson stared at him. "MacLean said we were both in trouble."

"I ... so what? You think I'm what? You think I'm running drugs for this girl?"

Patterson shrugged, glancing meaningfully at the stack of photos in her partner's hand.

"When did you meet this woman?" Wolf asked. "What did she tell you? I want to know everything. What is this?"

"Sir," Rachette raised his face to the sky, "she just said she had to take off to go to Denver, and couldn't wait around to return this backpack to her girlfriend. Said I was doing her a favor. That was it! She never told me what was in the damn thing."

Patterson popped her eyes. "And you didn't think to ask?"

"She said it was her friends overnight bag. Clothing and stuff."

Wolf snapped his fingers.

They froze and looked at him.

"I want to know who this girl is." Wolf's voice was a growl. "I want to know when you met her, exactly. Where, exactly. What she said, exactly."

Rachette swallowed, and began recounting his tale of a night in downtown Rocky Points that seemed too good to be true. A night when all of Rachette's bad luck with women had miraculously reversed its course and he'd become the Casanova of the local zip code.

Patterson watched Wolf as Rachette told his story. He was eerily still, staring across the pond. She noticed a blotch of blood spreading on his pant leg, but he was oblivious to it; his mind was elsewhere and, by the look of his flexing jaw, it was an angry elsewhere.

When Rachette was done, Wolf stood in silence a while longer.

Rachette shifted his weight. "Sir."

Wolf turned and looked over their heads. "What's that?"

Patterson pulled her eyebrows together and looked behind them, noticing for the first time that radios were exploding with voices.

"What's going on?" Wolf walked away, leaving Rachette glaring at her.

"They've found something up at Olin Heeter's house on the lake!" Baine had his radio pointed toward them.

"Thanks," Rachette said under his breath as he walked away.

Someone's scratchy voice on her handheld said something about blood, and a door. But her thoughts were too mangled to comprehend.

Wolf jogged to his SUV, still clutching the stack of photos in his hand. "Baine, you're with me!"

"Sir, I drove up here."

"Leave your vehicle for Patterson."

Baine shrugged and jogged past her, bouncing his eyebrows on the way by. "Keys are in the ignition. See ya up there."

Rachette ran to their SUV and got in without a glance back to her.

Wolf's SUV revved and bounded up the steep incline, past the other SCSD vehicles, and then out of sight. Rachette struggled to flip his vehicle around for a few moments, then peeled after him.

It took Patterson another few seconds to realize she'd been rooted to the same spot.

"Penny for your thoughts?" Lorber stared at her.

She shook her head. "Maybe some other time."

"Go get 'em, tiger," he said with a fist pump.

She smiled despite herself, and jogged to join the cavalry.

CHAPTER 34

WOLF STARED down at a blood smear on the doorknob of Olin Heeter's lake house, contemplating how he'd failed to see it the night before.

The mid-afternoon sun shone on the front porch, warming his back, which served to evaporate the cold from his body, which had lingered since his dip in the tailings pond.

The wind breathed through the trees surrounding the property, bringing the scent of pine and the faint noise of motorboats tooling around the lake below.

Patterson drove up to the property and scraped to a stop. When she got out, she pointedly ignored Rachette, who returned the favor.

Wolf sighed inwardly, knowing those pictures were the beginning of something big. The fact that MacLean had delivered them told him a full-blown scandal was imminent.

"I've got a key here." Yates stood up at the end of the porch with a key in his gloved fingers. "Was underneath this flowerpot."

Wolf nodded. "Let's go in."

"Sir." Rachette appeared next to him. "Kimber Grey was

behind me on the drive up. She's probably arrived at her place now."

Wolf nodded.

Yates gingerly inserted the key into the knob, not disturbing any of the blood smeared around the sides of it, and twisted.

The door opened a sliver, and Wolf pushed it open.

With a groan, it swung wide before hitting a coat rack behind it, sending a crumple of fabric to the wooden floor.

"Put these booties on," Patterson said, handing out pairs of shoe-coverings to everyone.

"You think?" Rachette grabbed a pair and put them on.

Wolf donned them and stepped inside the doorway.

The interior of the house was cool, almost cold, and dark, the air heavy with the scent of chemical cleaner. As he stepped inside, a honeybee dive-bombed past his ear and went down the hallway in front of him, disappearing around the corner.

Yates sniffed behind him. "Smells like some one's been cleaning recently."

Wolf flicked the light switch on the wall and a yellow bulb above his head brightened the entryway. At the end of the hall in front of him stood a dining table.

Walking after the buzzing insect, Wolf reached the end of the hall and turned into a wood-and-linoleum kitchen, where brass-colored pots and pans hung from ceiling hooks above an antique-looking stove. Black-and-white checked drapes covered a sliding glass door, blocking out natural light.

He flipped the light switch on the wall and squinted as the overhead lights glared on.

Yates was right: the smell of cleaner was overbearing and the linoleum countertops were spotless, the dining table shiny, and every nook devoid of dirt or dust.

The refrigerator hummed.

"Looks definitely lived in," Patterson said.

"Sir." Yates crouched next to a door knob. "More blood."

Wolf stepped closer and examined another smear of maroon on the brass fixture.

"Both these stains, the front door and this door, look fairly new," Patterson said. "Lorber would have to check with the spectrometer, but I'd say they're recent."

"Open it," Wolf said.

Yates studied the knob and then gingerly put his hand on it and twisted. The door swung open, revealing a cramped stairway leading down.

Wolf reached and flicked on another light switch. The overhead light illuminated brown carpet steps and beige walls, and at the bottom of the stairs hung a painting of a full moon over the lake.

Wolf walked down, and with each step the wood squealed under the carpet.

The air was dusty and colder still as they descended into a walkout basement. Wolf flicked a light switch at the bottom of the stairs and lit a wide-open space to the left.

A hanging lamp and canned lighting in the ceiling blazed bright, showcasing a covered pool table and a bar crafted of logs and lacquered boards. The drapes were all shut, covering a large sliding glass door and two windows that faced the back of the property.

The walls were covered in paintings, and it took little time to realize they were all of the moon: the moon waxing, waning, full above the lake, full rising through the trees, close-ups of craters as if seen from a telescope lens. There had to have been thirty of them, mounted all over the walls in neat rows. The artistry was impressive.

Wolf pulled aside one of the drapes covering a sliding glass door. Natural light streamed in, mixing with the harsh yellow coming out of the ceiling fixtures. Outside, the lake glittered diamonds beyond the wall of stacked rocks he'd stood next to the night before. Below, boats streaked in all directions, leaving white wakes.

He fished inside the fabric, found the cords, and pulled the drapes open. The room brightened with each yank until the glass doors were exposed. He pulled it open and walked outside onto the grass and dirt.

"What's up?" Patterson asked, following him out.

Wolf pointed down and to the right. "You can't see where we've been pulling up the bodies from this vantage. It's blocked by that land jutting out to the south, towards Kimber Grey's house."

Patterson followed his eyes. "Yeah ... so?"

He craned his neck and looked up through the slivers of light in the deck above him.

"Sir. Look at this." Yates pointed at a pile of red-clay bricks near the rear wall of the house. "Same type of bricks found in those bags."

Wolf picked one up and saw the Tracer Building Supplies logo.

"That's not good for Olin Heeter," Patterson said.

He dropped the brick back on the pile and turned back toward the lake, returning to his line of thinking.

"Sir!" Rachette called from inside. "I've got more. More blood."

They went back inside and found Rachette pointing to another closed door.

"Open it up," Wolf said.

Rachette waved Yates over. "You do it. I don't have gloves."

Yates twisted the knob and pushed it open, revealing a pitch-black void beyond. He clicked on his Maglite, took a deep breath and stepped inside. "What the hell?"

CHAPTER 35

PATTERSON WATCHED with mounting curiosity as Yates and Wolf shuffled into the small room.

Wolf stood blocking the doorway, then finally stepped forward, freeing up space so she could see what the commotion was.

She waited for Rachette to barge in front of her, but he stood still and held out a hand for her to go first, which she found deeply unnerving and out of character.

With guilt wriggling her gut, she stepped inside the room.

Wolf pulled on a string dangling from the ceiling and the room lit up, revealing a scene that made her skin crawl.

A cluster of photographs was affixed on one wall, every one of them of Kimber Grey. They were tacked to the wall tilted every which way, some on top of others. The whole montage, when looked at as a whole, was circular. Like a moon made of photographs.

Kimber chopping wood. Kimber milling around her boat. Kimber standing on her porch, looking directly into the lens of the camera, though from such a distance that it would've been impossible for her to know she was being photographed.

Yates leaned close to one of the prints of Kimber standing naked behind her yellow-illuminated window. "Can I keep this one?" he murmured, looking back at Rachette.

Rachette ignored him, not even cracking a smile.

Extremely unnerving.

"Kimber Grey is the moon." Yates stepped back and folded his arms. "And the moon is the world to Olin Heeter. Jesus ... obsess much?"

"Let's process that rifle," Wolf said, pointing behind Patterson.

She turned around and saw a midnight-black bolt-action rifle leaning in the crook between a bookshelf and a blank wall.

"I didn't even see that," Yates said.

A lot of reading material lined the small shelves, its subject matter seemingly suited for such a man as Olin Heeter: survival techniques, military history and tactics, at least a hundred hunting magazines, and several horror fiction novels. A box of .308 Winchester cartridges bookended one row. The cardboard was cracked open, revealing the box was less than full.

"There's blood on it," Wolf said, keeping his nose to the photo wall.

Patterson nodded and looked at the rifle. "Yes. I see that ... now." There was a smear of blood on the stock and on the trigger guard.

Wolf stepped back and put his hands on his hips. "There're bloody gloves on the lowest shelf."

Patterson saw the gloves.

"These photos were all taken recently," Wolf said.

When no one else spoke, Patterson asked, "How do you know that?"

"Kimber has the same hair in all of these. Same length, same ponytail, with a strand flipping out on the side. She has the same outfit on in these over here. The same jeans and shoes, but some with her long-sleeved shirt, others with the rain parka." He pointed to some of the photos scattered in different spots. "It's raining in these. Look here." He pointed at the corner of a photograph.

Patterson leaned forward and saw an unfocused blob. A few moments later she realized she was looking at a tiny droplet of water on the lens, which was causing the refraction. Then she realized what he was getting at, because it was in every single photo on the wall. "They were all taken on the same day?"

Wolf nodded. "Looks like it. And this is the outfit Kimber had on yesterday, when I came and talked to her. I think these were all taken yesterday."

"What the hell?" Yates asked no one in particular.

Wolf looked like he suddenly remembered something, then pushed past them and out of the room.

The remaining deputies exchanged a glance and then followed.

Patterson took the lead, catching up to him as he climbed the stairs.

"What's up?"

Back on the main floor, Wolf twisted, searching for something, and then walked to another door. With his rubber-gloved fingers he twisted the knob and looked inside.

The other side of the door was dark, but she saw a gleaming car bumper and smelled motor oil.

He flicked on a light switch, revealing a two-car garage.

An older-looking Chevy pickup truck was parked inside.

"That's Heeter's truck," Yates said behind them. "Those are his plates."

"It's clean, too," Wolf said. "No dust on it."

"So it hasn't been parked here long?" Patterson asked.

"I'd say no. Let's search it."

Wolf turned to the door and stepped around Patterson to go back inside.

She watched him go into the kitchen dining area and pull back the drapes, unveiling another sliding glass door that led onto the deck outside. Abandoning the garage door and letting it click shut, she walked after Wolf again.

With a whoosh, Wolf pulled open the glass, letting in cool, fresh air smelling like lake water and pine trees.

He walked out toward a blue tarp that was tented at shoulder height, grabbed it, and lifted it off, revealing a telescope that reflected the surroundings off its silver cylinders, knobs, and mounts. He got in front of the telescope and looked at it, as if he was staring down the barrel of a gun. "Here. There's a single water mark on the lens."

Wolf looked closely at the eyepiece portion of the telescope and pointed. "This is an adaptor to attach a camera lens, for taking photos through the telescope."

"What a perv," Yates said.

Patterson watched Rachette. He was taking in everything in perfect silence, and Patterson wanted to punch him in the face for it. She got the point. She'd betrayed him, and he was hurt. But in her defense, Rachette had betrayed her first. Or at least she had been led to think so at the time. And that was *if* Rachette was even telling the truth that he'd been played by that floozy in the pictures. *Screw him.*

Her face dropped when she realized everyone was looking at her. "What?"

Wolf gestured to the sky. "I asked if you knew anything about celestial coordinates?"

"Celestial coordinates? That's a big no. Why?"

Wolf pointed at the lake. "See how we can't see the diver boats out there?"

Patterson looked down at the shimmering water. She could

only see one Sheriff's Department boat, and knew it was there to keep a northern perimeter, making sure no other boats passed into the crime scene beyond as divers continued working.

"Yep. No diver boats. They're behind the trees on that rise."

"When my father spoke to Olin Heeter twenty-two years ago, he said he'd seen something suspicious on the lake the night of the sixth. Two nights after Nick Pollard's disappearance."

Patterson nodded. "Okay. And ..."

"Yates," Wolf said, "can you please get that report packet from my car?"

Yates nodded and bolted back into the house.

"Thanks."

Wolf leaned on the railing. "So, because of Heeter's interview, my dad and Burton spent a few days out on the lake with sonar and dive equipment. Looking in the exact spot that Heeter said he'd seen activity."

Thumping and jingling keys approached, and Yates reappeared, out of breath and packet in hand.

Wolf leafed to a page and read, "... the night of July 6, at eleven thirty p.m., Olin Heeter saw Parker Grey's boat go out in the water and stop. Olin says he got a clear view of the boat because it happened to stop in the stripe reflection of the full moon, which he was photographing that night. He saw (through his own eyes, not the telescope—the telescope was pointed at the moon) a splash, also heard it, and then the boat headed toward Parker Grey's property."

Wolf lowered the packet and looked back out at the water.

Rachette furrowed his brow. "I'm not pickin' up what you're puttin' down."

"The bodies we're pulling out of the water are out of view from here," Wolf said. "If Grey had dumped a body where we're finding them, Heeter wouldn't have seen a thing."

They stood in silence.

"So there's another dump site," Patterson said. "Right out there."

Wolf nodded, and then pointed at the packet. "It's right here on the page. My dad wrote some coordinates in the margins. They're celestial coordinates. The exact location of the moon on July 6th, twenty-two years ago, at 11:30 p.m."

Wolf turned to Rachette and Yates. "Get Lorber and his crew up here ASAP. You guys stay and give him any help he needs."

Rachette and Yates nodded and walked back into the house.

"And me?" Patterson asked.

Wolf handed her the packet and then pointed an arm into the sky above the lake. "Figure out exactly where that moon was, and let's get the sonar guys in the boat looking there."

"Okay, wait. Who says Olin Heeter could even identify the boat as Parker Grey's from this distance? It says his telescope was pointing at the moon."

Wolf looked out at the lake and pointed. "It's a coincidence, and one my father was willing to invest five days of his life diving into the water to check out. So it's good enough for me."

She sighed, wondering how she was going to accomplish such a task.

Wolf squeezed both her shoulders and gave her a reassuring smile. "Figure out where that moon was."

"Is that ..."—she looked at the telescope and then the lake —"even possible?"

"For you? Yeah."

"Wait." When he went back inside she followed after him. "I need a computer. Internet."

He kept walking. "Check and see if Heeter has one. If not, call the station and work with Tammy."

"There's no cell service up here!"

Wolf disappeared out the front door.

A landline phone hung on the wall next to her. She plucked it off the cradle and heard a dial tone.

She hung up and stared at the telescope through the sliding glass door.

"Fine," she said to no one.

CHAPTER 36

WHEN KIMBER GREY answered the door in a wet towel, Wolf couldn't help but glance down the length of her body, and then he couldn't help but think about her naked body underneath, the image of it still fresh in his mind from seeing the picture twenty minutes ago.

"Sorry." Wolf averted his eyes. "I just came over ... I heard you were back here, and I need to ask you a few questions."

"Please," she opened the door wide, "come in. I'm just getting dressed. You can wait in the living room."

Before Wolf could say, *No, I'll just wait out front*, she was already gone and the door was swinging open.

He stepped inside and shut the door, turning just in time to see Kimber's naked backside for an instant as it disappeared into the hallway and out of sight.

Wolf wondered how imperative it was for Kimber to pull her towel off and dry her hair an instant before she was back in the privacy of her own room.

He stepped to a bookshelf and studied the contents, cutting off any angle for a further view into the hallway.

A washed-out color picture of Kimber and her family

perched at eye-level. Her mother and father were standing arm in arm, Kimber next to them, all genuine smiles in the throes of laughter. They stood in front of a lake on a sandy beach, pine trees in the background. Kimber was young in the picture, no more than eight years old, with sun-bleached pigtails and a black void for front teeth.

Wolf saw the door to the room was open to his left, and he walked toward it and peered inside. Though he could only see the edge of the single bed from his angle, it was clear that the sheets were tousled, like it had been slept in.

"What are you guys doing up at Mr. Heeter's?" Kimber's voice came from down the hall.

Wolf cleared his throat. "That's what I'm here about. When exactly is the last time you saw Olin—"

Kimber walked in front of him and leaned on the wall between him and the room. She was fully clothed now in jeans and a button-up shirt.

"What happened to you?"

Wolf pulled his eyebrows together.

She pointed down. "Your leg?"

He looked down at the bloodstain on his thigh. "Oh. Swimming accident."

She looked confused.

"When's the last time you saw Olin Heeter?"

She shrugged, brought her towel back up to her damp hair, and walked out of sight back down the hall. "I don't know. A couple of weeks ago? He comes and goes a lot. I don't remember him coming up this weekend, though. He usually comes up on the weekends."

Her footsteps came closer and she stepped around the corner again. "He'll do that until winter hits, then he winterizes his place and stays away until the next spring. Sometimes he stays for longer than the weekend. Doesn't have anything to go home to, with his wife being dead. Not sure why he even goes home, actually."

"I'd like to get all the footage you have available on that Wi-Fi camera up there."

She raised her eyebrows. "Okay. Sure. I don't have much, though. The video is loaded onto an external hard drive every seventy-two hours, and then I go over it and erase it to leave room for the next seventy-two hours, or the whole thing shuts down."

He watched her, noting the way she brought her hand up to her neck. The vulnerable gesture was listed in textbooks as an indication of lying.

"What?" she asked.

"How much footage do you have now?"

She shrugged. "A couple of hours? I just did the memory dump earlier when I got home."

Wolf nodded. "Okay. I'd like to see it."

"Okay. I'll get it." She disappeared into the back rooms again.

Wolf twisted slowly on his heels, taking in the rest of the space. Paintings hung on the wall depicting mountain wildlife scenes: deer, elk, and bear foraging for food. The framed artwork was dusty, and add the pile of lint tucked in one corner and he saw she rarely cleaned.

She returned, holding out a memory stick. "Here you go."

Wolf took it. "Did you check the footage before you erased it?"

"Yeah."

"Was there anything?"

She shrugged. "Just a lot of you coming and going."

"Thanks. I'd like you to come back into town tonight, where we can more easily keep an eye on you. With cell service being shoddy up here, and our radio relays not reaching, it would be better."

"Keeping an eye on me, eh?"

He shrugged. "What we found up at Olin Heeter's house suggests it may be dangerous for you up here at the moment."

"Seriously?"

"Yes."

She pulled back her wet hair and twisted it into a knot. Then she stepped into *the room* and pulled the sheets off the bed, piling them on the floor.

"You sleep in this room?"

"I take naps in here." She wadded the sheets, came out, and stepped out of sight down the hall. "What are you doing tonight?" she asked.

Wolf frowned to himself and didn't answer. He walked back to the bookshelf and looked at the picture in front of a row of worn paperbacks.

Once again she appeared at the wall and leaned against it.

He saw her studying him from his periphery. "I like this picture. Where was it taken?"

Stepping close, she moved silently and put her hand on the small of his back. "Oh, that? I think in Tennessee. Near the commune."

"Oh yeah. The hippy commune. Must have been a fun time growing up there."

She pulled back and folded her arms.

Wolf looked at her. "I'm just saying it's an interesting way to grow up, is all. How many people were living there?"

She stared suspiciously at him, then seemed to relax. "Lots. It was the biggest commune in the world at one time."

He nodded, looking at the pine trees in the background of the photo. "I'm not too familiar with geography east of Colorado. What is that, the Appalachian Mountains?"

"I think so. I don't remember when or where that was taken."

He nodded.

"You want some tea?" She walked away to the kitchen.

"No thanks."

He set down the picture and looked at his watch. 2:45. He calculated he'd be back into the office at 3:30 p.m. if he left now, which would give him a couple of hours before the meeting with Senator Chama, a meeting that was making him more nervous than he was used to being on the job. And what if Senator Chama wanted to talk about the pension? The development projects of the resort village base? The future budget concerns of the bigger, consolidated Office of the Sheriff in the next four years?

Suddenly the urge to read through Margaret's packet sitting in his desk drawer trumped any and all work he had to do otherwise. Rachette, Wilson, Yates, and Patterson, even if some of them weren't speaking to one another, could handle Heeter's.

"Sheriff?"

Wolf looked at Kimber standing in the kitchen doorway.

"You okay?"

"Yes," he said. "Listen, I think it's a bad idea for you to stay here tonight. I'd like you to come down to Rocky Points, where we can keep an eye on you."

"You already said that."

"It bears repeating."

"I tell you what. You meet me for a drink and I'll do it. I'm sick of sitting in that hotel room and watching shit TV." She blushed and pulled a strand of hair behind her ear. "So?"

"All right. Eight o'clock. I'll meet you at the Pony Tavern. You know it?"

She nodded and opened the front door. "Okay then. Sounds good."

CHAPTER 37

THIRTY MINUTES LATER, Wolf's phone vibrated in his center console just as he was starting up Williams Pass. Not recognizing the number, he hesitated and hit the answer button.

"Wolf."

"You get my pictures today?"

Wolf switched phone hands and turned down the radio. "Yeah. And I have a few questions about them."

"I bet you do ... like what?"

The sound of wind buffeting MacLean's phone scratched in Wolf's earpiece. "Like what's the Byron County Sheriff's Department doing conducting an investigation in my county without my permission?"

"That's a delicate topic. We had a man deep under, and I had to make a call on the fly."

"You're conducting an illegal investigation. Those pictures of yours aren't going to do you any good."

A chuckle. "Aren't they?"

Wolf clenched his jaw.

"Listen, I'll let you think about those pictures some more,

but I'm actually not calling about that. I'm calling because I've got two dead bodies sitting in a burnt-up SUV with Sluice County plates. Only, when I checked up on the plates, they came up stolen. I just got off the phone with your dispatcher, Tammy. She's informed me the plates were taken from a car in the marina parking lot last night. At least that's what ... me."

"What?" Wolf slowed and stopped on the side of the road. "I didn't hear that."

"Which part?" MacLean scoffed. "Damn cell phones."

"The last part."

"I said your dispatcher tracked down the owner of the plates, and called them. They assured your dispatcher that they were indeed alive and well, which was good. But when they went out and checked their car, they realized that their plates were missing. They swear it must have happened the night before, up at the marina. They said they were up at that Tackle Box place."

Wolf shook his head. "This is the first I've heard of this."

"That's because you guys have all been incommunicado up at the lake. So instead of waitin' for your asses, me and Tammy had ourselves an investigation. Nice woman. Glad someone up there knows the score."

"What kind of car was it?"

"The burnt?"

"Yeah."

"It's an SUV. Mercedes Benz. One of those real expensive jobbers."

Wolf remembered seeing a black Mercedes SUV pull into the marina parking lot the night before. "Damn." He looked at his dashboard clock—3:15. "Where are you?"

"Me?" MacLean paused, and there was the sound of a door shutting. "I just got to my office. I've got a meeting with Senator Chama in a few minutes."

Wolf remained silent.

"But if you want to know where the vehicle is, I've got some deputies up there. I'll let them know you're on your way. Hello? You still there?"

"Yeah. Tell me where."

CHAPTER 38

WOLF PULLED up behind the Byron County Sheriff's Department vehicle, turned his keys, and looked at the dashboard clock —3:52. He did the mental math and figured he had about a fifty-minute drive back to Rocky Points. If Senator Chama was keeping his appointment, that meant he had to be out of here by five at the latest.

He stepped out of the SUV and zipped up his jacket. The densely-forested hillside he stood on was draped in afternoon shade and the temperature would be in steady free fall until the next morning.

"Sheriff Wolf?" A middle-aged deputy came marching down the dirt road beyond a bouncing line of crime-scene tape.

Wolf walked toward the deputy, stopping next to another deputy holding a clipboard near the tape.

"Sheriff Wolf, you say?" the clipboard holder asked, writing his name.

Wolf nodded.

"Come on, go ahead," the other deputy called, waving an arm.

Wolf ducked under the tape.

The other deputy was shorter than Wolf with a brick-house build. His cop mustache was full and blond, so thick Wolf wondered if the man could breathe out of his nose. He took Wolf's hand and his grip was firm and energetic.

"Deputy Fuller. Nice to meet you, sir."

Wolf nodded. "Sheriff Wolf. Nice to meet you."

"This way." Fuller marched up the road at a blistering pace, which Wolf was grateful for. "Twice in one day our departments work together. That's definitely a record. Guess we should get used to it."

Wolf smiled politely at the banter and concentrated on the surroundings. The land on either side of the dirt road was steep, higher on the left and plunging down to the right. Chipmunks chittered from the trees and there were blasts of static coming from distant radios ahead and below.

"Here we are." Fuller stepped to a widening of the road and went over the steep edge on the right side without slowing.

Wolf followed, digging his heels into the pebbled earth covered with inches of brown pine needles. He eyed tire marks off to their left, marked with yellow numbered evidence tents. There was no skidding on the forty-degree slope, which would have been a double black diamond if they were skiing it.

"Why didn't we hear about this earlier?" Wolf asked.

"We got the report a few hours ago. We just figured out the plates."

Wolf nodded.

Down the slope another fifty feet was the SUV, bent severely in the front and burned to the frame. At first glance, the make and model were in no way apparent. But as they got closer, he could see the Mercedes Benz three-pointed star and the Colorado plates covered in soot.

"You find a VIN?" Wolf asked.

"Yep. But had to get it from the engine block. Someone

scratched out the driver's doorpost VIN, and the windshield one was clearly destroyed by a blunt object before they dumped it down here."

"Dumped it?"

Deputy Fuller stopped at the rear of the SUV and put his hands on his hips. "Yep. We've got multiple gunshot wounds on each of the victims inside the vehicle. The teeth have been destroyed on both bodies. Someone was definitely trying to hide these two men's identities."

Wolf walked to the driver's-side door. It smelled like burnt plastic, gasoline, and cooked meat.

A woman clad in a white suit stepped back and pointed into the seat at a twisted, shriveled black body. The head was torqued back, mouth open in a mute scream.

"Got a gunshot to the head. African American male. Early twenties, I'm estimating. Next to him a Caucasian male. Mid-fifties. Autopsy will confirm. Tougher to tell with this one in the passenger seat, but I think he has multiple gunshot wounds to the torso. Massive trauma to the ribs that the fire damage failed to hide completely."

A man, clad also in a white suit, stood on the other side of the vehicle and nodded.

"Slugs?" Wolf asked.

"Gotta wait until the autopsy, but I'm guessing they're all through-and-through shots. High-powered rifle?"

Wolf nodded in thought.

"Vehicle's registered in the state of Idaho," Fuller said.

"Idaho." Wolf frowned.

"Yep. Registered to one William F. Van Wyke. Resident in Boise, Idaho. Coroner will start there with trying to ID the Caucasian. There's no telling who the African American is."

"Where's the coroner?" Wolf asked, looking up the steep hill.

"On his way," Fuller said.

"I'd like the VIN."

Fuller nodded, jotting it down in a pocket notebook. He tore off the sheet and handed it over.

"And your contact information."

"You got it." Fuller handed him a contact card.

"Any witnesses?"

"Nope. No one who lives around here for miles. There was a woman who was walking her dog on this road and she saw it. Lucky it's been so wet lately and it burned itself out without setting the mountain on fire." Fuller looked around. "Lot of beetle kill around here. Of course, that's most places now."

Wolf narrowed his eyes. "So when do you think this happened?"

"Our fire investigator said there were accelerants. Gas poured inside. He says it probably happened early a.m. He'll be back in a few minutes if you want to talk to him."

Wolf held up the card and the sheet of paper with the VIN and nodded. His watch said 4:25. "I've actually gotta get going."

Fuller nodded. "Okay, yeah. I can keep you posted with any developments. Don't worry."

"Thanks."

Fuller turned around and started the climb.

Breathing hard, legs screaming with fatigue, Wolf trailed Fuller over the edge and back onto the dirt road a minute later. Looking down toward his SUV, Wolf paused. A circus of activity was underway below, with two ambulances and three more police vehicles surrounding Wolf's SUV. An army of uniforms were digging into compartments, pulling out bags, preparing stretchers, ropes, and other equipment.

Wolf and Fuller walked down the road and ducked under the crime-scene tape.

"I see you're blocked in. I got this," Fuller said, and walked toward a man near the ambulance. They spoke in low tones, looking back at Wolf. The man, apparently the driver of the ambulance, looked up and nodded with annoyance, and then opened a side compartment and began pulling out orange bags.

Fuller came back, stepping quickly to Wolf. "They'll just be a minute." He stood next to Wolf and folded his arms. "So, how's the campaign going?"

Wolf nodded. "It's going."

There was a loud beeping and a tow truck came into view, driving up the road rear first.

Fuller nodded, and then stepped away again. "Hey, we gotta move these vehicles out, Ted. This is Sheriff Wolf from Sluice, and he's gotta get going."

The crew of men and women ignored Fuller, and any request he made seemed to have the opposite effect Wolf was hoping for.

Wolf turned to the deputy with the clipboard, and was surprised to see the man wearing a sadistic grin.

Eleven minutes later, Wolf's dashboard clock read 4:46 p.m., and he was on his way down the dirt road past the idling emergency vehicles when an SUV marked with the Byron County Sheriff logo came into view.

Wolf slowed and the SUV did the same.

MacLean's smiling face rolled up next to Wolf.

"You done already?"

Wolf nodded. "I think I've got all I need."

MacLean leaned back and checked his rearview mirror, as if settling in for a long conversation.

"I've gotta get going."

MacLean smirked. "Yeah. I know. Chama."

"Chama."

"Well, he knows what he needs to know about the way

you're runnin' your department up there." MacLean's mustache curled.

"Well, then, that's a good thing. I appreciate it."

MacLean chuckled. "You gonna play it that way?"

"Listen, like I said, I gotta get going."

"I thought you were a smarter man than that, Wolf. I'm really trying to envision where I might put you in the new department, where you would be a good fit. And I keep drawing a blank. I don't know, a jailer? You even got experience doing that? Hell, I don't know. Maybe somewhere a little less taxing mentally. Let's see ... I keep seeing a toilet brush. A mop. One of those big push brooms."

Wolf lowered his eyelids to half-mast.

MacLean raised his hands. "Easy, Sheriff. I'm just playing with you." He propped an arm out his window. "Listen, it's as simple as it gets. You end your campaign and I have cushy jobs lined up for you and your two little deputies. Whatever you want, whatever they want. It'll be one big happy family going forward. Either that, or you three look for new careers." MacLean finger-combed his mustache in the side-view mirror. "And I'm sheriff, anyway."

Wolf let off the brake and drove away.

CHAPTER 39

PATTERSON STOOD next to the tall rookie rescue diver she'd had the privilege to meet the day before on the boat. "Look, Jeremy," she pointed up at the cloudless sky, "there was the moon."

Jeremy looked up. "Yeah?"

"The reflection would have been a straight line on the water from the moon to the observer, which is us. Right here." She pointed down and stomped her foot, shuddering the deck.

"Okay," Jeremy popped his eyes like a dog in mid-poop.

"Look. Please. Can I just take the radio?" she held out her hand.

Jeremy peaked his eyebrows and handed it over. "Yeah. Fine."

"Thank you." She pushed the button. "I need you to move fifty yards south."

There was silence. "Who's this?"

"This is Deputy Patterson. I'm taking over radio contact."

After a pause, the voice said, "Copy that. Moving now."

The water behind the silver rescue boat below frothed white, and a split second later Patterson heard the distant gurgling of the outboard motor.

Patterson ducked underneath the telescope's main body, in front of the mounting tripod, and squinted one eye. She backed her head up until it touched the cylinder, and then looked at the weighted string she'd hung from the lens.

She was winging it, with no help from Einstein standing on the deck with her, but had effectively traced the path of the moon's reflection with the string, as it would have appeared that night. How wide a swath from left to right the reflection would have covered, she could only guess, but the boatmen said the sonar transducer covered a two-hundred-and-fifty-foot-diameter circle as it traveled. She hoped that was enough to catch whatever had dropped out of Parker Grey's boat. And that was only if Olin Heeter had been a reliable witness and something had actually been dropped out of Parker Grey's boat in the first place.

"Such a scientist," Jeremy said.

Patterson ignored him and pushed the radio button. "Okay, there! Stop."

"Copy that."

"That's right on it," Patterson said.

"All right. We have a bearing."

The engine of the boat started up again and it inched forward. Patterson squatted again under the telescope's main housing and the boat traveled a straight line along the string.

"Here we go," the voice said over the radio. "Let you know what we find."

Patterson stood up, satisfied. It had been a grueling hour or so, first trying to figure out how to point a telescope to precise celestial coordinates, with remote help, via a landline, from Deputy Tyler at the station, who had proved to be one of the least patient men she'd ever known. Then there was tracing the heading of the moon's reflection using the string, which was actually a thin strip of T-shirt that Deputy Wilson had offered up from his SUV. She was sure there was a better way to do all of it, probably some app sitting on her phone that could have helped, but all in all she was satisfied.

"So, listen." Jeremy's eyebrows were peaked again, his head tilted, smiling with one side of his mouth. "You live in Rocky Points, right?"

Patterson rolled her eyes. "Yes."

"What say you and I grab a bite sometime?"

"Sorry. Taken." Patterson leaned on the railing.

"Well, he's a lucky man."

"Thanks."

"I mean"—Jeremy leaned down, close enough to smell his dead-animal breath—"because I think you're cute. Shorter than most of the girls I tend to be attracted to, but ... cute."

Patterson frowned. "Thanks. Now, don't you have a boat to catch?"

Jeremy stood up, his eyes darkening. "You don't have to be a bitch about it."

Patterson straightened, startled by the man's sudden hostility.

"Hey, dickhead. She said she's taken."

Patterson and Jeremy both turned to see Rachette standing in the doorway.

"Now get the hell off this deck and off our crime scene, before I throw you off."

Jeremy smiled as he walked by Rachette, looking down. "Yeah, okay, Napoleon. You two make a good couple."

Rachette stood flexing his fists as he watched Jeremy leave. He turned back around and looked at the telescope. He stepped to the railing, touching the makeshift string on the way past. "I see you figured this out. No way I could have. I guess that's why Wolf told you to do it."

Patterson said nothing. Wilson walked underneath the deck, nodding up at them.

"No prints on anything." Rachette stretched his back. "Looks like the place was wiped clean, top to bottom. That's why it smells like a hotel maid's cart."

"Look," Patterson said. "Thanks. I could have kicked that guy's ass—you know that, right?"

"Whatever. I know." Rachette looked down at the railing and picked at a sliver with his thumb. "I've seen that guy out on the town a lot lately. Always has a bunch of girls hanging on him."

They stood in awkward silence for a full minute, and she watched the boats meander on the water below, the trees swaying in the wind, and the birds flying along the cliff face.

"Listen," she said. "I'm sorry. I know you think I betrayed you or something."

"Nah, it's just that partners are supposed to have each other's backs, you know? Like, remember that time I got shot three times that night? When I—"

"Christ, Rachette. Of course I remember that."

"Oh, really? Because when you took those photos straight to Wolf without talking to me first, it was kind of like I was some piece of shit you were scraping off your shoe, and not a partner who's taken *three bullets* for you."

Patterson inhaled deeply and closed her eyes. "We're both going to be lucky if we have jobs next month. Look at it from my perspective. MacLean—our likely future sheriff, if my aunt has it right—pulls me aside, gives me those photos and tells you and I are both in trouble. I saw those pictures and thought you were going behind my back, doing something stupid, putting both our careers in jeopardy. And, oh wait, that's exactly what you were doing."

"Is that what you think? How the hell was I supposed to

know that this girl was giving me the runaround. She gave me a backpack and asked me to give it to her friend. What's so bad about that? How the hell could I have known?"

Patterson shook her head and stared out at the water.

"Oh wait. I get it. You think I should have been alarmed when a cute girl like that was suddenly into me. You think I should have known she was using me. Because I'm just some Napoleon, who nobody of the opposite sex takes any interest in. Yeah, I should have known."

Patterson turned. "No, I'm not saying—"

"No." Rachette backed away. "I get it. Hey, I'm sorry, Partner. Sorry for screwing up."

"Rachette."

He disappeared into the house.

Patterson pressed her palms to her eyes. He was probably right, and admitting that Deputy Tom Rachette was right was her least favorite thing in the world to do.

"Deputy Patterson," the radio scratched. "Do you copy?"

"Copy, go ahead."

"We've got something. It's too deep to get to with divers, but we definitely have something."

CHAPTER 40

By the time Wolf pulled into the parking lot of the station, his dashboard clock read 6:13.

With a glimmer of hope, he spotted a shiny black Land Rover in the parking lot. Parking near it, he got out, slammed his door and jogged through cool air smelling of barbecue and into the station.

Tammy greeted him by shaking her head.

Wolf frowned, looking around the reception area. "Where is he? Is he still here?"

She nodded. "I've been stalling, and I've been calling your cell. He's in your office, drinking coffee. Looks a little impatient. What happened? You get caught in that blasting on the pass?"

"Yeah. Okay, thanks."

"I'm leaving to go home." She raised her eyebrows.

"Okay." The door clicked and Wolf stepped inside. After a step, he froze.

"Bullshit!" Baine was yelling at Senator Chama, who stood in front of Baine's desk. "That's what I told him."

Chama pulled his coffee from his mouth and leaned his head back, laughing. "Well, that kid probably had it coming."

Wolf walked over with his hand extended. "Senator Chama, I'm sorry I'm late. I see you've met Deputy Sergeant Baine."

"Yes, yes. Good man." Chama nodded, his smile fading to a contented look.

The senator was dressed casually in well-worn jeans and a button-up dress shirt rolled loosely to the elbows. In his mid-forties, he was a fit, tall man who looked like he took care of himself, and by the looks of his complexion, had a punch card at a tanning salon.

"Why don't we head to my office." Wolf edged away from Baine's desk.

"Ah yes. I've already acquainted myself with it."

Wolf nodded and led Chama. "Sorry. I was detained down south."

"Me too. Did you get held up with that blasting?"

"Just for a little," Wolf lied, thinking about how he'd been stuck for ten minutes and then ended up blowing through the entire zone with his roof lights flashing. He stopped at the coffee machine. "More coffee?"

"Please."

Wolf filled Chama's cup and poured himself one, and then stepped into his office. The lights were already on, the shades open. Wolf walked around the desk and glanced out the window. Margaret Hitchens was across the street, clearly visible inside her office with her nose pressed against the glass.

Wolf locked eyes with her and twisted the blinds shut.

"Thanks for agreeing to meet with me," Chama said as Wolf sat down.

"You're welcome. Please, take a seat."

Chama sat and took a sip of coffee, smiling with his eyes over the rim of the Styrofoam cup. They were gentle gray eyes, with crow's-feet grooves at the corners. Chama's hair looked like it had been trimmed around the edges with a laser, and a generous amount of gel locked his short black hair in place, looking like it would stay put in a nuclear blast.

Wolf ran a hand over his own head, feeling the lines in his hair from his ball cap along with particles of sand and dirt.

"To what do I owe this pleasure?" Wolf asked.

"I just wanted to stop in and say hi."

"Ah." Wolf sipped his coffee, put it down, and sat back.

"I wanted to commend you on a well-run campaign so far," said Chama. "I certainly think you're a good man for the job."

Wolf nodded. "Thank you. Is this what you told Sheriff MacLean earlier today?"

Chama chuckled, and then stared Wolf in the eye. "No."

They gazed at each other for a few moments, listening to the plastic tick of the clock.

"I saw your recent commercial. Nice move."

Wolf shrugged. "Not my move, but thanks."

"Ah, yes. Your campaign manager, Margaret Hitchens. She has the fire, doesn't she?"

Wolf nodded.

The silence returned and Wolf spread his hands.

Chama eyed his jacket on the chair next to him, and then dug into the breast pocket and produced an envelope. Without saying a word, he flipped it onto Wolf's desk, the contents knocking as they hit the wood surface.

Wolf drew his eyebrows together and grabbed it. It wasn't sealed, so he flipped it open and saw a USB memory stick. Wolf stared at it, let the envelope close, and dropped it back on the desk.

"And this is?"

Chama took a sip of coffee. "That's your insurance policy."

Wolf blinked. "And what does that mean, exactly?"

"I heard from MacLean today that he had some dirt on you, or one of your deputies. I didn't get the specifics, but he made it clear it would make you look bad. He wanted to make sure I knew whom I should be endorsing in this campaign. Which one of you two is the winning horse to bet on."

Wolf sipped his coffee.

Chama nodded and then stood up.

Wolf watched with mild interest as the senator stepped around his chair, pushed it in, and leaned heavily on the back with both hands. "I want to level with you, David. May I call you David?"

"Sure."

"You can call me Alexander."

Wolf shrugged.

"I would like to endorse you."

"What's on the memory stick?" Wolf asked.

Chama's sly smile made Wolf cringe. "Let's just say it's something that catches MacLean with his pants down."

Wolf raised his eyebrows, then leaned forward and put his hand on the envelope. "And all I have to do is blackmail MacLean with this. Is that right?"

Chama's smile faded. "That USB stick has something on it that you need to see."

"MacLean paying a hooker for a blowjob?" Wolf shook his head and leaned back, leaving the envelope on his desk. His teeth ground as he clenched his jaw. "I don't want to see it. You know, I rushed here from an important case. Had to leave my deputies all alone to handle everything, without me there to back them up. It's been the busiest Sunday I can remember, and there's still a lot of work I have to get done."

Chama stood straight and looked at his Rolex.

"We're working on a case my father started over twenty years ago. It stumped him, but we're making some good progress. And I should have known it was something like this you were bringing to me. Not an endorsement for the man I am, for the job I do, but an endorsement because there's shit out there that makes MacLean look bad. And you know the score. You're not going to back him with this out there. So you're here to tell me I'm your man, and you're giving me the dagger to take down MacLean. And for what? What will you want from me after all this is over?"

Chama narrowed his eyes.

"I can't even imagine the favor you already have lined up to call in on me years down the road. I bet it's a real good one. Well beyond my political IQ, that's for sure."

Wolf leaned forward and shoved the envelope across his desk. It shot off the edge, flew through the air, clanked against his closed office door, and landed on the carpet.

Chama lowered his eyes and smiled.

"Pick that up on the way out." Wolf swiveled in his chair and powered on his computer.

Wolf watched from his peripheral vision as Chama shook his head and picked up his jacket, then bent over and plucked the envelope from the floor.

"Nice meeting you, Sheriff. Good luck with your campaign."

"Good night."

Chama twisted the knob and walked out, leaving the door open.

Wolf stormed around his desk and shut it. With a sigh, he sat in his chair, the springs squealing as it leaned back. He pulled himself forward and leaned his elbows on the desk, rubbing his temples. He opened the top drawer and looked at the crisp packet of campaign cheat sheets stapled together.

He slammed it shut, stood, and opened his door again. "Baine!"

"Yeah!"

Wolf sat back down and waited.

"Yeah." Baine leaned in the doorway.

"Did you find her?"

"Yep."

Wolf stared at him. "So what are you waiting for?"

Baine looked lazily at his watch. "Seven thirty."

Wolf frowned.

"That's when she gets off work." Baine lifted his lips in a jackal smile. "Don't worry. I'll get what you need."

Wolf's skin crawled, but he stopped short of calling Baine off. Instead he nodded, and Baine disappeared around the corner.

Wolf jerked his head as his desk phone shrilled. He stared at it for two rings and then picked it up.

"Wolf."

"So?" Margaret's voice was just below a yell. "I just saw him leave. How did it go?"

"It went."

"Okaaaay. What did he say?"

"He wanted to endorse me."

"What?" She laughed. "Are you kidding me? Oh that's good!"

Wolf felt a ball of molten lava hit his gut as he pulled the phone away from his ear.

She blew into the phone. "Oh, my God. That's such good news. With this video going viral, and now Chama's endorsement, we're sitting pretty. Do you know the pull this guy has? Do you have any clue the contact you've just made for the rest of your career? Listen, I saw Sarah earlier today. Maybe we should all go out and celebrate. I'll buy dinner."

Wolf's gut churned some more. "No thanks. I already have something going on."

"Oh. Okay. Yeah, you and Sarah probably don't want me being a third wheel."

"Listen, I gotta go."

"All right. Great work, Sheriff. Remember to study your—"

Wolf hung up the phone and leaned back.

The clock said 6:40.

Politics, he thought. Whatever it took to be a politician, Wolf had not been endowed with it at birth. And the more time he spent with politicians, the less interested he was in developing the skill.

He closed his eyes and breathed deeply, letting the tension melt through the chair under him.

What seemed like five hours later, he snorted awake.

The clock said 6:51—an hour and nine minutes until his drink date with Kimber Grey. He had a VIN number to pursue, two burnt bodies to investigate, one being the possible owner of the vehicle, an old man with a hundred stalker photos plastered to the wall of a back room in his basement, missing and nowhere to be found, and eight dead bodies pulled from the lake, six of which were still unidentified.

His cell phone vibrated in his pocket and he pulled it out.

Sarah.

He snorted out loud, hit the ignore button, got up, and left for the bar early.

CHAPTER 41

"I TELL YOU WHAT ELSE." Rachette stepped over a downed log, his foot crunching on dead branches. "She's got another thing coming if she thinks Scott Reed is some sort of saint."

"What's that supposed to mean?" Wilson asked.

Rachette concentrated on his steps.

"Are you saying Scott's been cheating on Patterson?"

Rachette tilted his head from side to side. "Well, no. But I wouldn't be surprised if he was. Good-looking guy like that? Always shuttling women off the mountain in that snow cat? Men can only hold back for so long."

Wilson stopped and looked at him with a sour face.

"What?"

Wilson rolled his eyes and started walking again. "I don't know what you want from me here. You want me to start bad-mouthing Patterson?"

Rachette shook his head. "Never mind." The big man just didn't get it.

"Good idea."

They walked in silence for another few seconds, and then Wilson froze with wide eyes.

"What?"

"Shh."

Rachette tilted his head and listened. It was probably another squirrel, chipmunk, or deer. They'd been hiking zigzag patterns in the woods for over two hours now, and hadn't found anything of interest. But Wilson was a big man and hardly excitable, so this had definitely got Rachette's heart going.

"What?" he whispered again.

There. A branch snapped in the distance, somewhere up to the left.

A century of fire suppression in the area had made the forest so thick it was impossible to see further than fifty feet from where they stood.

"I think I saw movement." Wilson's eyes popped.

"I didn't see anything. Probably another deer."

"No. I saw ... I don't think it was an animal. I think it was a person."

Rachette pulled his gun without thinking, his pulse racing now. "You'd better be sure. You've got me freaked."

A second later came the sound of footfalls, the rhythm of a person running at a fast jog, traveling west up the slope ahead of them. They looked at each other.

"Let's go." Rachette started running toward it.

Sheriff Wolf had sworn he'd encountered a person a couple of nights ago, and Rachette was determined to prove his boss right. After his debacle with Jessica and the backpack, or *Gail*, or whatever her name was, he was desperate to redeem himself. This was his chance.

They were west of Kimber Grey and Olin Heeter's house, way up in the virgin forest with the lake at least a mile behind them.

Saplings scratched against his jacket, his lungs pumped, blood rushed in his ears, and he pushed harder. But the light was fading fast now, and he'd not seen anything in the first place. Before he got too far he stopped and listened for the footsteps again.

Wilson came up a few seconds later. The big man put his hands on his knees and huffed.

"Shh." Rachette cupped his ear.

Wilson closed his mouth and a squeak came from his nose as his chest heaved.

Nothing.

The sky above was turning orange, and despite there being at least thirty minutes of light left, the forest around them was turning pitch black. Though a flashlight would give away their position, Rachette saw no choice. He pulled his Maglite and clicked it on and Wilson did the same.

Wilson's breathing normalized, and the forest went silent once again.

They stood motionless for another minute.

Rachette flicked his head and they continued west up the mountainside.

"I don't hear anything anymore," Wilson whispered.

Rachette ignored him. He stepped between the dense pines, the trunks as thin as his forearm and no more than five feet apart. They needed to burn this part of the forest to the ground, damn it.

Five minutes later he stopped, breathing hard out of his mouth to try to catch his breath, happy to rest his legs, which ached from the incline.

Rachette shone his beam on Wilson's face and saw he was clearly the worse for wear. The forest had thinned out considerably, and it seemed a good spot to get their bearings.

They stood still for another minute, listening to crickets and a mourning dove.

Behind them, down the hillside the way they'd come, branches smacked, and then there was a thump on the ground.

"What the hell was that?" Rachette swept the forest with his beam, seeing only pine trunks.

"I don't know. Sounded like something falling from the trees." Wilson pointed his flashlight. "That direction. Probably a hundred feet."

They crept toward the noise, keeping pistols aimed and flashlights pointed.

Rachette darted the beam left and right, wondering what they were getting into. It had not been a natural sound. If palm trees on a desert island had surrounded them, then something falling and thumping to the ground would have made sense. But barring an owl dropping dead and hitting the forest floor, that noise was man-made.

Blood swished in his ears. His breath quickened. His limbs felt clumsy with the excitement pulsing through his veins, but his pointed pistol gave him all the courage he needed.

"Who's there?" Rachette called, realizing they might accidentally shoot one of their own. But they were the only ones out here. Patterson and Yates were down at the Heeter place. He wasn't thinking straight.

Wilson led the way, and then they reached a clearing. Wilson swept the forest floor with his flashlight beam and homed in on a rock.

"I think this was it." Wilson leaned down and picked it up.

Rachette swung his flashlight in a circle. There were a few more rocks twenty or so feet away, but they had clearly not been disturbed in ages. Pine needles were naturally laid on top of them, parts of them settled into the soil.

Wilson twisted the rock in his beam. It was caked with mud on one side, but it had not been embedded in the ground. It had been sitting on top of the pine needles.

"Someone threw it," Rachette whispered. He swallowed, wondering what the hell was going on. Had someone thrown it for a diversion, escaping in another direction while bringing them to this spot? Or had someone lured them here? If so, why? Rachette couldn't help but think that the person who'd decapitated seven people and sunk them in the lake was literally a stone's throw away.

Olin Heeter? A seventy-one-year-old man? It didn't seem likely, unless Heeter was a fitness buff, but the pictures they'd found of the man said otherwise—one of him holding fish, and another with his wife—showcasing quite a gut on the man. He was the kind who spent hours on end fishing on a boat, not wandering the dark forest.

Wilson dropped the rock and swept his beam in a circle.

Rachette did his own sweep, trying to peer deep into the woods, but it was no use. The beam only went so far in the surrounding dense pines.

"I vote we get the hell back down." Wilson's voice had an edge. "Come back in the day time."

Rachette nodded, taking a shaky breath. "I agree."

CHAPTER 42

THE PONY TAVERN was a boxy log structure on Main Street, known for its pool tables and craft beer. Located a few blocks to the south of the station, it stood across the street from the Edelweiss, where Kimber was holed up for the second night in a row.

Wolf parked his SUV and crunched across the parking lot, eyeing Kimber's black Chevy Blazer across the street. It was just like her father's old missing one in Wolf's report, but not identical. It was her mother's old truck, a final gift before ditching out on her daughter.

Stepping inside, he was surprised to see her talking animatedly with the bartender.

He sat next to her and ordered a double whiskey.

"You're early and going for the hard stuff, huh?"

He smiled.

"You know they have the best selection of beer in Rocky Points here." She pointed to the sign that said *We have the best selection of beer in Rocky Points* hanging on the wall.

"I'm in the mood for something with a little more bite."

"I'll take one of those, too." She pushed her beer aside. "Too bitter anyway."

Wolf's first sip was like gasoline going down his throat, but he enjoyed the immediate warmth traveling through his torso.

They sat in silence for a minute, watching muted baseball highlights on the screen above the bar, the soundtrack, instead, of two men shooting pool, the clack of their balls piercing over the faint country music coming out of the jukebox in the corner.

"This place is rockin' tonight." Kimber swiveled on her stool.

Wolf watched in the bar mirror as one of the men missed his eight-ball shot. "It's perfect."

Wolf watched Kimber's reflection as she studied the place. Her hair was pulled back, a thick brown ponytail resting in between her shoulder blades, a cream-colored silk blouse shining in the yellow overhead lights.

Her perfume was subtle and flowery and she was wearing more makeup than he'd ever seen on her.

He felt a tinge of self-consciousness looking like he was making zero effort in the self-presentation department. His jeans were dirty and he wore the T-shirt that he'd been wearing under his uniform all day, both probably smelling less than breezy.

"You eat yet?" he asked.

"No. You?"

"Nope."

They ordered burgers and he another whiskey, and then ate the meal in silence. She seemed to have something on her mind, and Wolf certainly had plenty to think about as he ate.

She swallowed the last bite of burger and said, "Wanna talk about it?"

"About you?"

She frowned. "What do you mean?"

"I thought you were asking if I wanted to talk about what I was thinking about."

She blushed and ducked into her drink. "Really? About me?"

He nodded. "About you and your family."

She set down her drink. "Pretty screwed up, right?"

His phone vibrated and he fished it from his pocket.

Rachette.

"I've got to take this." Into the phone he said, "Hey."

"There's definitely someone up there." Wolf could hear wind buffeting Rachette's cell.

Wolf stood and headed toward the jukebox, glancing over his shoulder at Kimber. She sat still, sipping her whiskey and staring at him in the mirror behind the bar.

"Where are you?"

"Up at Heeter's. Wilson and I were out in the woods, looking for whoever you saw the other night, and we're certain there was someone out there."

Wolf leaned on the jukebox with one hand. "Did you see them?"

"Nope. Wilson thinks he saw someone, but just a glimpse."

"Description?"

Rachette paused. "None. He just saw, you know, a person. But we heard him. Running pretty fast away from us, then he threw a rock to fool us."

"A rock?"

"Yeah. He threw a rock. Freaked us out."

"So it's a he?"

Rachette paused again. "We both think so. We think it was a young male. The person moved fast. And then he threw the rock."

"What happened at the house? Any prints?"

"Whoever left that blood everywhere was wearing gloves. Otherwise, they found a few usable prints inside the house. Heeter's ex-military, so they got a quick hit on those. All prints were his. But like you know, someone went to town scrubbing the place clean."

Wolf rubbed his face and stepped away from the jukebox as it exploded with sound. "And the rifle?"

"It's a Thompson Center ICON .308. Looks like it's been fired recently. Registered eleven years ago to Olin Heeter. A few of the cartridges were missing from that box. No prints on any of it. Just blood. Lorber's working the samples now, but he says it could take a few days to see a hit in CODIS. Says 'work is piling up faster than elephant shit.' His words. Not mine."

"And what about Heeter's truck? You find anything of interest?"

"We found a gas receipt from a week ago in the center console."

Wolf paused in thought, looking over at Kimber, who was laughing with the bartender. "A week ago?"

"Yep. From the Pumapetrol station."

"Where are you?"

Rachette hesitated. "We're at the marina. We were thinking of heading back to the station."

"Good. I don't want you guys poking around up there in the woods at night. You might have been lucky. We still don't know what we're dealing with. We'll get up there with the cavalry in the daytime and do a thorough search. Let me talk to Patterson."

A pause.

"Where's Patterson?"

"She headed back by herself. I'm with Wilson."

"Okay. What did she find out?"

"The rescue divers found something. Say it's just the right size to be a body, right where Heeter told your dad he saw some-thing dumped. They say they can't pull it up until tomorrow. Too deep. The equipment they had today wouldn't reach."

Wolf eyed Kimber again. "I put a VIN on yours and Patterson's desks. We need to know everything about the owner. And I want you to look deeper into Heeter. His business. His wife's death. His children. His business partners. His potential enemies." Wolf looked at his watch. "Do what you can tonight and then get some rest. We'll get back on it tomorrow morning."

CHAPTER 43

WOLF HUNG up and walked to Kimber.

She raised her watch and made a show of looking at it. "Work never ends, eh?"

Wolf sat and sipped his whiskey, grateful for the melted ice diluting the taste.

Staring at the muted televisions in silence, Wolf made more progress on his drink than she did on hers, so he ordered another one. When it came, he took a generous pull and looked over.

"You've never gotten the sense that someone is up in those woods? I mean, besides you or your neighbor, Mr. Heeter?"

Something like fear flashed in her eyes, but she shrugged and it disappeared. "No. Not really. I mean, I get alarms all the time. But there's all sorts of animals in those woods, and I just got so sick of being scared that I started ignoring everything."

"And you said it's been a couple of weeks since you've seen Olin Heeter?" Wolf asked.

She nodded. "Yeah. Not that I keep tabs on him or anything, but I can usually see when he's up there. You know, lights on at night, and he goes out in his boat a lot."

Unable to tell whether she was lying, Wolf turned back to

his drink and took a slurp. "You got sick of being scared, you just said. So you've been scared before?"

"No, not really. I mean, I used to be scared about being all alone at first, but I got used to it."

Wolf watched a tough person who'd been abandoned by both her parents, at least that's how she'd perceived it all these years. It was clear she had built up a wall around her feelings and it was thick. Or she was hiding something and this was her poker face.

After a sidelong glance she turned and looked at him. "Why? Do you think someone's up there?"

Ice tinkled in Wolf's glass as he stirred it. "I came across someone up there Friday night, and my deputies just had another encounter tonight."

"With Mr. Heeter?"

Wolf shook his head. "We don't think so. From what we've gathered about Olin Heeter, he's not exactly the picture of health. He's over seventy years old and out of shape. The person my deputies encountered was fast."

She blinked and stared into her glass.

"Tell me about the day your father left. When was that again?"

She gave him a sidelong glance. "The sixth. The sixth of July. I've told you this."

Wolf nodded, feigning recollection.

She looked up at the ceiling. "Geez. I don't remember much, I mean, I don't know much. I was locked in that damn room until late morning. When my mother let me out, he'd left us."

He scrunched one eye. "So on the night of the fourth, he locked you in the room. And then the next night, the night of the fifth, our Sheriff's Department came and asked if you and your family had seen Nick Pollard."

She nodded.

"Then your father locked you back in the room that night?"

She nodded. "Yes. He was angry again. He seemed completely gone after your father and that other deputy came to talk to us."

Wolf nodded. "And then you say he left on the sixth."

"Yeah. Like I said, I woke up late, my mother let me out, and he was gone. He'd left us."

"And the bag of bloody clothes. It was gone."

"Yes."

"And then you and your mother came down to Rocky Points and talked to the Sheriff's Department. Talked with my father."

She nodded.

Wolf raised his eyebrows. "But your father *didn't* leave you."

Kimber nodded and took a sip of her whiskey. "I know."

"So," he stared at her, "knowing now that your father was shot in the head and dumped in the lake instead of driving away in his truck on the morning of the sixth, do you want to revise your story?"

She looked at him and shook her head. "For what? That's all I know."

He stared at her.

"I don't remember hearing a gunshot. It's silent up there. I would have heard a shot."

Wolf watched a tear trickle from her eye down her cheek, past the mole on her upper lip, and drip off her chin.

"I don't know. I think maybe ..."

"What?"

She sniffed and looked up at him. "I think that maybe my mother killed my father."

"But like you said, you didn't hear the gunshot."

"But I didn't hear the gunshot," she whispered.

Wolf shook his head and took a sip. "Yeah, and your father killed Nick Pollard. Anything could have happened all those years ago, and all I have is your word for it."

She leaned back and stared at him. After a few seconds, she pushed her drink forward, making to get off her stool.

"Please, sit," he said.

She leaned forward and deflated back onto the stool.

"Look, you have to look at this from my point of view. All we have is your word, and that's not good for you."

"But you know someone called my father from the gas station. That person put Nick's blood on the phone. I was at the fireworks show at that exact time. There's phone records."

"So? That tells me nothing. Unless we can somehow prove Nick Pollard died in that window of time that you were at the fireworks show, then I don't give a shit what you were doing that night."

"Ooookay." She slid off the front of her stool. "I think this was a bad idea."

Wolf flipped a hand in the air. "Fine. Leave."

She leaned nearer. "I had nothing to do with Nick Pollard's death."

Wolf nodded, looking into his drink. "What about the night of the sixth?"

She picked her jacket off the back of the chair and paused. "What?"

"The sixth. The fourth, you were at the fireworks show and then locked in the room. The fifth, the Sheriff's Department comes and talks to your family, and then you were locked in the room that night. And the sixth? Your father's gone, and then you say that a couple of days later your mother went missing."

Wolf watched in the mirror while her brain ran calculations.

She nodded. "That's right. So?"

"So what did you do the night of the sixth?"

"The sixth?" She shook her head. "I don't know. Nothing."

Wolf stared at her and narrowed his eyes. He stopped short of mentioning Olin Heeter's testimony of seeing something dumped in the lake. Instead he shrugged and said, "Okay."

"Okay." She stared at him and then put her jacket back down. "So what?"

"So sit down." He studied her beautiful face, and again at her liberal and unnecessary use of makeup. He tilted his glass back and ended up sucking ice. With a roll of his neck, he sat straight and realized he was way past okay to drive.

"I have to use the restroom." He got up, leaving her dumb-founded, standing in place.

When Wolf was done, he returned to the bar and realized he'd been moving unconsciously for the entire act of voiding his bladder and washing his hands, because his mind was whirling with possibilities.

Wolf walked slowly, half in a trance towards Kimber, who had now sat back down, apparently shrugging off their harsh exchange. He watched as the bartender lined up another drink on the bar, and realized for the first time that Kimber had been sipping the same drink all night.

Sitting down, he snapped out of his thoughts as a commotion ensued at the entrance. A few men barged in, howling with laughter, and headed to an open pool table, pushing aside chairs like they owned the place.

Wolf twisted on his barstool and narrowed his eyes when he recognized the tallest of them as Carter Willis.

Carter removed his Armani jacket and the other two took off their hooded sweatshirts. The two men wore tight T-shirts, showcasing their bulging tattooed arms. Carter rolled up the sleeves on an expensive-looking button-up and looked over, locking eyes with Wolf.

Wolf stared back.

The two other men eyed Wolf with smirks, and then Carter mumbled something to them and walked straight over.

"Okay. Who the hell is this guy?" Kimber shifted forward on her stool and eyed Wolf.

Wolf turned back to the counter and stirred his drink.

Carter stood next to him and leaned on both hands. "Can I get two pitchers of Bud and three glasses?"

The bartender nodded and got to work pouring. "Hey, what was it, Sheriff Wolf?"

Wolf ignored him.

"All right. Dave? Can I call you Dave? Listen, I've heard all about you."

Wolf kept silent, resisting the urge to clench his fists.

Carter shook his head. "Have it your way. I just wanted to apologize about the other night. I know you and Sarah are involved and were out to dinner, and I was a little rude barging in like that. And I just wanted to say sorry."

He looked up at Carter's reflection in the mirror.

Carter slapped him on the shoulder, sending Wolf's hand into his drink, spilling a dollop onto the bar.

Wolf clenched his teeth as the sharp sting from the blow on his skin dissipated to a warm, tingling ache. He took a deep breath and looked at the liquid as it spread into a comma, reflecting the baseball highlights above.

"It's just hard to forget a piece of ass like that once you've had it, you know?"

Wolf twisted and punched as fast and as hard as he could with a backhand left, connecting with air where Carter's head had been a split instant before.

Carter ducked easily and jabbed once into Wolf's nose with lightning speed.

Before Carter's hand had left Wolf's skin, Wolf jerked back and connected an uppercut to the chin, sending Carter sprawling back with fluttering eyes. With a crash and tumble, Carter knocked over two barstools and landed on them. As Wolf stepped over a downed stool, he blinked away stinging tears as a gush of blood flooded his throat.

Carter finished bouncing off the wooden legs and put his hands down to push himself up, a move that left him vulnerable.

Wolf kicked and it connected with Carter's nose.

"Watch out!" Kimber yelled.

Wolf turned, hearing more than seeing a pool cue hurtling toward the side of his head. His skull thumped and he landed hard on top of Carter.

For a split second, Wolf was incapable of moving, his consciousness ebbing into darkness as he lay on top of Carter's wriggling legs. With the sound of ripping clothing, he was yanked to his feet and then another blow hit him square in the jaw. The last thing he saw was a shotgun and Kimber grabbing tattooed arms; then he went to sleep.

CHAPTER 44

PATTERSON LISTENED to the eighth purring ringtone in the earpiece. The digital clock read 10:25 p.m. and her eyes were stinging, losing the fight against gravity. This was the perfect end to the longest day on the planet.

"Jesus Christ, don't they have employees on duty on Sunday ni—"

"Boise County Sheriff's Department," said a bored voice.

Patterson straightened in her chair. "Hi, this is Deputy Heather Patterson from the Sluice County SD in Colorado. We found a burned vehicle yesterday with two yet unidentified bodies inside. The VIN came back registered in Idaho in your county. I'm doing a follow up call—"

"Please hold."

The line clicked and a recording of a man talking about Boise Sheriff Department's commitment to serving and protecting the people of southwestern Idaho crackled in her ear.

She leaned back and blew out through her nose.

Her cell phone lit up and started dancing across her desk.

She leaned forward and read the screen with a sigh. Scott. She had missed three of his calls today, and when she'd called him back he hadn't answered. Now she was going to have to leave him hanging yet again.

The phone stopped vibrating and darkened, plunging the room into silence once again, save for the recording in her ear.

The squad room was black, the only light the red flash of computer-monitor switches and the small cone of photons under her desk lamp. The ground outside the windows was painted with moonlight.

The recording went silent in her ear. "Deputy Michelson speaking."

"Hi." Patterson introduced herself. "I'm trying to get some information on a man we might have found down here. Looking to see if you have a rap sheet on him."

"Rocky Points, Colorado, huh?" The man's tone was breathy, couldn't-give-two shits-but-I'm-still-asking.

"Yeah. The name is William Van Wyke. I'm looking for priors, anything you have on him."

A long exhale. The squeak of a chair. Finger taps on a keyboard. "Yep. Here we go. A licensed private investigator. Registration is current with our department. Other than that, squeaky clean. Looks like he's working on the right side of the law. Wait, what did you say happened to him?"

"We found him burned up in a car, shot four times. Or at least we think it's him. Someone made sure his teeth weren't going to tell us, and he was a piece of charcoal after the fire."

The deputy gasped into the phone. "Hey, Rocky Points. They're talking on the news today about a bunch of bodies being pulled up from a lake near there, aren't they?"

"Yes, they are."

"In your county?"

"Yep."

The deputy let out a long whistle. "Well, have fun with that. That's some messed-up—"

Patterson jumped as the station line rang shrill and loud on her desk.

"Look, thanks for your help. If you find anything else, please give us a call. Again, it's the Sluice County Sheriff's Office, and I'm Deputy Patterson."

"Got it. Have a good one."

Patterson hit the button and switched to the main line. "Sluice County Sheriff's Department."

"Hi, my name is Doug Orden. I live up on Bear Hill Road. I'm pretty sure I just heard three gunshots."

CHAPTER 45

WOLF WAS HOT.

With exertion that made his head throb, he squinted to see. But the light was too bright and the images were washed out.

He heard the chopper in the distance, and by the sound of the rotors it was ready to lift off. Everyone was almost on board, and he was supposed to be sweeping the perimeter of the jungle, but he couldn't see a thing.

He was hot and his pack was heavy. So heavy he couldn't move.

The rotor of the chopper thumped, thrumming in his skull, but the wash didn't reach him. He was so damned hot.

As he looked back toward the jungle line, his earpiece roared with distressed yells, almost rupturing his eardrums. His head shrieked with pain from the sudden cacophony, and he was flooded with panic.

"They're dead, and it's all your fault!" someone screamed at him.

With a loud bang, he was slammed by a wall of heat as the helicopter exploded.

━━

Wolf grunted and tried to sit up, but something was on top of him. Something heavy and unmercifully hot was pinning him down.

He opened his eyes and saw a twirling ceiling fan, and then a face inches from his.

As he laid his head back, he was shocked by the sudden thud of pain that hit the back of his skull. His vision twisted for an instant, and then he blinked and looked again at the face in front of him.

"Are you all right?" it asked in a soft voice.

His chest heaved as he tried to normalize his breath. His nose was plugged, blood draining down the back of his throat. He closed his eyes and relaxed, realizing it was Kimber.

But wait. He opened his eyes again. That was his fan mounted on his bedroom ceiling.

The pressing heat on his body. Without having to move he realized that Kimber was lying stark naked with her full weight on his left side, her leg draped across his crotch. The sweat trapped between their bodies made the scrapes on Wolf's upper thighs itch.

"What's going on?"

She peaked her eyebrows and smiled. "You're at home. You got beat up by a bunch of thugs last night. And a little drunk to boot."

He reached up and touched the side of his head, sucking in a breath at the sudden pain. "Ah."

"Don't touch it. If it feels half as bad as it looks then I'm sure it hurts."

Wolf took a few deep breaths as he ran his fingers over the goose-egg bump above his ear, all the while feeling the sheets as they pulled across his naked skin. Suddenly it was all too much, and nausea rose from within.

"Get up." Wolf pushed her off and closed his eyes. "Get up."

The sheets rustled and the bedsprings rose as she got up.

After a few more breaths the nausea abated and he looked over and saw Kimber standing fully nude.

"What happened?"

"I just told you, you got beat up by—"

"No. I mean with us." Wolf wiped sweat off his forehead.

She looked genuinely confused. "You don't remember?"

He shook his head. The motion felt like a sledgehammer to his temples.

"The bartender, he had a shotgun. Got those guys off you. You got up and said you were all right. He was wondering if he should call your deputies, but you said no, and then you told me to take you home." She looked down at the sheets, and then she bent down and pulled up the comforter to cover her breasts. "And so I took you home."

Wolf closed his eyes. He remembered the fight with Carter, and he remembered what the man had said to him. In fact, Wolf felt rage course through him again just thinking about it, and it only served to make his head pound further.

"I'm sorry," she said.

Wolf cracked an eyelid and looked over at his nightstand. There was a wad of bloody gauze and bandages, and next to it was a bottle of peroxide.

"You were bleeding pretty bad. I got it to stop. I didn't think you needed stitches. It's just those head wounds won't stop sometimes."

He blinked. "And after you patched me up? We ..."

She smiled sheepishly. "You don't remember?"

"No I don't."

"Maybe you do need to get that checked out." She rolled her eyes and put a strand of hair behind her ear. "Jesus. I'm sorry. I had no idea."

He was thirsty as hell, like he'd swallowed some of the gauze and it was stuck in his throat. With immense effort he sat up, feeling dizzy as he looked around the room.

The light outside was dim. Was it morning or evening? He swept his legs off the edge of the bed and sat. The nightstand clock said 6:14.

"This is going to sound like a stupid question, but it's morning, right?"

She chuckled. "Yeah. Who the hell were those guys, anyway?" she asked.

He stood up, feeling too dizzy to worry about his nakedness. He paused to look out the window and saw an elk grazing under a pine. The window's cold aura got him walking again. "Nobody to worry about."

He walked to the bathroom and saw his clothes from the night before hanging on the shower-curtain rod.

"There was quite a lot of blood on your shirt, and some on your jeans. I washed them for you."

He looked at her and nodded thanks.

She returned the gesture.

He looked in the mirror, tilting his head to check out his wound. It was a bump the size of a golf ball with a red T-shaped split on the tip, clearly visible through his hair. The slightest touch sent a current of pain through his entire skull.

His nose was swollen and the skin was darkening in between his eyes. He wondered whether he was going to have two black eyes for the ... *shit. The debate.* Life came back at him like a slingshot.

"What is it?" Kimber stood next to him, still naked, staring at him in the mirror.

He looked down at her and frowned, thinking of the absurdity of the situation. "How did you know how to get to my house last night?"

She shook her head. "You told me how."

"I'm going to take a quick shower. Then you can take one if you want and we'll head back into town."

She narrowed her eyes and then, without a word, turned and closed the door behind her.

Wolf stood transfixed in front of the mirror, staring at the doorknob, wondering what the hell just happened, and what the hell had happened last night. Thoughts and snippets of his and Kimber's conversation before the fight flooded back into his brain, like a wave that goes out only to join forces with another and come crashing in even harder.

He remembered that after the pool cue had snapped against his head he'd gotten a good shot in on Carter, and then had been leveled by one of the other two men. And, yes, he remembered telling the bartender to hold off on calling his deputies. He didn't want the embarrassment of being caught out drinking with a person of interest in the case, and he never liked being broke and beaten on the ground.

What he did not remember was getting home, or anything else beyond that. Had he drunk that much? Apparently so.

The truth was, he wondered whether he should feel like a rape victim, or perpetrator.

There was one thing he did remember, though. Closing his eyes, he thought about the end of his dream.

They're dead and it's all your fault.

CHAPTER 46

ROILING clouds above slid by and the tops of the pines bent in the wind as Wolf walked across the station lot. Looking at the darkness to the north was all the forecast Wolf needed to know that it was going to be a miserable Monday. Fitting, he thought, still waiting for the Advil to deaden the miserable pounding in his skull.

Tammy glanced up at him and the door clacked.

Wolf almost made it by her. "Wait, what the hell happened to you?"

"Hello, Tammy." He grabbed the door and pulled.

Tammy stood, making to meet him on the other side through her own door.

"I don't want to talk about it," he warned as he stepped through the squad room.

She pulled her eyebrows together and watched him pass. "Let me know if you need anything."

"Will do. Thanks."

Wilson stood from his desk as if ready to refill his coffee and paused. "What happened to you?"

Wolf ignored the question. "What's going on? Where is everyone?"

"Rachette and Patterson just left to go up to the lake. Baine, too. Rachette and Baine were talking about going into the woods, and Patterson about the rescue team trying again to get what they found at the bottom of that lake. Oh yeah, and Baine says he left something on your desk?"

Wolf nodded. "Okay. Thanks."

"And, sir, Patterson got two calls last night from people who heard shots fired. Both said they heard three shots, but we haven't found anything yet, haven't heard anything. We had two units on patrol last night who couldn't find anything out of the ordinary either."

Wolf frowned and nodded. "Okay. Let me know if anything comes of it."

"Yes, sir."

He stepped down the hall and into his office. With a twist of his fingers, he opened the aluminum blinds, letting in the subdued light from outside. Margaret Hitchens was outside her office across the street, bundled in a knee-length dress coat and talking to three other professionally dressed people.

He narrowed his eyes as he watched Margaret signal toward his office, and the other three looked his way.

He turned and sat down. The squawk of the chair springs jabbed his brain. After a few seconds of staring dumbly at the wall, he stood and got a bottle of water from the mini-fridge in the hallway and downed it. With another half a bottle down his throat, he felt some vitality returning.

He heard his desk phone's digital trill and walked back into his office and picked it up.

"Wolf."

"Hey, it's Lorber. Have you checked your email yet?"

"No, just a second." Wolf woke up his computer and logged into his email.

As he waited for the screen to load he noticed a sticky-note on his desk.

Done. Check your email—Baine.

Wolf ripped up the note and put it in the trash. "All right. I'm clicking on your email."

"Look at the attachments. There're three pictures."

Wolf clicked on one. "Okay. I'm seeing a watch."

The sound of Lorber sipping coffee filled Wolf's ear. "I found this watch in Nick Pollard's truck. Notice the way the strap is severed at an angle. I'm calling this the smoking wrist watch."

"Mmm," Wolf said.

"This is a Swatch watch," Lorber continued," popular in the eighties and nineties. Some models are water resistant. Lucky for us, this one was not. Also lucky for us, this watch is made exclusively from plastic parts, which resisted corrosion from the particular vat of chemicals you bathed in yesterday. By the way, how are your genitals doing this morning?"

Wolf clicked on the second picture. It was a close-up of an arm of one of the murder victims pulled from the lake. "I'm on the second picture."

"Okay. The second picture is a close-up of Nick Pollard's left wrist. Do you see that vertical slash on it?"

Wolf leaned into the screen. "Yes, I do."

"And it just so happens that the angle of the cut on the wrist lines up exactly with the severed watch strap."

Wolf clicked on the third picture. It was a close-up of the watch face.

Lorber coughed into the receiver. "And the third. I give you ... the smoking wrist watch."

Wolf shook his head, allowing a small smile to reach his lips. "It's stopped at 8:25."

"Eight ... twenty ... five. There's even a cute little date and day underneath all that gook that I cleaned off, and it says Thursday, July 4th."

"So there's our time of death," Wolf said. "Or, correction, the time his truck was dumped in the lake."

"Yep. And there are eleven other stab wounds from the same knife on Nick Pollard's body, and three tears in the vinyl seat of his truck seat that were made by the same blade."

Wolf leaned back. "You'd bet your hair on it?"

"Yes, I would. It's safe to say that by the time Nick's truck was dumped in the pond, he was dead." Lorber made a kissing noise. "And there's the sound of Kimber Grey's alibi sealing tight."

Wolf stared at the picture on his computer screen, and then up at Wilson's head peeking inside the office.

"Sir? You have some company," Wilson said.

"Who?"

"Who what?" Lorber said in his ear.

"Lorber, I have to go. I'll talk to you later."

Wolf hung up and looked up to see Wilson gone and Margaret poking her head around the corner with a surprised grin on her face. "Howdy, Sheriff."

He needed to have a talk with Tammy.

"Sheriff Wolf, we're sorry to bother you." She stepped into the doorway and looked over her shoulder.

We?

Two men and a woman stepped up behind Margaret and craned their necks to see. He raised his chin and smiled politely, recognizing one of the men and one of the women from somewhere that escaped him now.

"Hello." Wolf walked around his desk.

"David," Margaret stepped aside, "these are all members of the Byron County Council. They were in town this morning and wanted to meet you. You might remember Chairwoman and President Teresa Ball. And Vice Chairman Phillip Henley. And this is Council Member Andrew Kensington."

Halfway through the second handshake, Margaret's face dropped. She stared closely at Wolf's injured scalp. "What happened to you?"

Wolf gave a sheepish smile and pointed a finger at his wound. "One of the hazards of the job."

Margaret and the council members shared an exasperated look with one another.

"Can we come in?" she asked. "We'd like to talk for just a few moments."

Wolf looked into his office. "Sure. But I only have two chairs. Let's go into the situation room to talk."

He led the way and held the door open. They funneled past him, trailed by their strong fragrances, and took seats on the plastic chairs inside.

Wolf pulled out a chair on the opposite side of the white table and sat down.

Chairwoman Teresa Ball leaned forward on a thin forearm. "I'd like to congratulate you on your recent popularity."

She flashed an attractive smile and smoothed her hand over her gray sculpture of a haircut. "We were just in the neighborhood, up from Ashland, checking on the new county building that's going up."

Wolf pulled down the corners of his mouth and nodded. "They're getting close."

She nodded. "They say they're going to be done by the end of the month."

"Just in time." Wolf smiled.

"Just in time." Her smiled faded. "I want to get to the point,

Sheriff. We're here because we want us all to be friends, here in this room. We have some great things already planned for the sustainable growth of this new county, and for this beautiful resort town of Rocky Points, and I think we can all help each other out with the trajectory our respective careers are taking."

Wolf leaned back and smiled. "The trajectory our careers are taking? We'll have to see about me. They still have to count the votes. At least I think so. Isn't that how it works, Margaret?"

Margaret's face froze for a second and then she smiled. "Ha. Of course, David." She looked at the three council members and then shot a dagger glance at him.

"And what about you three?" Wolf gestured to them. "You don't have to be voted in?"

The two men relaxed in their chairs and exchanged a glance. The chairwoman looked down at her hand and tapped a finger. "Yes, we do have to be voted and sworn in, but unlike you we are all running unopposed for the positions we will hold in the newly formed county council."

"Ah." Wolf nodded with genuine interest. "And if I were to be elected sheriff, the bylaws state I would have voting power in many of the council matters."

"That's right." The chairwoman nodded and her bangs bounced. "You would, on certain issues."

He spread his hands. "Just trying to 'get to the point' as you say."

The chairwoman leaned back.

The door clicked and creaked open, and Wilson peeked his head inside. "Sheriff?"

Wolf held up a finger. "I'll be right out. We were just finishing up."

Margaret's nostrils flared as she white-knuckle-gripped the armrest of her chair.

"Sir, we have a"—Wilson looked at the four guests and then back at him—"10-79."

He popped his eyebrows. "Sorry, folks. I've gotta get going." He got up and left the room.

The sit-room door latched behind him and Wilson stood staring with a strange expression. "Did you just say we have a dead body?"

Wilson blinked.

"What?"

"It's ... Beacon Light Road, sir. Two 10-79s on Beacon Light."

Wilson's sad eyes answered Wolf's question before Wolf could line up his words.

He sagged against the wall. "Who? Who is it?"

CHAPTER 47

WOLF TOOK his time getting to the black BMW sedan. The scratch of radios muffled and the rain seemed to pass through him. As he rounded behind the passenger side and ducked under the makeshift tent, he was laser focused on the alabaster hand dangling from the car.

It was clenched in a half fist, a single stripe of red on the palm to the first knuckle of the slender pinkie finger.

The two white-clad deputies stepped aside as Wolf approached.

A bare arm and leg came into view, and Wolf slowed to a halt. For a few long seconds he stared at her muddy feet, and then his eyes traveled from the bare foot, up the impossibly white skin of the knee to the thigh, all the way up to the side of her buttock, then to the waist and the slinky black nightgown pulled up to her belly.

For just an instant he allowed himself to look at her exposed black panties. It was unclear whether the movement of being ruthlessly murdered had raised the material above her waist, or whether it had been something or someone else. He moved forward and then stopped before raising his gaze to her face. *There are some things you don't need to see.*

He turned and walked around the back of the vehicle. Tinted windows. Colorado plates. Gleaming black paint covered with orbs of water.

He ducked under the edge of the tent. A white-clad deputy stepped back.

The open driver's-side door.

Wolf tracked his eyes from the man's shiny shoes, muddy and scuffed on the top of the toes, up his pressed black slacks, and paused at his fly. The crotch zipper was up and Wolf blinked with something akin to relief.

The rain slapped the top of the foldout canvas tent as he bent for a closer look at the dead man in the driver's seat.

Carter Willis's face was scratched and bruised, and there was a neat hole in his temple. His eyes were open, gazing into the void.

Wolf stared, his eyes transfixed on Carter's groomed hair. In his peripheral vision, he saw Sarah's face twisted toward him, blonde hair across her face; and though he did not look directly, he could see two white specks and knew that her eyes were open. The most beautiful blue eyes the world had ever seen, and would never see again. *There are some things you don't need to see.*

Wolf backed out of the tent and walked past Sergeant Yates, who stood silently at the rear of the vehicle.

"Sir." Yates stepped up behind him. "We found a receipt for the Pony Tavern from last night in the center console."

Wolf stopped and faced him.

Yates looked down at his feet. "Sir, I was on patrol last night, and I saw your truck there. You were there last night, weren't you?"

"Yes."

Yates held out his hand. "Sir, I gotta ..."

Wolf stared at his hand for a second, his mind too numb to comprehend what his deputy was doing, and then it hit him. He unholstered his service pistol and held it out, butt first. Yates took it with a rubber-gloved hand and ejected the clip. He held it up, counting the rounds, and checked the chamber. Wafting the barrel in front of his nose, Yates flared his nostrils and stared into the distance. He shook his head, jammed home the clip and handed the pistol back to Wolf.

"Good enough for me."

Wolf took it with a nod, his gut churning from the exchange.

He looked back at the BMW and then down the road that led down the mountain toward town.

A quarter mile away, barely visible through the rain, Wolf saw a figure alongside the road. Pacing. Back and forth. Back and forth.

The wriggling in his gut became a thrashing wild animal, a gorilla trying to break out of a cage. *Jack.*

He began walking.

CHAPTER 48

PATTERSON GRIPPED the ceiling handle and held her breath as Rachette sped up Beacon Light Road. The SUV's wheels skidded on the wet asphalt, catching just before they slid out of control.

"Careful," she said, but she wasn't about to tell him to slow down. Halfway to the lake, they'd received a call from a freaked-out Wilson. The news had been nothing short of a mental bomb detonation.

She and Rachette had not spoken on the way to the lake for one reason, and now they were silent for another.

Sarah was dead.

She closed her eyes and swallowed. Three gunshots, the two calls last night had said. At the memory, her eyes welled again. This time she let the tears stream down her face like the water across her passenger window.

"God damn it," she said.

Rachette reached over and squeezed her arm.

Flashing lights marking their destination came into view through the mist, and they sank back in their seats as Rachette revved the engine.

A figure standing on the right shoulder came into view, and Rachette swung into the oncoming lane to give a wide berth. As they passed, Patterson gazed out through wet eyes, seeing a curious look on a teenaged face framed by a cinched hood.

Her head whipped back. "Shit. That was Jack."

"What?" Rachette let up on the gas.

"Yeah. That was Sarah's new house we just passed. Jack doesn't know yet?" She looked at Rachette.

Rachette looked in the rearview mirror. "Damn. I don't know. What do we do?"

"There's Wolf." She pointed out the windshield.

Rachette jammed on the brakes and stopped in front of Wolf, who was marching down the edge of the road.

Patterson's breath caught when she saw Wolf's eyes underneath his hood. They were blood red and swollen, unblinking, staring past their vehicle.

She hit the button and lowered the window.

Wolf sidestepped the front of their SUV onto the muddy shoulder and walked past without pausing.

"Sir ..." The next word was impossible for her to choose. She looked back at Rachette and rolled up the window. "There's nothing we can do. Let's go up."

They drove on, parked behind a flashing SCSD vehicle and got out.

Patterson stepped into a patch of mud straight out of the SUV and slipped, barely catching herself on the door before she went down. With spread legs, she shut the door, zipped up her jacket against the cold, and then gingerly walked around to the asphalt.

Rachette stopped next to Yates at the top of the driveway. They stared down the road at Wolf's receding figure, now barely visible through a passing bank of fog.

"What the hell happened?" Rachette asked no one in particular.

Yates gestured to the black luxury sedan. "The homeowners discovered the car this morning. They live in Denver and this is their second home. You can see for yourself."

Patterson followed Rachette. Dread pressed down harder with each step she took, and she focused on Rachette's unwavering steps to get her there.

He went to the driver's-side door where Deputy Tyler was collecting forensic evidence.

Patterson ducked into the tent, determined to work the scene as she would work any other.

She flinched at Sarah's vacant stare, and it threatened to turn Patterson's resolve to rubble, but she pressed on. She had a job to do. She noted the trickle of blood that had oozed from a neat hole in her forehead. The rear of her skull was misshapen, but there seemed to be no exit wound. A wound on the upper right of Sarah's chest had bled profusely, running down her right arm, which dangled off her exposed right thigh.

Patterson tried to cloak herself in professional detachment, and to ignore the coppery scent of blood and death. She studied the scene from various perspectives: the gunshot wound on Carter Willis's head, the scuffmarks on his shoes, the lack of shoes on Sarah's muddy feet, and her nightgown outfit.

"Where are the keys?" she asked.

"Center console." Deputy Tyler cleared his throat. "Cup holder. It's a push-button start motor."

She looked down to the concrete driveway. "No brass?"

"Nope."

She reached back and Tyler handed her some gloves. She put them on and pulled open Carter Willis's jacket, exposing the empty inner pocket.

"I already checked his pants. No wallet. No ID. Insurance

card and registration in the glove compartment say Carter Willis. We're confirming his ID."

She nodded. "I met this guy. He introduced himself by that name." She noted the powder smears throughout the interior of the car where prints had been found and lifted.

"We've got at least four separate sets of prints so far," said Tyler.

Rachette walked away shaking his head. His face was pale and his lips shiny with saliva.

She listened to his footsteps quicken as he ran, and then his retching. The soundtrack of Rachette heaving drew no glances from anyone.

"Did you call Lorber?" she asked.

Tyler nodded. "He's on his way."

She looked around the interior of the car and at the scuffs on Carter's shoes. "Looks like they were shot outside the car and put inside."

"That's what I'm thinking," Tyler said. "There's no spatter inside. We'll scour the area with the K-9s."

She stood straight and walked up the hill to the top of the driveway.

Her eyes welled up again when she saw Wolf holding Jack in a bear hug and rocking back and forth, his son trying to escape to no avail. Then she flinched for the second time that morning when a distant wail reached her eardrums.

CHAPTER 49

RACHETTE STARED at his computer monitor, listening to the patter of rain on the squad-room windows. Despite the late afternoon hour, it was almost dark as evening outside and he needed to turn on his desk lamp, but he had too little willpower to reach up and twist the switch.

He felt a tinge of regret that he wasn't out scouring the scene of Sarah's murder for clues with Patterson. He felt like he'd betrayed Wolf once by getting caught unknowingly running drugs ... running drugs for Christ's sake! And now, instead of trying to crack Sarah's case, he was staring at the seizure-inducing glow of his computer screen, trying to find a damn match for at least one of these bodies pulled up from the depths, something he was also failing at.

"Rachette." Tammy was leaning out her door.

He looked up.

"There's a Kimber Grey here. Says she wants to talk to you."

He sat straight, his curiosity piqued. "Okay." He walked to the reception door and opened it.

Kimber Grey sat on the edge of a chair, her thick brown hair bundled at the back of her head, eyes big and wide and looking up at him.

"Hi," he said.

"Hi." She stood up and pulled down her sweatshirt. "Can I talk to you?"

"Sure. Come on inside."

She smiled gratefully and walked past him into the squad room.

Rachette took a deep inhale of her flowery scent as she passed and couldn't help stealing a glance at her butt.

"I've been sitting at the hotel all day, and I just wanted to see how things were progressing."

He nodded and motioned for her to sit in front of his desk.

Patterson's desk phone began to trill.

"With things up at the lake?"

She nodded and sat down. She crossed her legs and pulled a piece of escaped hair behind her ear.

He sat down behind his desk. "Yeah. Well, we had a little incident in town, and haven't gotten up there today. The rescue divers have been up there, though, trying to fish a ... trying to exhume something they found yesterday."

"Really?" She narrowed her eyes. "Another body?"

"Well, I don't want to speculate. It's not in the same spot we found the other bodies. Uh, and your father."

"Ah." She nodded and looked down at her hands.

Her eyelashes were so long, her lips so smooth. Even after so much time, over two years now, he recalled the way she kissed. So hungry and passionate, and then so quick to switch it off. He remembered it like it was yesterday. It was a typical shoot-down of the variety he'd endured many times before—one second he'd been making out with them, the next they'd come to their senses. But her shoot-down had stung badly, and he still remembered exactly how he'd screwed up the moment. They'd gotten into his car in full steamy mode, and he'd had his uniform in the back seat. He'd pointed at it and told her, *See that? I'm a man in uniform. You like men in uniform?*

Apparently she didn't. Because that had been the end of their kiss, and the end of any sort of meaningful communication they'd had with one another until the present moment.

He stood up. "You want any coffee?"

"Sure. Hey, have they found anything interesting in Mr. Heeter's house?"

He walked out from behind his desk. "No, I mean I can't really talk about it." He paused at the coffee machine and frowned. "So when is the last time you saw him?"

"Geez, I don't know. It's been a couple of weeks, I guess. He usually spends most of his weekends up there during the summer, but I didn't see him this last weekend, or the one before that, I guess."

"You want cream and sugar?"

"No thanks. Black."

He walked over and sat it down in front of her.

Patterson's desk phone rang again.

He jerked his head towards it and then got up. "Just a second. Someone keeps calling her damn phone. Hello?"

There was shuffling on the other end and then a man clearing his throat. "Hello. I was looking for Deputy Patterson."

"Yeah. Are you the one that keeps calling?"

"I called just before this, but I didn't leave a message. Then I contacted your dispatcher and got your fax number. I was just ringing back now to let her know that I was going to send over some files of interest we have."

"I'm sorry, who is this?"

"This is Deputy Michelson, Boise Sheriff's Department."

"Boise?"

"Idaho."

"Yeah, I know where Boise, Idaho is. I'm just wondering why you're calling."

"I'm calling because Deputy Patterson called last night about a VIN number. And we got to talking about the bodies you've been pulling up from that lake down there."

"Yeah?"

"I just got off the phone with a retiree from our department, a guy who lives up-state. He called, talking about an unsolved case we have from twenty-four years ago. This retiree worked the case back all those years. Anyway, he saw the news stories they're plastering all over the TV about those headless bodies you're pulling up down there, and he swears there's a connection to his case way back when. Looks like they had a body that showed up, killed with the same MO."

Rachette leaned on the edge of the desk. "In Idaho?"

"That's what he's saying."

"Same MO? You're sure?"

Deputy Michelson cleared his throat. "Yeah. I'm looking at the pictures. I don't envy you guys with eight of these bodies."

"Seven. One of them was killed with a shot ..." Rachette looked over at Kimber and stopped talking. It looked like she had been staring at him with wide eyes, and now she turned away.

Shit. He was being an insensitive bastard talking about her father like this right in front of her.

He stood from the edge of the desk and turned away. "Anyway ... sounds like we need to hear about this."

"That's what I figured. Like I was going to tell Deputy Patterson, I'm sending it over, so keep an eye out for it."

Rachette looked absently at Kimber and nodded. "Sounds good. We'll look forward to it. Thanks." The line clicked and he hung up.

"Hey, Wilson. We've got an important fax coming in from the Boise Sheriff's Department."

"Idaho?"

Rachette held out his hands. "No, California. Yes, Idaho."

"What do you want me to do about it?"

Rachette exhaled. "Just make sure it comes through."

Wilson shook his head and kept his eyes on his computer screen. "Yeah, sure."

Rachette felt his face blossom red.

"Deputy Rachette?" Kimber looked up at him with puppy-dog eyes.

She was gorgeous.

"Yeah?"

"Can you do me a favor?" She smiled sheepishly.

"Sure. What?"

"The reason I came in here ... to talk to you ... is because I have to go up to my house, and I heard from Sheriff Wolf that you guys have seen someone up there."

Rachette sat down. "Nobody's seen anyone. But someone is definitely up there."

Her eyebrows creased together and she looked at her hands. "I have to go up there. I have to get some things, but I don't want to go alone. Do you think you could go up with me?"

"Now?"

"I have to go. I left my laptop computer up there and it's driving me crazy."

He shook his head. "If you need to, you can use one of our computers in here."

She sagged in her chair. "I also don't have enough money on me to stay another night in the Edelweiss. I don't use credit cards, so I have to go get more cash. Listen, I'll buy you a drink on the way back."

Without even trying, he gave her an awe-shucks smile that lit up her face. "If you need money, I can spot you, Kimber."

Her face dropped and she scooted her chair back. "No, thank you. I'll just drive up by myself. I'm sorry for bothering you." She stood up.

"All right. All right." He raised a hand and stood up. "Geez, I'll go with you. Don't worry."

She smiled and tilted her head, her eyes softening with unending gratitude that made him blush.

"But I'm driving," he said. "I don't want to be listening to Madonna all the way up there in that Blazer of yours." He picked up his jacket and put it on.

She rolled her eyes. "Thank you. I feel so much better."

He smiled and hooked his thumbs on his duty belt. "No problem. Hey, Wilson, I'm heading up to the lake for a little bit. I'll be back."

Wilson eyed them for a second and then nodded. "All right. I'll be sitting in this dark room sifting through databases."

Rachette pursed his lips and thought about Wolf. Where was he? Patterson had said after he'd talked to Jack, Wolf had driven away without a glance or word to anyone.

He felt sick thinking about the grief the two Wolf boys must have been feeling right now.

"Could be worse," he said.

Wilson looked up and nodded with closed eyes. "Yeah. Could be worse."

CHAPTER 50

PATTERSON WALKED into the squad room and took off her jacket, being careful not to flip water all over the papers on her desk.

Easing around to her seat, she looked out the rain-splotched window and read *Debate Cancelled Tonight* in black capital letters on the town-hall sign across the street.

"You see all those reporters outside?" she asked Wilson.

"Mmmhmm."

She slung her jacket on the chair and sat down, feeling an ache in her shoulders as she reached for the mouse to wake up her computer. The screen for the National Missing Persons Database materialized on screen.

"Any luck?"

Wilson gave her a sour look. "What do you think?"

She opened another internet browser tab and checked her email.

"So what have we got up there?" Wilson's tone softened.

She leaned back and rubbed her eyes, trying to vaporize an image of Sarah's exposed dead body from the back of her eyelids.

"Nothing yet. None of the neighbors saw anything. The two people who heard the gunshots were over a mile away, on the other side of thick forest, over on Bear Hill Road. They didn't see anything. No brass at the scene. Fingerprints are Carter Willis's, Sarah's and another two sets that aren't matching in IAFIS."

Patterson and Wilson turned to the sound of the reception door slamming closed. Wolf was already halfway through the squad room, head leaning forward as he marched.

She swallowed. "Sir."

Wolf ground to a halt at her desk and dropped a plastic bag that knocked against the wood.

Looking down, she saw it was a brushed nickel doorknob. With raised eyebrows, she looked up.

"Where's the Pollard case packet?" he asked.

She snatched it off her desk and held it up.

Without a word, he pulled it from her fingers and flipped to a page. "I want you to check the prints on this doorknob against these. And then"—he flipped to another page—"these."

She took the packet back and pulled her eyebrows together. "You want—"

"Wilson, help her." And with that, Wolf left the room.

"Yes, sir," Patterson said to no one. She looked up at Wilson and they exchanged puzzled looks.

"Now!" Wolf's voice boomed from around the corner.

She jumped in her seat and stood.

"What the hell is going on?" Wilson stood up.

"Follow me." She grabbed the plastic bag and case file and marched out of the squad room, down the hallway past Wolf's office and into the tiny box of a room they called a lab.

Wilson was breathing excitedly on her heels. "What's going on?" he whispered when they got inside.

"We have to check for a print match on this doorknob to these or these." She got busy.

"But ... the first prints are Kimber Grey's."

"Yep." Patterson flicked on an overhead lamp and bent it down.

"And these are the prints on the payphone."

"Yep."

"I don't get it."

"Me neither. Now stop wasting time and hand me that brush."

Ten minutes later, Patterson stood over the white sheet of paper and pasted the clear tape on top. An array of charcoal-colored prints crowded the small area like a cloud of swirling smoke.

With a magnifying lens, she bent over and studied the patterns, looking for specific indicators. There were dozens of fingerprints, smudges on top of smudges, and most were warped because of the shape of the knob.

Her lower back ached from bending over. The humming light was hot and making her palms sweat even more than usual under her gloves. Wilson's nose-breathing and shuffling feet weren't helping the overall atmosphere inside the tiny room, especially knowing Wolf was outside waiting with what looked to be a biblical temper flare up happening.

Then she came up with a result. And it confused the hell out of her.

Wilson stood straight, studying her expression. "What's the matter?"

She picked up the print-covered card and held it next to Kimber Grey's print sheet. "The fingerprints on this doorknob do not match Kimber Grey's."

"Okay. So, what's the matter?"

She picked up the print sheet from the bloody handset of the payphone at Pumapetrol Gas. "The fingerprints on this doorknob match these on the payphone from twenty-two years ago."

CHAPTER 51

"MacLean," the voice barked in Wolf's ear.

"I need to know what bullets were used in the Idaho vehicle fire."

"Sheriff Wolf? Hey, listen. I was so sorry to hear about your ex-wife. My God, I can only—"

"I need to know."

"Yeah, yeah. Just a second." The phone line clicked and there was silence.

Breathing out his mouth, Wolf sat listening to the pulse pounding in his ears. A trickle of clotted blood slid down his throat and he made a face as he swallowed.

"You there?"

"Yes."

".308 FMJ."

Wolf hung up and rubbed the sandpaper stubble on his chin. Sarah and Carter had been murdered with a nine-millimeter hollow point. A pistol.

Up at Olin Heeter's, there'd been a box of .308 Winchester full metal jackets, half empty, sitting on the bookcase next to a rifle. It was looking like that rifle had killed those two burned men.

With growing impatience, Wolf stood and walked to the hallway and saw the lab door was still closed.

For ten minutes, he'd been waiting on Patterson and Wilson, and on Jake Wegener, his friend from his football days who worked for the Carbon County Sheriff's Department. Wegener had promised to send over all he had on Aspen's Carter Willis, but the fax machine at the end of the hall sat dormant.

The lab door flew open and Patterson came rushing out. "Sir, the prints on the doorknob you gave us match the ones on the payphone receiver."

Wolf snapped the sheet out of her hands and walked into his office.

"Where did you get that doorknob?" Patterson was on his heels.

"My house," Wolf said, laying the sheet on his desk.

Patterson shook her head. "What do you mean, your house?"

Wolf nodded. "Kimber Grey was over at my house last night."

"Sir." Patterson spoke slowly. "I talked to Lorber today and he said the watch they found in Nick Pollard's truck proved Kimber Grey was telling the truth about being at the fireworks show when that payphone call was made."

Wolf nodded.

"And I just confirmed those are not her prints."

The fax machine hummed and Wolf walked past them out into the hall. "I've been thinking about those doorknobs at Olin Heeter's place for a while now. It was so out of place that every-thing was scrubbed clean, except for those knobs. It was like someone was trying to lure us in there." Wolf paused at the fax machine. "In fact, that's exactly what it was."

"I ... sir, I'm not getting it."

A page marked from Carbon County Sheriff's Office spit out the slot.

Letting the machine do its work, he turned back around. "I was out with Kimber Grey last night. I don't want to talk about it, but she ended up staying at my house. I took that doorknob from my bathroom, which I watched her touch."

Patterson lowered her voice and spoke slow again. "But, sir, the doorknob prints at your house did *not* match Kimber Grey's."

The fax machine finished and Wolf turned and picked up the pages from Carbon County. He was surprised to find a hefty stack of paper already in the incoming fax tray.

With mounting curiosity, he picked up the entire stack. The heading on one of the pages read Boise County Sheriff's Department.

As he flipped through the sheets one by one, he held his breath. With a toothless grin, he pulled out the third sheet and held it in front of their faces.

CHAPTER 52

PATTERSON STARED at a picture of two teenaged girls standing side by side, arm in arm on the shore of a lake. The black-and-white photo was poor quality—a copy of an original that had been faxed—but she could see that the two girls were of identical height, with identical haircuts, wearing identical sweatshirts.

With a sinking stomach she looked up. "They're identical twins."

Eyes glassing over, Wolf nodded and twisted his lip in a satisfied snarl. "Identical twins who are sadistic killers. That's who was out murdering Nick Pollard at the same time she was at the lake watching fireworks. That's why her father left that night. Because it was Kimber's sister in trouble. She had a dead body to dispose of."

Wilson frowned. "What the hell ... let me see that." He stared at the paper. "But if she killed Nick ... why would she call her father about it?"

Wolf walked slowly past them toward his office, staring at the fax from the Boise Sheriff's Department.

Patterson and Wilson followed.

"It's all here," Wolf said, flipping to another page. "The family disappeared from Idaho twenty-five years ago, right after a similar killing happened. Near decapitation. Mutilation. Took place in McCall, Idaho. A neighbor of the *Kiplings*. A teenaged boy found murdered in the woods near his boat shed. Stabbed nineteen times, head almost severed clean off, a slice from the pubic bone to the ribs."

Wolf dropped a page with four photographs of the gruesome killing printed on it and turned to the next sheet. "Here are their real names: Parker Grey was actually named Dustin Kipling. The twins are Hannah and Rachel. The mother is the same name: Katherine."

"That's why the Greys' past never checked out with the Tennessee commune," Wilson said.

Wolf paced in a circle, reading farther down the page. "Dustin Kipling used to own a chain of boat dealerships in Idaho. Kipling Boats was the largest statewide seller and buyer of watercraft and fishing boats, with four dealerships. Says here he sold every dealership in the span of a single day for pennies on the dollar to a casino owner in Wendover, Nevada, named Gabriel Sithro. In the middle of the night of that same date, their house in McCall, Idaho, burnt to the ground, and the family went missing. Suspected arson. No bodies were found in the fire, and the family cars were in the garage ... and then the family was never heard from again."

Patterson leaned against the wall with wide eyes. "So they were fleeing ... trying to disappear, because of their murdered neighbor?"

Wolf held up another sheet and read.

Patterson's curiosity boiled over. "What?"

"Looks like a family friend, a psychiatrist, came into the

Boise station after the Kiplings disappeared. He had recently prescribed anti-psychotics for Dustin, or Parker, as we know him. Learning about that, Idaho law enforcement has assumed all along that Dustin murdered the neighbor, but the Kiplings' whereabouts stumped them."

Patterson frowned. "That was the same story Kimber and her mother told about Parker Grey. He was psychotic and needed meds."

Wolf perused the next page. "Here's a statement from a school psychologist taken a few months after the Kiplings disappeared. She reported two incidents involving Hannah Kipling at Duck Mountain Middle School. First, Hannah received minor injuries while fighting a boy. Hannah said she was just sticking up for her sister, Rachel. A few months later ..."

"What?" Patterson asked.

Wolf shook the sheets of paper. "Hannah retaliated against that same boy, beating him with a baseball bat until he was unconscious. The kid was hospitalized with a fractured skull, broken ribs, and a broken arm, and she was expelled from school."

"Wow," Wilson said.

"She had extremely violent tendencies according to the class psychologist," Wolf said. "It was the girls. It's always been them, not their father. They killed that teenager in Idaho, and that's why the family left. It makes sense now why we found Parker shot in the head. A girl called from the payphone that night. It was one of Parker Grey's girls, sorry, Dustin Kipling's girls, who killed Nick. She'd killed him and had his blood all over her hands, and called her father to help clean it up. There must have been a family meltdown after that. Think about it— they leave Idaho because of their psychotic, violent daughters. They literally burned their old life to the ground, and now the girls are starting up again."

Patterson nodded.

"After my father and Burton went up to the lake and talked to them on the fifth, maybe Parker had had enough. Maybe he threatened to hospitalize them. Turn them in. Who knows exactly? But the family all knew what had happened to Nick Pollard that night. And in the end, Parker Grey was a threat to the girls. So they shot him and dumped him out in the lake, right next to Nick."

"And Katherine Grey?" Patterson gasped with realization. "She would have known about her husband's death. And she came in and did that interview knowing he was dead, killed by the hands of her own daughters. But she stood there and lied to your father."

"She looked like she was hiding something in that interview. She had a tell," said Wolf, "and now she's at the bottom of the lake in front of Olin Heeter's place."

"What?" Patterson asked.

"I think Katherine's daughters killed her that night after the interviews with my father at the station. Maybe they were skittish about whether or not Katherine would crack under the pressure. Whatever the reason, they killed her and dumped her body out in the lake, but in a different place the following night, and Olin Heeter had a front-row seat to watch it, complete with a spotlight, thanks to clear skies and the moon's reflection." Wolf stared out the window.

"So Katherine leaving to go back to Tennessee was all a big—"

"Shit-shit-shit." Wilson blurted.

Patterson and Wolf looked at him.

"Rachette took a call from the Boise Sheriff's Office earlier, and they said they were sending a fax. He told me to keep an eye out for it. He was talking with Kimber Grey at his desk at the time, and took the call at Patterson's desk. At your desk."

"Okay," Patterson said. "And?"

"And Rachette hung up and left with her, said he was going up to the lake with her and would be back in a while."

"So she knows we know." Wolf darted past them toward the door.

CHAPTER 53

RACHETTE SCANNED the woods on either side of the dirt road as they crept down the slope towards Kimber's cabin.

The wipers squeaked across the windshield and Rachette turned them off. The rain had finally abated, but the clouds were still low and thick. Though it was only late afternoon it looked like dusk outside.

He leaned back in his seat, wondering where someone lurking in the woods would have taken shelter in a storm like this. A cave? A tent? Heeter's place? They needed to get back up here with the cavalry. Tomorrow.

Kimber eyed him from the passenger seat. "What is it?"

He shook his head and tried to look calm. "Nothing. Just thinking."

"Slow down here. Your back bumper will scrape."

"I know. I've been here a few times myself the last couple of days."

The SUV rocked back and dropped down as Rachette eased into the giant pothole between the two over-sized rocks.

Rachette stopped at Olin Heeter's turn-off and looked up

the road. The dirt was undisturbed, or, if it had been agitated, the earlier deluge of rain had smoothed it over.

He let off the brake and wondered whether the rescue divers had made any progress out on the lake today. Then he decided since he'd not heard anything, that they hadn't.

The dashboard clock said 5:12—a few minutes past a normal workingman's clock-out time. With such a full day of gut-wrenching trauma that had transpired, he could have used a beer. He decided he was going to take Kimber Grey up on buying him some suds on the way back.

A few minutes later, Rachette parked in front of the cabin and stomped his foot on the parking brake. "Here we are. You want me to wait here for you?"

She smiled. "No. Why don't you come in? I'll make us some coffee before we head back."

Rachette felt lightness in his chest as his heart fluttered. Was she hitting on him?

He twisted the keys and got out. A drop of moisture slapped him in the face from his roof and the soggy dirt gave way beneath his boot. The air was thick and moist, and he zipped up his jacket all the way against the chill.

The lake was a magnificent sight to see, so calm, lead color from the reflection of the clouds above. A crow sailed by and over the edge of the cliff that severed the land to the rear of her house.

"Geez, you aren't afraid of heights I take it."

She chuckled. "No. In fact I climb that face most days. Got a top-rope set up. You should try it."

"No, thank you. I'd have a chain-link fence along the top of that thing if I lived here. I couldn't ever trust myself after a six pack. Probably fall trying to take a leak off it."

She scrunched her face and walked up the stairs.

Shaking his head at his own last comment, he followed her.

When he got to the top, his boot slipped on the wet wood and he almost went down. Regaining his balance without slamming into her, he stood up straight and felt his face reddening, but Kimber's soft smile disarmed him and he smiled back. "I'm a klutz. What can I say?"

For a second she leaned towards him, like she was going to kiss him or something. Then she stopped, looked down at the deck, and dug in her jeans pocket. She produced a key and opened the door. Stepping inside, she turned and beckoned him in with a bashful look.

Rachette swallowed at the sight of her beautiful eyes and took a deep breath to calm his thumping chest.

"Let me take your coat." She took off her own jacket, revealing her slender body, and turned to him.

He unzipped his jacket and sloughed off one sleeve, nice and slow, then the other.

Like she'd been kicked from behind by an invisible foot, she lurched forward and bumped into him, sending him off balance.

"Whoa, easy ..."

He let the words die on his lips when he found himself staring down the barrel of a pistol. His stomach dropped an inch when he realized it was his own Glock 17, pulled from his holster.

He quickly regained his composure. There was no doubt in his mind that he was going to duck and grab for the weapon, but before he could make his move she stepped back with lightning speed and fired a deafening round into the ceiling.

"Ah!" Rachette's hearing became a thousand ringing bells. "What the hell."

"Don't think about it." Kimber's lips were raised like a rabid dog's, her beautiful face twisted into pure rage.

"Yeah, you got it," he said with raised arms.

He stared at her through crumbs of drywall falling from the

ceiling, knowing instantly this woman had murdered and decapitated seven men with a knife. How had he been so duped? How had they all? Strangely, he felt detached from the moment, like he was watching a scene in a horror flick.

Kimber took forced breaths through her nose and looked at the floor beneath her. Keeping the pistol aimed steadily at his chest, she stomped her foot down on the wood, and a boom echoed through the house. "Get up here!"

He frowned. "Who are you talking to?"

Closing one eye, she brought her other hand up to the pistol and aimed. "Keep quiet. Or I will shoot you in the head."

There was a creaking sound below the floor, and then a door shutting.

Listening intently, he stood stock-still and heard nothing more. A few seconds later, footsteps creaked on the wood outside, and Rachette eyed the closed front door.

Kimber waved the gun. "Step over here."

He stepped forward into the living room as she stepped back.

"Back there. Lean against the wall."

He did as he was told, keeping his hands motionless above his shoulders.

Kimber stepped to the door and opened it. "Stay out there. We're coming out," she said, and then she turned to Rachette.

"What's going on?" a female voice called from outside.

The sound of the voice was familiar.

"Out." Kimber came back into the family room and waved him toward the open front door.

He obeyed. The air flowing in the door penetrated his uniform shirt, making him shiver as he stepped onto the porch. At the top of the stairs he froze and widened his eyes. "What the hell?" With a quick jerk of his head he looked over his shoulder, making sure he was seeing correctly.

Kimber stood behind him, thrusting the barrel into his face with renewed vigor. "Keep walking."

He turned around and walked, almost falling down the stairs as his mind whirled with the reality of the situation. "There's two of you?"

"I said shut up or I'll shoot you in the head and throw you off that cliff."

He quickened his pace down the stairs, noting the specificity of this woman's threats.

The other Kimber stood out of the way at the bottom of the stairs, wearing a jacket that matched her doppelganger sister's.

"Over there. Against your car."

Rachette leaned up against the ticking front end of his SUV, grateful to feel the warmth streaming out from under the hood. He turned to look at both women, who now stood next to each other. In every way they looked alike, from the amber eyes to the smooth lips, to the wavy thick brown hair that was too much to tame.

"Wow. You guys are so much alike."

Kimber whipped her glare toward him and marched with the muzzle raised. "I said shut up!"

He lowered his gaze submissively and waited for ten long seconds for something to happen—hoping that something involved him not getting shot.

"Why are you with him?" Her sister broke the silence.

Kimber backed up and lowered the gun. "They know, Rachel. Or at least they're gonna know. Boise sheriff called them this afternoon."

Rachel, Rachette thought, trying to pick out a feature on the women to tell them apart. Back in Nebraska, he'd gone to elementary school with twin brothers, and he remembered they were easy to distinguish. But not these two.

"Oh, my God." Rachel gripped her thick head of hair and

began breathing hard. She paced with crunching footsteps and looked at the ground, her lips moving without sound. She crouched into a ball and sat on the first step of the stairs.

Rachette's pulse was escalating with each breath. He was thinking about the dead bodies in the morgue, and how they generally matched Rachette's description.

It had been one of them in the woods last night, he realized. Wolf had encountered one of them, too.

With immense effort he took a breath through his nose, trying to calm himself.

"What's our plan here?" Rachel raised her head.

Kimber shrugged. "We get in that cop car and drive."

"And then what? Don't they have GPS trackers on those things?"

Rachette nodded, but neither of them noticed.

"They'd find us in minutes. And then what?"

Kimber refocused on Rachette. "We bring him."

"And then what, Hannah?"

Hannah.

"Then we what? Ransom this cop for a helicopter ride somewhere? Yeah, that's going to work."

"I don't know!" Hannah paced a few steps, rubbing her nose. "Then we'll just go into the woods."

"And then what?"

Hannah looked into the forest behind Rachette. "We don't have a choice."

Rachette heard the rolling hiss and pop of tires somewhere in the distance. He flicked his eyes left and immediately caught movement—a white SUV with roof lights flitting in and out of the trees along the lake's edge.

Hannah looked and raised her pistol at him. "Shit. Go see."

Rachel stood up from the stairs and jogged down toward the cliff. She skidded to a stop and looked left, then shook her head and walked back fast. "It's the frickin' cops. What are we going to do?"

Rachette cleared his throat and lowered his hands a fraction. Whatever was going on was apparently all explained in the fax message that the Boise Sheriff's Department had sent. Rachette blinked, pausing to clench his eyes with a prayer that whatever it was, Wolf and Patterson had figured it out, had found the fax message, and were coming to his rescue. He prayed that Wilson had done as he'd been asked and had kept an eye on the fax machine.

Amen.

When he opened his eyes, Hannah was sneering at him, walking slowly in his direction, the pistol rising with each step.

"Please don't do it, Hannah," Rachel said.

He swallowed, unnerved by Rachel's tone. It was like she was pleading, but knew her sister too well, and it was no use trying to stop her. She'd seen it all before, and she was going to see it again. Because it was starting to make sense to Rachette. It was like Hannah was the uncontrollable one who killed. Who murdered her father. And Rachel? She was the one who sat back and watched in horror.

"Please." Again, he lowered his gaze submissively. "You have to tell me what's going on. I can help you guys. I can help you out of this."

Hannah's footsteps crunched all the way to him and the cold steel of the pistol barrel pushed against his forehead, forcing his chin up.

She bared her teeth. "What the hell are they—"

With a lightning-quick move he ducked to the right and swatted up with his left arm. The gun fired, deafening him and sending a blast of heat onto the side of his face, but the shot missed, just like he'd known it would. Nobody could react fast enough to such an unexpected, ballsy maneuver. An instant later he gripped her gun arm with both hands and pushed his full weight back into her, knocking her back and to the side.

With a whimper, she fell sideways and before she'd even hit the ground Rachette had twisted the gun from her grip.

"That's right!" he screamed at the top of his lungs, elation filling his body.

Gripping the pistol and twisting to raise it toward Rachel, he flinched when he saw she had her own pistol aimed at him already.

There was a lance of fire, and his gun-holding shoulder was wrenched back like he'd been clipped by a semi-truck. He twisted and his feet slipped out from under him. Stutter stepping, he tried to keep his balance, but slammed head first into the tire of his SUV.

For an agonizing eternity, he convulsed on the ground, trying to take a breath that would not come. All the while, a warm pool of blood spread underneath him.

A throat-tearing scream filled his ears, and he felt powerful arms pick him up and drag him away over the wet ground. The next thing he knew he was rolled onto his back and staring at the leaden sky.

Hannah's face appeared in front of his, her eyes bloodshot and evil. She stepped over him and sat hard on his chest.

With a squeal, his lungs finally opened, and a cold breath of wind rushed into his chest.

And then Hannah's cold hands locked on his neck and squeezed.

He tried to struggle, but the strength in him was already gone.

The last thing he saw was Hannah's drooling snarl, popping stars in his vision, and then Rachel wrapping her arms around her sister.

CHAPTER 54

PATTERSON SLAMMED THE BRAKES, fishtailing to a stop, and then stuck her head out the window.

Cursing as the engine fan kicked on, she craned her neck, trying to catch the echo of sound waves she thought she'd just heard, but heard nothing.

As she ducked her head into her cab again she heard it again. This time the gunshot was clear as day, without the rumbling tires drowning it out. Wrenching the radio off her center comms console, she thumbed the button.

"This is Patterson. Come in."

She leaned out the window again and listened.

The radio scratched and then a loud whining noise blasted out. "... ahead."

Whatever Wolf had just said had been mostly drowned out by the sound of the boat and rushing wind.

"I just heard a gunshot."

A pause.

She let off the brake and eased forward down County 74. She was almost to the County 16 turn-off that led to the Grey and Heeter places. The Kiplings, she corrected herself. But what was this development? Did they need to change their plans?

Damn it. The response was taking too long. She brought the radio up to her lips but it barked before she pressed the button again.

"The plan stays the same." Wolf's voice was distorted as he yelled over the din.

"Copy that. I'm almost at the turn-off."

"Let me know when you're there."

"Copy."

She dropped the radio and hit the gas. The road climbed, and for a moment, she saw over the tops of the trees and caught a glimpse of the motorboat slicing through the smooth water. It was actually ahead of her.

Looking back at the road, she'd barely straightened before she careened off the steep edge on the left.

"Pay attention!" she yelled at herself. Her breathing was borderline hyperventilation. The whole time she'd raced up here with screaming sirens—at one point reaching one hundred twenty miles per hour on a straightaway, passing every and all vehicles in a blur—she'd been gripping the wheel with white knuckles, all the while going through scenarios in her mind, none of which were ending well in her imagination. And now there were gunshots?

She slapped the wheel. Maybe they were Rachette's gunshots, and he was standing over injured killers right now.

Or maybe he was lying on the ground bleeding out.

Damn it! She had to think positive.

She white-knuckle-gripped the wheel again and bared her teeth. These bitches were going down.

"You there yet?" the radio squawked.

Her pulse jumped even higher. "No. Not yet. A few more minutes."

"Okay. We're approaching fast. We saw Rachette's vehicle. Make the call."

"Okay."

She twisted the dial to Channel 14, the designated vehicle-to-vehicle communication channel their department used, and pressed the button. "Deputy Rachette, do you copy?"

"Come on. Come on," she whispered.

There was no response.

She pressed the button again. "Unit 3, this is Unit 8, do you copy?"

She waited five Mississippis. No answer.

She flipped the switch back to the encrypted channel and pressed the button. "No answer."

"Okay." Wolf's response was immediate. "We go in."

Patterson pressed the gas and the engine screamed, pulling her back in the seat.

CHAPTER 55

WOLF PRESSED the soft rubber eyepieces of the high-powered binoculars to his eyes again. The water was glass, making for a smooth boat ride, but the wind proved too much to steady the image of the cliff-top cabin. He saw Rachette's SUV, and any other details were a blur.

Tucking the binoculars behind the passenger-side windshield, he sat down in the sheltered seat and zipped up the rear of his wetsuit.

Wilson looked over at him with a wary eye.

Wolf gave him the thumbs-down signal and Wilson pulled back on the throttle, bringing the speed to half, raising the nose of the boat. The engine noise lowered in pitch, though not in volume.

He took the radio and shoved it in the ten-by-seven-inch dry bag, and then slid his Glock in after it. Zipping the bag shut, he tied two half-hitches in the nylon line around his wrist, and, just to be safe, secured the free end with an overhand knot to keep the half-hitches from slipping.

That finished, he twisted in his chair, feeling the dive knife against his flexed calf as he stood up. With a few hard pulls, he tightened the climbing harness around his legs and waist, making sure the Grigri—a belay device—he'd borrowed from Baine was solidly affixed and the carabiners were locked.

The wind pushed against his chest as he turned forward, chilling him to the bone. He looked up at the granite cliffs and shook out his arms, doubting he was in shape for the climb ahead. It had been years since he'd had experience on any sort of rock face. But adrenaline and perseverance would get him where he needed to go, he assured himself. The cam inside the Grigri would pinch the rope, arresting any fall should he slip while climbing, and the device would give him ample opportunities to hang and rest his muscles on the way up. Of course, time was of the essence. There wasn't going to be much rest.

Wilson eyed him again. "You know, people don't normally leave climbing ropes anchored for days on end. Those things are expensive, and there's a damn good chance it'll be gone."

Wolf had already brought up the same objection with himself. It'd been Friday evening when Kimber, *Rachel*, had pointed out the rope dangling over her backyard cliff.

"And killers don't normally have their stack of mutilated bodies discovered by the cops. I'm willing to bet they've had other stuff on their minds besides bringing in the climbing ropes."

Wilson shook his head, clearly unconvinced at the entire plan, but that failed to faze Wolf.

"I'm just saying," Wilson pressed, "if there's no rope, I don't want you going up that cliff."

"I'm not looking to die today. I'll skirt to the south and find another way up if need be."

That seemed to satisfy Wilson.

"Okay." Wolf looked off the starboard side at the small island in the distance. "You know what to do. Stay on the other side of that island until you hear otherwise. Keep everyone else back. I don't want another unit traveling down that road."

Wilson nodded with wide eyes. "I know, sir."

Wolf pulled the hood over his head. As he straightened the edges around his face, the pathway up the hillside from the Grey's dock to the cabin came into view.

Without another word, he clutched the dry sack in his left hand and dove off the back of the boat.

CHAPTER 56

RACHETTE WAS YANKED out of unconsciousness by a stabbing pain in his shoulder.

"Ah!" he cried.

Opening his eyes, he saw Hannah was still on top of him.

The pain ebbed, and he saw she was concentrating on his shoulder. He felt another explosion as she leaned on his wound.

"Keep this on it," she said.

Rachette wondered who she was talking to.

"Here." She took Rachette's left hand and put it on his right shoulder. "Press."

His jaw bounced uncontrollably. He was so cold. "Kimber?"

She sat up and looked over her shoulder. "Yeah, sure. Kimber."

"Hannah?"

She rolled her eyes. "No. It's Rachel. Whatever. Now don't mess with my sister when she comes back." She gripped some rustling fabric and pulled it up to his chin. "Keep this pulled up."

Rachette looked down at his jacket, which was now draped

over him. He croaked an unintelligible word and then gave up on responding.

She stood and walked away, her rain jacket swishing as she moved toward the stairway to the front porch.

Rachette shook his head and blinked his eyes. His shoulder was cold, and when he looked down he could see that the shirt had been ripped away. Rachel had done some first aid and now he was holding a wadded-up piece of fabric on the wound.

The other one barged out of the front door holding an open laptop computer and trotted down the steps. *Hannah.* The anger in her eyes told him as much. The two were not identical in every way, after all.

"You fix up your boyfriend?" she asked without looking at him.

"Yeah. He'll live."

She clicked a button and scoffed. "We'll see."

Rachette pulled away the fabric on his wound and looked underneath. An oozing red hole with striated muscle bulging out stared back at him. He shut his eyes and took a breath.

Slowly, he propped himself on his elbow and looked around. Instinct was telling him he needed to elevate his upper body to slow the bleeding. His shoulder throbbed with each micro-movement, but he managed to shuffle over to his tire with his ass and good arm. When he reached it, he collapsed backward and panted, sweat streaming down his face, his teeth sounding like a jackhammer in his skull.

The two women were glancing between the laptop screen and his sideshow performance.

"Not sure if you want to be awake for this. Your little partner just showed up. She's been trying to get hold of you on the radio."

Rachette looked at Hannah, the memory of the white SUV

with roof lights on top coming back to him in a flash. "Don't you dare hurt her."

Eyes locked on Rachette's, Hannah handed the laptop to Rachel and stepped toward him. Her face was twisted in rage, and Rachette knew this was probably the end, but she slowed to a stop and turned toward the lake.

"What is that?" she asked, jogging away. She ran all the way to the edge of the precipice and looked down at the lake.

Rachette frowned, watching Hannah's strange actions. Then he heard a faint thrumming sound of an engine, and he saw why she'd run.

A blue motorboat, out far enough that he could see it under the drop-off, slid by lazily, the wake spreading out into a white V behind it. With a smile, he remembered wakeboarding with his sister in Omaha, growing up.

She used to suck. Could never get up. Had to resort to waterskiing with two skis.

"What are you laughing at?" Hannah was back in his face.

He looked up under heavy eyelids. "What?"

"I asked what you're laughing at."

He squinted, trying to figure out who was talking to him.

CHAPTER 57

THE SHOCK of the cold through Wolf's eighth-of-an-inch wetsuit was overshadowed by the violent wrenching of his body as he landed in the wake of the boat. He'd landed wrong, too vertical, and the momentum of the water sliding by rotated him, arching his back and twisting his neck like he was caught in a blender.

As his body stilled, he opened his eyes and let himself float to the top of the water. Poking his head out, he took a soundless breath and swam toward the shore.

Panic arced through his body when he realized his arm was gliding too effortlessly through the water. The added resistance of the tied dry sack was not there.

Treading with strong kicks that were less than effective with climbing shoes on, he twirled, desperately searching for the yellow sack.

There.

Twenty feet away, a bright-yellow bag, now with a frayed nylon string slithering on the surface, was just below the top of the water.

In an instant, he saw that it was sinking.

Ducking his head, he pulled and kicked with all his strength. A few strokes later, through his blurry vision, he saw a yellow rectangle plunging down, fluttering back and forth as it sank out of sight.

His ears plugged and squeaked as he dove down after it, but it was no use. He was too slow, and it was gone. With a burst of bubbles, he cursed at the top of his lungs and then broke the water in silence once again. Without looking back, he swam towards the shore in a silent breaststroke.

CHAPTER 58

RACHETTE FELT himself moving and emerged into half-consciousness again. With a head-rattling scrape, he felt himself being pulled by his legs across the ground. He looked up and saw that it was Rachel pulling him toward the steps to the house.

He opened his mouth and croaked.

"She's here. Wait. She's stopping," Hannah said.

Rachel dropped Rachette's legs and his body rocked to a halt. There was less pain now, and he knew that was a bad sign. With mild interest he watched Hannah and Rachel huddle at the laptop screen.

"She's stopping right at the camera."

Their concerned identical faces glowed from the laptop screen's light.

"Into the woods?" Hannah frowned and shook her head, looking into the forest over and beyond Rachette. "They know we have motion and vibration sensors everywhere. What the hell is she doing?"

Rachel looked down at Rachette. "She's coming for him."

Hannah put the laptop down hard on the stairs. She pulled

the gun from her waist and racked the slide. "You take this. Keep him covered. I'm going in to cut her off before she gets here."

"Don't!" Rachette's shoulder exploded in pain as he yelled the word. "Patterson! Patters—"

His teeth slammed together and his head jerked back, and then Hannah stepped on his shoulder and disappeared.

He doubled over, his mouth open in a silent scream. Between gasps, he heard footsteps receding into the distance. "Patterson," he said again, and then he closed his eyes.

CHAPTER 59

PATTERSON TWISTED the keys and got out.

With a glance over at the wildlife camera nailed to the tree, she slammed the door and ran around the front of the car and up the slope to the woods on the right-hand side of the road.

With quick, powerful strides she climbed the dirt embankment and before too long was swerving between tight pine trees. Her lungs beat a steady rhythm, and her left earpiece thumped with every movement. For minutes, she kept the steady pace without struggle, and she thanked herself for taking time out of every single day for the past two years to exercise.

Jumping over a downed log, she slowed and stood behind a thick pine. She leaned on it, catching her breath with long pulls of air, and then, with slow deliberation, she ducked down and peeked around the edge of the trunk.

The road veered down and away from her below, and in the distance was a partial view of the Greys' cabin. She saw the white paint of Rachette's SUV parked in front, and the wood two-story structure to the right of it. Past that, she saw slivers of the gray lake water beyond. A row of wake waves rolled along its otherwise still surface.

Where the hell was Wolf's radio signal?

If that was their boat's wake, Wolf was undoubtedly on shore by now. Judging by the height of the waves, he should have completed his swim and short hike to the base of the cliff by now.

"Wolf, do you copy?" she whispered into her wrist mic.

There was no response. Quickly she checked her belt and made sure the dial was turned on. It was. The green light was solid next to the power knob and she was on the agreed channel.

Damn it.

In an instant she forgot the radio, because a branch had snapped loudly somewhere down the slope between her and the cabin.

Again she leaned out, and she still saw nothing in the forest below. For ten full seconds she scanned the area below, doing methodical horizontal sweeps with her eyes, adjusting the distance downward, and repeating the process. If someone was there, they were waiting her out.

What was her next move? It was impossible to make a choice without Wolf's signal. She was there as a decoy, to bring their attention up the hill while Wolf snuck up from behind. Was the climbing rope that Wolf had been expecting not there? Was he hurt? Had he been seen?

Even if things were still going to plan, if Wolf was nowhere close to finishing his climb up the cliff face behind the property, she was not in position to start banging pots and pans.

Damn it. Wolf was silent, and the sisters had the edge. They knew the forest. According to Wolf, they had sensors, and as far as she knew they signaled her position right now.

She leaned back against the tree trunk and shook her head. Something must have happened to Wolf's radio, she thought. Otherwise he would be communicating. That was the only thing she could think of.

What if he's fallen off the cliff face and is lying dead on the ground right now? Then what?

"Shut up and move," she hissed to herself.

She needed a better view of the property below. Scanning straight across the slope, she found a group of old-growth pine trees below that would give her an improved vantage.

With a quick breath she gripped her pistol, then sprinted for it, trying to keep her footfalls as silent as possible. She swerved and ducked, jumped a downed log, and baseball-slid through pine needles to a stop at one of the thick trunks.

For five seconds she steadied her breath and then poked her head out. *There!* She cheered silently to herself as she saw that Wolf was already up the cliff and making his way across the property to Rachette. Something must have happened to his radio. Then her face fell and she gasped in horror, because what was about to happen next she could see as clear as Rocky Mountain air.

CHAPTER 60

Wolf was only halfway up the rock face when his forearms started giving out.

The rope had been there, just as he'd hoped. The Grigri was doing its job—the cam inside the device pinching the belay side of the rope, arresting his downward motion when he needed.

And now he was using his full bodyweight on the rope, stretching his forearms, staring alternately between the rest of the climb ahead of him and the trail below. He stared longingly at the path, and then the stairs that led up the cliffs, but he knew to take the route was too exposed.

Wolf's father had helped set up the security system surrounding the property, which meant the trail from the dock, and the stairway up the rocks, would have been equipped with at least one sensor. To not do so would have been negligent.

Steeling himself for another push of exertion, he sucked in a breath, gripped a thin hold with his right hand and hauled himself up. Then he pulled the slack of the rope through the Grigri. He changed hands, heaved himself a foot up the rock, and pulled the slack of the rope.

The light was fading fast, like he'd suddenly entered a cave. The skies would open up with rain again soon.

He pictured himself summiting. He envisioned himself doing it in one continuous burst of energy.

With clenched teeth, he reached up and grabbed another handhold.

Pulling up with shaking biceps, he thought of the two deputies' lives at stake on top and it fueled his muscles with another burst of energy. And a minute later, when that wasn't enough, he thought about Sarah's dead body, and how he was sure now that one of these twin sisters had shot her dead.

Two minutes later, Wolf summited the top of the cliff and collapsed onto his front, panting for oxygen. Feeling exposed, he quickly gained his composure and ducked behind a wind-warped scrub oak. On the way to his cover, he saw the two women he now knew as Hannah and Rachel Kipling at the front of the house.

Chest heaving, pulse pounding in his temples, the muscles in his biceps feeling like they'd been torn in half, Wolf watched in silence.

Blood trickled out of his nose and onto his teeth. When he wiped it, his right-hand middle finger flexed against his palm as the tendon in his forearm cramped with agonizing pain.

He froze as the two sisters looked toward him, but they turned and looked back up the mountain the opposite way.

Studying the two women, he saw they were identical physically, but surely not the same mentally. One sat on the front steps of the house, looking defeated, while the other glared into the trees above with a raised chin. He thought about the makeup on Kimber's face last night. How it had seemed overdone. That had been Hannah, he knew now. The picture from Boise had shown she was without a mole on her lip, and she was the one who had taken a baseball bat to her classmate in middle school. It made sense that Hannah would not be sitting defeated, she would be standing, ready to fight as she gazed into the trees up the mountain.

Wolf snapped out of his thoughts and moved silently to the trees to his left.

The rope scraped across the top of the cliff below him. He stopped and dropped to his knees again, watching in horror as a fist-sized rock dislodged and rolled before stopping a few inches from the edge. If he'd raked the stone with his rope any harder he would have sent it crashing over the edge, giving away his position.

He flipped the line over the stone and crouched behind a thick pine trunk. The cabin above was built perpendicular to the edge of the cliff, with the front of the house on Wolf's right, where Rachette's SUV was parked and the stairway climbed to the upper-level deck and front door.

The rear of the cabin had an upper-level deck and a door to a ground level underneath it. The side of the house was straight ahead, and Wolf recognized the kitchen through the windows on the upper floor.

He watched as Hannah walked away from him along the front of the house. She paused and kicked something on the ground, then continued in a jog into the woods.

He sagged with relief to see she'd kicked Rachette, who in turn writhed in pain. His deputy was hurt, but he was alive.

Any doubt he had of that sister being Hannah was gone now.

Wolf's anxiety ratcheted up a notch when he realized what she was doing: going after Patterson.

He pulled his dive knife and severed the rope below the Grigri, then watched the frayed end disappear over the edge.

Gripping the rope above the device, he paused before cutting it, thinking he might be able to use the rest to restrain one of the sisters. The multi-colored nylon weave ran from his Grigri, through two carabiners attached to the top anchor lines, and then back over the cliff all the way to the bottom. Instead of slicing it, he jammed the knife home in its sleeve and reeled the rope hand over hand, up the cliff, and through the two carabiners until he had thirty or so feet of it coiled on his arm.

He took the coil, slung it over his head, and sprinted silently to the rear of the house.

Once up against the side of the house, he walked toward the front and peered around the corner. Rachette was near his SUV, fluttering his eyes as he barely held onto consciousness, his shoulder covered in blood and his face looking ghost white.

The sister who'd stayed behind, Rachel, paced short steps at the base of the stairway that led to the second floor. She looked eagerly in the opposite direction toward her sister, who made her way past the front of the house and out of sight.

Patterson was coming from up and from the right. Hannah was clearly going to try to flank her from the left.

"Be careful," Rachel hissed. "She could have a rifle!"

Wolf ducked back around the corner, knowing he had to act fast.

He peered out again, and then with light feet stepped around the corner, keeping the stairway between himself and Rachel. Without slowing he bent down, picked up a stone, and lobbed it high in the air and over the back of the SUV, all the while moving forward at the same silent pace.

The stone landed with a splat and Rachel turned toward the noise and pointed her pistol. He sprang up from behind at the same instant, clubbing her on top of her head as hard as he could with the butt of the knife handle.

His fist was a sledgehammer with a solid-plug center, and the muffled knock on her skull dropped her to the ground face first, unconscious.

He sheathed his knife, and then took her pistol and tucked it into the waist of his harness. He grabbed her under her arms and pulled her back the way he'd come. Tossing her into the dirt on the side of the house, he went back up to Rachette.

Rachette looked up at him and smiled.

"Don't say anything," Wolf whispered.

He grabbed Rachette under the arms and dragged him backwards, scraping his heels along the dirt and wet grass, down to the side of the house next to Rachel.

"Drop the cop, and drop the gun."

His stomach sank. With a slow squat, he laid Rachette down and held up his hands.

"Slowly. Pull the gun out of your harness and toss it to your side."

He gritted his teeth and did as he was told.

"Thank you. And now the dive knife."

He pulled the knife and tossed it next to the gun.

Quick, soggy, footsteps approached behind him, and he turned to see Hannah picking up the weapons.

"Hannah?"

She raised her eyebrows and tucked the pistol into the back of her jeans; then she picked up the knife and stared at it, as if the blade was a medallion hanging from a hypnotist's chain. Then she turned, hauled back, and threw the knife across the lawn and over the cliff. With a sour smile, she faced Wolf and pointed the gun.

An icy raindrop slapped the back of Wolf's neck and trickled down his wetsuit. Another one smacked the wood side of the house, and a cold breeze drove up over the edge of the cliff.

Hannah glanced at Rachette and then raked her eyes up and down Wolf. "Nice outfit. I got to thinking just now, why the hell did that midget deputy of yours stop in front of our camera and go into the woods? And then we saw that boat go by. I almost didn't put it together." She twirled a finger in the air. "But then I did, and I came around the house."

Wolf glared. "Why did you kill Sarah?"

She narrowed her eyes. "I killed Sarah? Oh yeah, we heard about that." She shrugged. "You're better off without that slut, believe me."

"What the hell do you want?" he asked. His chest heaved, and despite the cold wind that howled up the cliff, he was sweating under the wetsuit.

Hannah's cool façade cracked for an instant and she thrust the gun at him. "To be left alone!"

"Then"—he waved a hand—"go. Get out of here. Leave me and my deputies, and you and your crazy-ass sister get the hell out of here."

"She's not crazy."

"Ah, right. That's you."

Hannah peered around the corner to the front of the house and then pointed the gun at Rachette. "Tell your deputy to come out with her hands up or I shoot this guy again. She's at the back of the house."

Wolf glanced toward the rear of the property.

"Do it!"

Rachette stared up at Wolf from the ground, shaking his head in defiance.

"Patterson!" Wolf yelled. "Come out!"

Wind whooshed through pines and more raindrops knocked on the side of the house.

"Patterson!"

"Here." Patterson came around the corner with both hands in the air, her pistol aimed to the sky.

"Drop it!" Hannah pushed the gun closer to Rachette. "I

swear to God, I shot him once, I'll shoot him again. I'll shoot him in the face. Drop it."

Patterson threw her gun to the side and walked toward them. Her eyes were half closed, eyeing Hannah with burning hatred.

"Okay, you got us," Wolf said. "Now what? What's your plan, Hannah?"

She backed away from Rachette and walked to her sister, who lay motionless next to him.

"Rachel." She slapped her cheek. "You okay?"

Rachel groaned and rocked her head back and forth.

Hannah glared at Wolf and raised the gun. "You two, back up. Towards the cliff."

CHAPTER 61

RACHETTE STARED at Patterson and Wolf's drawn faces, and felt the hope that he might live to see another day, like the blood that seeped from his shoulder, drain from his body. He no longer had the strength to press on his own wound, and he no longer cared. He was on the way out and he knew it. The cold was absolute, but his chin no longer bounced from shivering. That had to be a bad sign.

All he cared about now was the wellbeing of his two partners. Now that he sat on death's door, he could see so clearly now that these two people were everything to him. Nobody else came close.

And now the barrel of a gun was pushing his two friends toward the edge of a cliff.

And now he knew what he had to do.

Patterson was saying something, her arms raised, probably trying to bargain their way out of it somehow.

He looked at Wolf. Such a God among men was this sheriff. Such a man of honor and dignity. Such a ... Rachette did a double take, because Wolf had just slung the rope from his neck and dropped it on the ground.

For a moment it was like Rachette was watching nothing of significance, like he was staring at water swirling down a drain. But then he squinted, because *Wolf was doing something*, he realized. Because the rope was on the ground; but that was not everything, because Wolf was grasping the end, and he was twisting it in his fingers.

Hannah was preoccupied with talking to Patterson, noticing none of it. But how long could that last? He had to act.

With all his might, Rachette pushed air through his lungs. "Hey!" He looked at Patterson and winked.

Patterson frowned and shook her head

Hannah stopped marching toward his friends and turned to him.

"You know what?" Rachette cleared his throat, tasting blood in his mouth. That had to be a bad sign. "You know what I told these two, Kimber, Hannah, or whatever the hell your name is?"

Hannah walked away from Wolf and Patterson and stopped at Rachette's legs, tilting her head.

"I told them you were a crazy bitch. And I was right!" Rachette let out a long, contrived laugh that turned into genuine mirth. "Remember when we made out that time?"

Hannah shook her head. "No, I don't."

"Because you're a crazy bitch." Patterson lifted her chin. "My partner's rarely right, but this time he's spot on. A crazy bitch."

Hannah stopped and looked at Patterson, frowning like she'd just taken a bite out of a lemon. With a shake of her head, she curled her lip in amusement. Then her face dropped.

Rachette watched in sickening horror as Hannah raised her pistol.

"No!" Rachette screamed as fast as he could. "Me! Me! Me!"

It was no use. Without hesitation, Hannah pointed her pistol at Patterson and pulled the trigger.

The gun roared and Rachette turned his eyes away at the last second, seeing the bright flash of light illuminate the side of the house, like lightning. As the echo of the shot faded into the distance, his eyes instantly welled up.

He inhaled and stretched his mouth, and then he screamed. "Ahh—"

"What the hell?" Hannah yelled.

Rachette blinked and looked down. Patterson was still standing. Unharmed.

CHAPTER 62

WOLF, Patterson, and Hannah stood in a more-or-less equilat-eral-triangle formation, with Hannah at the point nearest the house, swaying her pistol between the two of them, pushing them ever closer to the cliff, all the while keeping a safe distance.

When Wolf had found the end of the rope that was coiled around his neck and started tying the knot with his right hand, he'd exchanged a glance with Patterson. *I need a diversion*, he'd screamed with his eyes.

He could only assume that Patterson had read the situation correctly, because without a second's hesitation she began sniveling.

"Please," Patterson spoke with heart-stopping pain and passion in her voice. "We didn't bring up the rest of our squad because we want to help. Listen. It's the—"

"You know what?" Rachette squirmed to life from his posi-tion on the ground. "You know what I told these two, Kimber, Hannah, or whatever the hell ..."

Dammit.

Apparently Rachette had come up with a plan of his own.

Hannah turned her gaze from Patterson to Rachette.

Wolf blocked out everything and concentrated on the knot in his fingers. Easily enough, he twisted the rope with one hand into a regular knot and tightened it, but he needed two hands for the pretzel twist, the push-through of the end of the rope, and the final cinch to complete the slipknot.

Hannah's expression changed, like she was about to act, and by the looks of it, Rachette had seconds to live.

Abandoning stealth, Wolf looked down at the end of the knot, cinched it tight, making it complete and ready to use, and then pulled open the loop with a quick motion that burned his thumb.

As Wolf dropped the climbing-rope loop to his side and twirled it once, Hannah aimed at Patterson.

He stepped toward Hannah and let the rope fly with a side-armed toss his father would have been proud of. The loop wobbled and widened at the perfect moment, as if guided by a higher power, and encircled her gun arm and her torso. He pulled back as hard as he could, cinching the lasso tight and yanking Hannah off balance.

At the same instant she shot, she stumbled toward him and landed hard on her knees. "What the hell?"

Wolf had no time to attack.

Without hesitation, she raised the pistol and aimed it at Wolf's center mass, and then squeezed the trigger.

CHAPTER 63

SOMETHING BOUNCED in front of Rachette, a line of rope or a cord, and for a second he blinked through the tears, trying to focus on what it was. He felt a surge of excitement, because it was the rope that had been in Wolf's hand. One end was a loop, now cinched tight around Hannah's upper arms and torso, and the other end was in Wolf's hand.

A lasso, he realized. Wolf had thrown a lasso made from the rope and pulled her down.

Before Rachette could form a smile, Hannah's gun roared and spat fire once, twice, three times. Her teeth were bared as her arm kicked back with each shot. Then she dropped her gun and grabbed at the rope with both hands, wriggling like it was a piranha biting at her skin.

Rachette turned to look at Wolf, but he was not where Rachette expected. He was zigzagging, running away as fast as he could.

But he's going in the wrong direction.

And then Wolf was gone, twisting as he flew down and out of sight over the edge of the cliff.

The rope was fluttering limp, and then with the sound of a

tightening guitar string it pulled laser-beam straight, one end scraping the top edge of the cliff, the other contracting around Hannah's torso.

Hannah let out a panicked squeal as she was flung in a blur towards the cliff's edge. Rolling in a thumping tornado of limbs, she barked like an animal as she smacked back-first against a tree. For an instant she was velcroed to the trunk of the pine, her body on the right side of the tree and the rope stretched around to the left. With a slack mouth, she stared vacantly at Rachette, blinked, and was then pulled over the edge and out of sight.

CHAPTER 64

As Wolf leaped head first off the cliff, as the wind rushed past his ears, as his stomach floated, and as death rushed up at him at 9.8 meters per second squared, he thought about a man named Claus Vaadner.

For the past six years, Claus had been a legend in Rocky Points. Because everyone in town knew the story of how, one day, Claus had cheated death with the aid of dumb luck, and a pallet of ceramic roof tiles.

Six summers ago, Claus had been installing Italian clay tiles twenty-five feet above the ground, working on the roof of a two-story luxury house in the hills to the west of Rocky Points, when he slipped and fell over the edge. Luckily for him, he was tied off, but unluckily for him, he had tied himself to the pallet, which was more than half empty and weighed less than he did.

With the aid of a few beers, fellow workers still told the tale of how Claus had dangled over the rocky ground, screaming frantically as the pallet had given way and slid toward the edge of the roof above.

Claus had been spared a horrific fall, however, because the resistance from the sliding pallet had effectively lowered him at a gentle rate, depositing him on the ground completely unharmed, as if he'd stepped off a three-foot step-stool and not just tumbled from a twenty-five-foot-high roof. Luckily for Claus, he'd watched as the pallet had flown off the edge, and he'd avoided the cataclysmic explosion of ceramic by diving out of the way.

With a wrench of his body, Wolf twisted one hundred and eighty degrees and pulled his legs to his chest, completing three quarters of a front-flip-half-twist, waiting for *his* pallet of tiles to slow his fall.

Now parallel to the ground and face down, he watched as the steep grade beneath him rushed up through his blurry vision. Just when he began to wonder whether his makeshift lasso had held, the slack in the rope pulled tight and his outward trajectory shifted downward.

He was halfway through the fall when the rope pulled again against the Grigri cam system, which was still locked on the rope and attached to his harness, changing his trajectory once more, this time sending him slamming chest first into the side of the cliff.

The collision was so fast and violent that he felt no pain, but he heard muffled crunches beneath his skin and felt the blows to his body as he tumbled down the rock face.

Disoriented, he sensed the ground nearing as his descent came to a complete stop.

The rope ripped at his harness, wrenching him around so that he faced the sky. He grunted as his body arched backwards and folded in half, and he felt his feet kick the back of his head. Then, an instant later, he was laid gently onto his back, on the cool, wet ground.

As the bright world tunneled in from the edge of his vision, he watched the rope drop in an angry coil next to him, and then he felt a rush of wind and a spray of warm blood as Hannah landed next to him.

Somehow amid the numbness, he found the muscle coordination to turn his head and look.

Hannah was next to him on her back, her neck twisted unnaturally, her face pointed toward his—eyes wide open but devoid of life. A web of blood trickled from her temple across her face.

Wolf's lids fluttered, and then he closed his eyes and felt nothing.

CHAPTER 65

Patterson stared dumbstruck at the precipice. Wolf had been planning something, she could tell that, and part of her was wondering just what exactly he could do to right the situation, but never in a million years had she expected to witness what she'd just seen.

After snapping out of her initial shock, she realized there may have been method to Wolf's suicidal move. By pulling Hannah over the edge, had he slowed his own momentum enough to survive the fall?

She turned to Rachette with wide eyes.

"Go," he said.

She sprinted to Rachel, handcuffed one of her wrists, pulled her semi-conscious form to the side of the house, clamped it on a water pipe, and ran to the top of the wooden stairway descending the cliff.

"All units move! Call Summit County and get a medevac helicopter up here now. Sheriff Wolf and Deputy Rachette are down and injured badly. Get the bus over here stat! I repeat, we need ambulances, and we need medevac!"

With thumping footfalls on the creaking wood, she ignored

the eruption of voices on the radio, keeping her eye on Wolf's unmoving form at the base of the cliff. She got to the bottom, jumped off the trail, and flailed across the steep incline.

Slipping onto her hip as she stepped on loose scree, and slamming her elbow on a rock in the process, she breathed through the pain with bared teeth, not slowing a second. When she reached Wolf, she pressed her fingers on his carotid, feeling the slick warmth of his blood on her fingers, and then the weak rhythm of his pulse.

"Medevac on route," she heard the radio squawk.

A boat was roaring toward the dock beneath her, Wilson standing with fluttering hair above the windshield.

As she panted, she looked down at Hannah's body. Her face was turned toward her and Wolf, but she was on her back and it looked like her neck had been twisted almost two hundred and seventy degrees. Her head rested in a growing pool of blood, and her face was completely red. She was as dead as it got.

Patterson thought about the concussion of air she'd felt against her face as Hannah's bullet missed by inches; then she thought about Rachette's pale face; then she looked back down at Wolf.

"It's going to be all right," she said with little conviction.

CHAPTER 66

5 DAYS LATER ...

Patterson squinted and gazed up at the sky, feeling the sun warm her face. The cotton-ball clouds above hung motionless, painting the water below with dark circles of shade, and the breeze brought the smell of freshwater and the whir of distant motorboats.

She popped her eyes open and sucked in a breath, remembering the zip of the bullet as it had passed inches from her face.

Perched atop the cliff below Hannah and Rachel's house, Patterson was mere feet from where she'd dodged certain death almost a week ago. She took a deep breath, reminding herself that that night was over.

"That was depressing."

Patterson turned around at the sound of Rachette's voice. "You got that right. Jesus. What are you doing up here?"

Rachette stepped next to her, thumbing the sling on his right arm that hung over his formal khaki uniform top, which bulged at his right shoulder as if he'd stuffed a pillow underneath.

Patterson knew there was a mass of gauze hiding a line of staples covering internal scars from reconstructive surgery on his joint, a large divot in his clavicle bone, two shredded ligaments, and severe muscle trauma from the bullet that had hit him.

"Seriously. What are you doing here?"

Rachette tried to shrug, a move that make him bare his teeth in pain. "I got a ride up with Wilson after the funeral, since you ditched me."

"I thought Wilson was taking you home. You should be in bed."

Rachette ignored her and gazed into the distance. "Did you see Jack?"

"Yeah."

It was an unnecessary question. Everyone had seen Jack at his mother's funeral earlier that morning. It had been the saddest thing she'd ever seen in her life.

Patterson had felt no sense of closure with the lowering of Sarah Muller into the ground, and she had not shed so many tears since her grandmother's death six years previously. But with her grandmother's funeral, she had at least felt resolution. Her family had been sad, but they had celebrated her life at the house later. *Grandma lived a long, full life, and then she died.*

The funeral earlier that morning had been the antithesis of her grandmother's.

Wolf's son Jack had stood next to Sarah's parents, never once lifting his gaze from his mother's coffin, a tear never once escaping his eyes—a sight that had blown Patterson's heart into a thousand pieces.

Wolf's absence had been the elephant at the funeral, but it had been impossible for him to attend, because he'd been in surgery at County Hospital, and when they were done with the third operation on his fractured hip, he remained unconscious, recovering from a ruptured spleen, three broken vertebrae, and an assortment of ten other shattered bones, ranging in severity from a cracked femur to a broken thumb. His absence had been necessary, but it made the whole thing that much more difficult.

Then there had been Sarah's parents. They had been a sniveling mess, and every time Patterson had looked at them during the funeral she'd broken down into a sniveling mess herself. *Sarah Muller lived a short, troubled life, and now she was dead.*

"Hey." Rachette nudged her with his good arm.

She looked up and wiped a fresh tear from her cheek.

"It's gonna be all right."

She nodded. "Yeah, right."

They turned around at the sound of an approaching car. "Looks like the Idaho boys are here."

A Caprice Classic with a Boise Sheriff's Department paint job crunched on the gravel into a tight spot between a swarm of five SCSD vehicles. The vehicle rocked to a stop and both doors opened.

A younger man climbed out of the driver's seat, dressed in a dark-brown uniform, and an older man dressed in civilian clothing pulled himself up with the passenger door.

Wilson was there to greet them and shook hands. They spoke for a few seconds and then he pointed toward Patterson and Rachette.

The younger, uniformed man raised a hand, and though it was far away, he looked like he beamed an attractive smile from under a black ball cap with a gold embroidered BSD on it.

Patterson raised a hand in greeting. For days, she'd been speaking to Deputy Michelson often while liaising with the BSD in order to close the file on the Kiplings. To her surprise, just like a pen pal from Japan she'd had in elementary school, she found she had connected on a deep level with the young deputy.

Now, as he followed the older man down the grass slope, she was seeing Michelson for the first time. He was dressed in a gray uniform, and she could tell he was young, probably no more than five years her senior—fit, medium height, brown hair—and moved with sure feet.

The older man next to him was dressed in jeans and a flannel shirt rolled up to the elbows; a trucker cap lay askew on his head. He waddled with a limp, and when Michelson offered a helping hand the man waved it away impatiently.

Michelson looked up at Patterson and smiled again, and it was enough to make her blush, which caused her stomach to twist with a pang of guilt thinking about Scott. What the hell was she feeling?

She turned to Rachette, determined to distract herself. "You hear anything about his surgery this morning?"

"Nope." Rachette checked his wristwatch and began walking to meet their two guests. "He's still in it right now. We should be there, damn it."

Patterson nodded. "Don't worry. We'll go later today, all right? Maybe check you back in, for God's sake. You need to sit."

"Pssh." Rachette took a breath through his nose. "I'm all right. Howdy," he called out.

Deputy Michelson smiled with squinted blue eyes surrounded by a bloom of dark eyelashes.

Patterson returned the smile, feeling her face flush again. "Deputy Michelson."

"Patterson, I take it?"

She nodded.

Michelson's hand was callused and warm, and he gripped firmly with a quick shake.

"And you must be Rachette. We heard about your injury." Michelson took Rachette's left hand and shook his head with a sympathetic look.

"That's a bitch, son." The older man's voice was gruff as he shook Rachette's left hand and then took Patterson's. His eyes were glimmering slits beneath leathery folds.

"Sheriff Dudley, nice to meet you," Rachette said.

The man nodded and poked the underside of his trucker hat. "Used to be. Now you can call me Fred."

Sheriff Dudley pointed past them. "Hell of a view up here."

They twisted and looked at the lake, and Patterson exchanged a glance with Michelson.

"There's quite a lot of activity up here." Michelson turned around and motioned to the five SCSD vehicles parked in front of the house.

"We had a K-9 unit find Olin Heeter's body yesterday," Patterson said. "Buried in a fresh, shallow grave up the mountain. We have all available units checking the area now for more bodies."

"You find anymore?" Sheriff Dudley asked.

Rachette shook his head. "Nope. But we've got some interesting stuff inside, that's for sure. Or"—he pointed at his sling —"everyone else found a hell of a lot. I've been laid up in the hospital."

Dudley squinted one eye and appraised Rachette, then nodded at Patterson. "Why don't you two give us the tour?"

Patterson gestured and they followed her around to the back of the house. Memories of that evening clawed at her with each step, and she had to steel her thoughts as she rounded the corner and faced an open door at the rear of the house.

Deputy Yates stood sentinel, stifling a yawn. He raised his clipboard. "Go ahead inside."

"Thanks, Yates." Rachette stepped aside and gestured for

Patterson to take the lead. Just like the two men from Idaho, she realized, Rachette had not yet seen inside the lower level of the house.

She walked through the door into a large rectangular room with a smooth concrete floor, which was lit brightly with an uncovered bulb hanging from the ceiling. She walked halfway across the space to the left toward a doorway on the far wall and stopped at a yellow plastic evidence tent.

"This spot is blood, and the rest underneath has been confirmed as the same," she said, gesturing to the floor.

"My God," Michelson said. "It's huge."

Fred Dudley pointed at the rust-colored smear on the floor. "This the most recent?"

Patterson nodded. "Our ME did a DNA analysis on it, and it matched William Van Wyke's profile, which was in CODIS from his Idaho private investigator's license registration."

Dudley pointed at the brown spot beneath the smear. It was roughly circular in shape with a diameter of at least ten feet. "This is where she killed, I take it?"

"Looks that way. There's a lot of old blood here, and check out that wall." She pointed behind them and they all twisted.

There was an old workbench against a wall covered with pegboard, and hooks of various sizes hung from the holes.

"We've removed everything and put it into evidence, but when we came inside here, there was a razor-sharp machete, hunting knives, and a few filet knives. They all had traces of blood on them."

Michelson shook his head. "And we heard that you've identified three of the other bodies you recovered."

"Yep. All runaways, all reported missing from their hometowns. All three were boys in their late teens, with one or both of their parents deceased. People figured they'd run away. No evidence suggested foul play. The other four seem to fit the same mold, but we don't have definitive IDs. I'm not sure if we ever will."

"Hitchhikers," Michelson said softly, his eyes glued to the floor stain.

"That's what we're thinking," Patterson said. "It makes sense. Highway 734 down the valley is a good place to find them. Even today, most people with their thumbs in the air will be late teens, early twenties, male, traveling solo."

Dudley pointed at a closed door on the far wall. "And what's in there?"

Patterson walked over and pushed it open. The bottom scraped along the top of high pile carpet, revealing a room with a couch, an old television, and a wood coffee table. Paintings of mountain scenery hung on the wood-paneled walls, and to the right was a stairway that led up to the second floor.

Dudley, Michelson, and Rachette craned their necks to see past her.

"Just a normal basement," Michelson said.

"Minus the fact that it's next to a killing room," Sheriff Dudley said, turning around and walking back to the bloodstain. "William Van Wyke, eh?"

"Yeah." Patterson stepped next to him and looked down. It thoroughly creeped her out every time she looked at this spot, and she was glad to be doing so with so much company this time. "A kill that definitely doesn't fit the mold. You know him?"

Sheriff Dudley and Michelson exchanged a glance.

"Yeah," Dudley said, "I do. Let's get the hell out of here and we'll talk about it."

CHAPTER 67

PATTERSON LED them out onto the back lawn and from the deep breaths it was clear that everyone was glad to be back outside.

Dudley stopped and put his hands on his hips. "Let's see. Where do I begin?"

"Why don't you start with the cat?" Michelson said.

"The cat?" Patterson asked.

The old man leaned his head back and closed his eyes against the sun. "Twenty-five years ago, I was a police officer in McCall, Idaho. McCall's a resort town a couple of hours north of Boise. There's Payette Lake right there, and McCall is a town on the south shore. Anyway, back then, during the summer, we got a call from a family. They'd found their pet cat in the woods. Decapitated, gutted from asshole to neck."

Patterson and Rachette exchanged sidelong glances.

"I was first on the scene, and I was shown the animal by one Mrs. Katherine Kipling." Dudley dragged his words. "This was the Kiplings' cat, you see?"

Patterson nodded.

"We were concerned, naturally, and so were Mr. and Mrs. Kipling. Hell, everyone knows what the textbooks say: Anyone who could commit such an act on a household pet was border-line homicidal to humans. So for two weeks we were on edge. My partner and I spent more than a few days and nights out there in the woods. But … we never saw anything unusual. Never had any leads, and the interest in the incident just sort of faded away.

"Until a few weeks later. The Kiplings' neighbors, about a mile away, had a teenaged son named Reggie. One morning a woman was walking her dog, and the dog ran ahead and into the woods. By the time she caught up with it, he was found licking something on the ground. She came up and saw that it was the neighbor kid, his head severed almost clean off." Dudley paused and rubbed the back of his neck. "Cut along the front the same way the cat was. Stabbed all over the rest of his body, including the eyes."

Patterson shivered.

"Well, needless to say, we were all freaked the hell out and on a manhunt after that. The news spread quickly, and the whole town was hysterical. Everyone was afraid of one another. Nobody went out after dark. We were working around the clock, but coming up empty on leads. If we saw anyone out after dark we would bring them in for questioning. You were the unluckiest soul alive if we caught you hitchhiking near McCall that week. We were using that interrogation room a lot for a few days.

"Then a week later, after the kid's body was found, the Kipling house caught fire in the middle of the night, and that's when all hell broke loose again. The fire burned hot, and there was nothing firefighters could do to save the structure. They had to stand back and watch it burn, along with a few acres of the surrounding woods.

"When it finally burned itself out, investigators determined that accelerants had been used, a whole lot of them, clear arson, and we assumed the worst for the family. When we ended up not finding any bodily remains inside, we were beyond puzzled. Even stranger, the two family cars were still in the garage."

Dudley coughed and pulled his trucker hat off, revealing a shiny dome. He rubbed his hand over it and put the hat back on. "Nothin'. Couldn't find the Kiplings. Dustin Kipling was kind of a big shot around town, with his statewide boat dealerships and all—Kipling Boats—and news traveled fast around the area about their disappearance. It was all the rave for a while on the news channels.

"Their disappearance, along with the news of the murder out in the woods, brought a few people of interest into our station, and things got more complicated, or *clearer* I guess, now that we have hindsight.

"The first visitor was a man named Dr. Lewis, a psychiatrist from Bend, Oregon, who was an old college friend of Dustin Kipling. Dr. Lewis told us that Dustin Kipling had come into his office a couple of days before his disappearance, looking for a prescription for anti-psychotic meds. When Dr. Lewis asked why he needed them, Dustin Kipling told him a story, confessing how he had killed their house cat, and how he was scared of what he might do next. Dr. Lewis was extremely concerned, but stopped short of detaining his old friend and putting him under psychiatric watch, which was within his power. Instead he wrote him the prescription with the caveat that Dustin come back and see him regularly."

Dudley looked at Rachette and then Patterson. "When we heard about this after the family's disappearance, our running theory was that Dustin Kipling had murdered the neighbors' kid and fled with his family. Perhaps he'd even taken the family under duress.

"And then a second person came into our station—the child counselor at the twin daughters' middle school. This counselor was talking about how she thought one of the daughters, Hannah, was highly unstable. She told us about Hannah attacking a boy with a baseball bat earlier that year. Vicious stuff —she was even expelled from school—but no formal charges were filed. And there were two other incidents of fights she'd gotten in before that were particularly violent, so said the counselor."

Patterson nodded. "Yeah. We saw that in the BSD report."

Dudley nodded. "We figured, like father, like daughter. But there was no way a teenaged girl could do the horrific things done to that boy, we thought." He shook his head and glanced at the door behind them.

"And what about William Van Wyke?" Rachette asked. "Why is an Idaho PI's blood smeared inside this house, while his charred remains are inside a Mercedes SUV in the next county?"

Dudley nodded and held up a finger. "We had a third visitor. A Nevada casino owner, who told us he'd seen Dustin Kipling a single day before the family's disappearance. It turned out that Dustin Kipling had sold his entire business to this guy from Nevada for cash at an extreme discount. Three million dollars in cash, to be precise, which was apparently pennies on the dollar for what all those boat dealerships and the inventory inside 'em were worth.

"This casino owner wanted to make sure that he was in the clear as far as we were concerned. And it turned out that he was. His story checked out. Kipling came to him with the deal, insisting it be all cash. We could find no connection with this casino-man to Kipling and his family other than purchasing the boat business at a fire sale price. No pun intended."

"And Van Wyke?" Patterson pressed.

"Van Wyke had apparently brokered the business deal. He was present and, as a witness, had signed the business-transfer agreement the lawyers had drawn up. His payment for facilitating the deal was the deed to Dustin Kipling's lakefront property in McCall."

Rachette frowned. "The property that burned down?"

Dudley nodded. "The property that burned down."

"So," Patterson narrowed her eyes in thought, "Kipling burned down the property before Van Wyke could have it? Why?"

Dudley raised an eyebrow. "I might have a good explanation for that now that we know the truth about Hannah and Rachel. Twenty-five years ago, we found some forensic evidence at the teenage boy's murder scene, some skin under the nails, and a few hairs that we could never match to anyone. It was public knowledge that we'd found these two pieces of evidence. When the Kiplings disappeared, we scoured Dustin Kipling's offices for matching hair and DNA, and found a few usable samples, but there was no match. That process alone took over a month. Tracking down samples for Katherine Kipling? We never found any usable hair or skin samples for her. The two daughters, Hannah and Rachel? By the time we were done testing Dustin's samples, we were stumped on where to get any usable samples for the girls. Maybe that was Dustin Kipling's plan all along with burning the house—to destroy any and all forensic evidence on his family, make it as hard for us as possible."

Patterson nodded. "That makes sense. Everything Dustin Kipling did was for the wellbeing of his daughters. That's why they were here in the first place. But you could have gone to the girls' middle school, right? Checked their lockers for a forensic match?"

Dudley shrugged. "We did. Didn't find anything. A month

later those lockers had been cleaned and disinfected inside, and different students were using them."

Michelson cleared his throat. "We think Van Wyke must have heard about the bodies being pulled up from the lake here and put two and two together. He came over here looking for Dustin Kipling, perhaps looking for revenge against him for burning down the house and getting snubbed on payment. Our preliminary look into Van Wyke shows that the guy was involved with some shady people in regard to some of his business dealings." Michelson shrugged. "When Van Wyke got here, he must have met up with Hannah."

Rachette blew air out of his nose. "And with a few bullets, some gasoline, and a match."

Dudley eyed Rachette and nodded. "When I saw the story on the news, I knew we'd finally found Dustin Kipling. The MO of the killer, with the heads severed and everything, was too perfect a match. Van Wyke must have seen the same stories and thought the same thing."

"What about the second body found burned in his car?" Rachette asked.

Michelson nodded. "We think that's a man named Darnell Dawkins. He's been Van Wyke's personal assistant, or something akin to that, for the last three years. Our department can't find him, and it seems nobody has seen him in the last week up in Boise."

They stood in silence for a few moments.

"Have you talked to Rachel Kipling about any of this?" Michelson asked.

All eyes fell on Patterson. "She's been mute for five days. Won't talk to anyone. But we'll keep at it, that's for sure."

"Where is she?" Michelson asked.

"Our county hospital, under lockdown, recovering from a

fractured skull. She'll be put away for a long time when all is said and done."

They stood quietly and then Michelson shook his head in exasperation. "And she's not talking? Not giving any explanation about any of it?"

Rachette scoffed. "You think there's a good reason behind it all? They were both crazy, and that's that."

Dudley and Michelson looked at Rachette, and then his shoulder, and nodded respectfully.

Patterson cleared her throat, breaking the silence. "As you probably heard, we found Katherine Kipling in the lake as well, dropped in a different place than the other bodies. The neighbor, Olin Heeter, saw Hannah and Rachel dump their mother's corpse overboard all those years ago. We think they must have known how Olin Heeter had reported what he'd seen to our sheriff's office, but they'd left him alone all these years until now.

"Whatever the reason they, or Hannah, were killing these boys and dumping them in the lake, it looks like it all came to a head with the Kipling family after Nick Pollard's murder, and the girls had to get rid of their mother and father.

"Things went cold for SCSD for twenty-two years and then, when we started pulling up those corpses last week, it looks like they were thrust into crisis mode. They killed the neighbor, Heeter, planted some pictures to make him look crazy and throw us off their scent. Then Van Wyke and this Darnell Dawkins showed up and they killed them." She shook her head. "I think Deputy Rachette puts it succinctly: they were crazy."

"And they were cornered," Dudley said. "Not a good combination."

They stood in silence for a few seconds until Patterson held up her hand toward the house. "Shall we?"

Slowly they walked to the side of the house, and Michelson stepped next to Patterson. "What about the sheriff's wife?"

Patterson and Rachette exchanged a glance.

"*Ex*-wife. And as of yet, we can't connect Hannah or Rachel Kipling to those two murders. And, of course, Rachel's not talking to anyone ..."

Patterson let her sentence die. She didn't feel right exposing details about the violent crime that had caused endless whispering and speculation among the locals, and who knew how much pain for Jack, Wolf, and Sarah's family.

At the very least, the department had a responsibility to keep it in the SCSD family, didn't they?

"Yeah," Rachette piped up, breaking her thoughts. "Something is totally off about Carter and Sarah being together in the first place. And why in Rocky Points? It makes no sense to me. Supposedly that guy was a gay interior designer from Aspen, so why's he here? Because he and Sarah worked together in the past? Margaret said she hadn't known anything about him coming into town, and if it had been for one of Sarah's real-estate deals, Margaret would have been in the know." He looked over at Patterson. "And if Carter was gay, why was he putting his hand on her leg that night, like you said? If you ask me—"

Patterson stomped her heel on Rachette's foot.

"Ah! What the hell are you ..." Rachette read her death glare and shut his mouth.

She shook her head and walked, leaving the men following silently behind her.

Reaching Michelson's Caprice Classic, she turned, hoping the red in her face had dissipated.

Michelson eyed her kindly and broke the silence. "I hope we've been able to shed some light. I'll give you guys whatever you need at your station, and I'll need everything you have to bring back to my department."

She nodded. "Of course. I'll see to it."

"Maybe you two would like to come get lunch in town?" Michelson asked, clearly directing the question more to her than Rachette.

"Sorry, I have some other things to attend to. I'll follow you guys back to Rocky Points and get that report for you, though."

Michelson nodded, taking the rejection in stride. "Yeah, sure. We'd appreciate that. We'll head into town and see you when you get there."

The two men from Idaho walked to their vehicle doors and got in. The engine fired up, and Michelson backed away. With a wave and a nod, he drove off in a cloud of dust.

Patterson had no clue why she'd let herself mislead the man so much on the phone the past few days. She'd needed someone to talk to, someone besides Scott, someone in the business, and Michelson had been there for her. To think for a second that she could have jeopardized what she'd built with Scott over the past year—for what? An out-of-state flirtation?—was ridiculous.

She shook it off and eyed Rachette. "How you feeling?"

"Like shit."

"Get in my car. I'm taking you home."

He nodded but he didn't move.

"What's up?"

"You know," he said, "I don't know what's going to happen in the next month with our jobs and everything, but I want you to know that I've enjoyed working with you more than anyone else on the force. You're a good cookie."

She narrowed her eyes. "Thanks. I've ... liked working with you, too."

"I know I've been a pain in the ass to you over the last couple of years. And I'm thankful for your loyalty despite every-thing. I know that was a bad situation with those pictures of that girl and me. And I know you didn't want to get on the wrong foot with MacLean, and I'm going to talk to him this week. Make sure he knows loud and clear that you had nothing to do with any of that BS."

"You don't have to do that, just—"

"No, I do. And I'm going to. I've already called and made an appointment with him down in Ashland."

She nodded.

Rachette took a deep breath. "You know, there was this time way back, when I was a senior in high school, when I really liked this girl, and she really liked me too. We even said the L-word to each other, you know? It was that kind of thing."

She lifted her chin. "Look, Rachette, you don't have to tell me this. Whatever it is."

"I know. I just ... want you to know where I'm coming from, all right?"

"Yeah. Okay."

"So me and this girl, her name was Libby, we were tight. My dad used to be real tough on me growing up, and she was always there for me. Helped me through the bad times. She even helped me realize I wanted to be a cop."

Watching Rachette speak, Patterson swallowed back a tear when she realized this was the first time she'd ever seen her partner open up.

"But after a while, I suspected she was cheating on me. So I put an audio recorder in her car. You know, to try and catch her in the act?"

Patterson tilted her head.

"And then I caught her. Got her right on audio tape, getting it on with some guy from the marching band." Rachette glared into the distance. "I beat the crap out of that guy. And I had a topless picture of her on my phone, you know, from earlier, so I sent it to every—"

"Okay, okay." Patterson closed her eyes and held up a hand. "Listen, are we good?"

Rachette blinked. "Yeah. We're good."

"Okay. Then that's all I need to know." She stared at her partner and smiled.

"What?"

"Nothing. Let's go."

CHAPTER 68

THREE WEEKS LATER ...

Wolf started at the knock on his front door. He looked over at the roll table next to him and reached over for the TV remote control, pushing it further away.

"Shit." He gripped and wheeled the table closer, sending the almost empty bottle of Scotch thumping to the carpet.

The second knock was more insistent.

He picked up the remote and lowered the volume. "Come in!"

The hinges squealed and there was a shaft of morning sunlight, and then the silhouette of a man with a cowboy hat stood in the doorway.

"Come in and shut the door."

MacLean did as he was told. "It's pitch black in here."

Wolf screwed his eyes shut, his eye sockets throbbing as MacLean hit the light switch. "Shut it off."

There was a soft flip and the room went dark again.

With the sound of shots ringing out, he opened his eyes in

time to see The Rifleman squeeze off five rounds from his customized Winchester.

"You look like shit." MacLean walked to the hospital bed set in the middle of Wolf's living room, crunching a plastic cup with his boot on his way over. "Jesus. Really. Don't smell much better either. Don't you have someone to come give you a sponge bath? I can probably get someone up here to do it. A girl if you want."

Wolf pushed the mute button and glared at his visitor.

MacLean held up his hands. "Or not."

"Sit down."

MacLean looked around and turned up his palms.

"There's a chair in the kitchen. Grab me a glass of water while you're in there."

MacLean eyed him for a second and walked away.

Wolf picked up a plastic bottle and rattled out two pills into his left hand. Cupping his fingers around the tablets, he felt a lance of pain in his purple-and-yellow middle finger.

"Where's that water?"

MacLean appeared and held out a glass to his right hand.

Wolf stared at it and raised his left.

MacLean smiled and walked around the rear of the bed to the other side.

Wolf popped the pills in his mouth, grabbed the glass, and tipped it back. Some water streamed off his chin, down his chest and onto his crotch beneath his hospital gown, but the pills hit the inside of his stomach.

"You're not gonna sit?"

MacLean shook his head.

"Can you pick up that bottle of Scotch and put it back on the table please?"

MacLean snorted and smiled in response.

Wolf stared at him.

MacLean walked around the back of his inclined bed and picked up the bottle with a grunt. With deliberate steps that squeaked the floorboards under the carpet, MacLean moved back into the kitchen and rattled around in Wolf's cabinets. There was the sound of a glass slapping on the counter, a cork being pulled, and the glug of the bottle.

A second later MacLean strolled back in, put the full glass of Scotch down his throat and slapped the empty glass on Wolf's plastic roll table.

"That's enough dicking around now." MacLean walked to the front of the bed and assessed Wolf. "How would the voters like it if they saw their favorite candidate now?"

Wolf felt a drip of water leave his chin.

"You've been ignoring me, Sheriff. And since you garnered the sympathy of the voters with your personal tragedy and"— MacLean quoted his fingers—"*heroics* of late, your numbers have surpassed mine. And you didn't even have to speak in front of a podium."

Wolf gazed at the television.

"Well?" MacLean bent in front of him and jutted out his lower jaw.

Wolf blinked and let his eyes land on MacLean.

"Fine." MacLean waved a hand in the air. "That was your last chance. Your time is officially up. I've called a press conference today up at the resort, where I'm going to let our voters know about everything—your drug-running deputy, and the way you covered it up. And it's really a shame what you're doing. I actually liked Deputies Rachette and Patterson. They're good kids. Deputy Rachette had the balls to come down and apologize to me about the whole thing. And Patterson? She seemed like she would have been a good addition to my department. But, thanks to you, they'll both be packing up and looking elsewhere for work. And with that on their record, I doubt they'll find anything in the field of law enforcement."

MacLean turned toward the door and stopped. "Oh yeah, and I've decided to add a few more pictures to the mix. I'm not going to show them to you now, but I can describe them if you like." He raised his eyebrows, and when Wolf kept silent he continued. "They're of you and that dead serial-murderer woman. A few pictures of you and her coming into your house, and then a few of you two coming out the next day. All within the time period of your investigation. Good stuff."

"I'm out."

MacLean stood straight. "What?"

"I'm out. I'm officially out of the race, as soon as you fulfill your end of the bargain. I'm out."

MacLean's laugh boomed in the dark space, and after making a show of forming his hat he wiped his eyes. "I'm afraid I don't care. Any sympathy I had for you or your deputies is long gone, and I think the voters of our new county need to know what kind of fraud you really are." Pulling his thumb and fore-finger down the corners of his silvery mustache, he turned and walked to the front door.

"I'll be releasing what I have to Renee Moore," Wolf said, "from Channel 8, down in Denver. The FBI will also be inter-ested in what I have to say."

MacLean stopped and turned. "What are you blabbering about? What do they have you on there? Percocet? Hydrocodone?"

Wolf lifted a finger and pointed it toward a manila envelope laid conspicuously on the otherwise bare coffee table. "That's yours."

MacLean walked over and looked at it.

"That's right." Wolf smiled. "I have an envelope for you now."

"What is it?"

"Pick it up."

MacLean picked it up and pried it open. With a frown he pulled out the single sheet of paper. "What the hell is this?"

"My demands. I admit my handwriting is less than stellar, but I've been barely conscious for almost four weeks now, and when I'm awake I'm usually pretty buzzed on pain pills and Scotch. And since I can't get up to use my printer, I had to write it."

MacLean shook his head with impatience and reached into the envelope. Burying his arm to the elbow, he pulled out a USB memory stick.

"My Deputy Baine—you'll want to keep a good eye on that guy by the way—tracked down your friend, Ms. Gail Olson. He brought her into the station and had a little chat with her, and you'll see he's a persuasive guy with his technical and legal jargon, and the way he uses cuss words. He had her spinning, and then shitting her pants, and then spilling everything, about how she was coerced by you to first seduce Deputy Rachette, then to carry out a drug transfer with him in the pre-arranged place and time, where we all know your photographer was in waiting. It's all there on that USB in your hand, the interrogation video, her confession that she took your payment, everything."

There was a thwack as MacLean dropped the USB into the envelope. His eyebrows slid down and one side of his mouth turned up. "Bullshit. It'll be her word against mine."

"And expunging her record? Did you go through the official court procedures for that? Or was it you and your pal, Lieutenant Bentman in the Ashland PD records department, who made that deal happen off the books?"

MacLean's eyes darted back and forth.

Wolf lifted his eyebrows. "You and Bentman will be looking

at hard jail time for that little move. Gail Olson put us onto that track. She told us about that carrot you hung on the stick in front of her in addition to the two-thousand-dollar payment. Again, it's all on the video."

MacLean blinked. "Touché." He looked at the crumpled piece of notebook paper and frowned. "And what's this chicken-scratch say? Because I can, in fact, not read a single word of it."

"That's just saying that once you're sworn in as sheriff you'll hire deputies Rachette, Patterson, Wilson, Yates, and Baine into the department at their current rank or higher. I'll be adding names to that list as I see fit in the coming two weeks, and the employment contracts will be looked over by my associate, Margaret Hitchens. When I get the word that all has been done, I'll continue to hold myself back from releasing this information."

MacLean shoved the paper into the envelope and dropped it to his side. With a puff of air from his lips he looked at Wolf. "You'll continue to *hold back* from releasing this information?"

Wolf nodded. "And I've already told Deputy Rachette that you've had a change of heart about the photographs, and you'll have to tell him the same as soon as possible. He doesn't know anything about you setting him up, and I don't want him to know. That would only damage the relationship going forward, and cripple his ability to do a good job for the department. But, as far as I'm concerned, you owe him. You owe him big time. So you'd better tell him something that makes him feel off the hook for good, like he never even made a mistake. I don't care how you do it, just do it.

"Deputy Baine, however, can't unlearn what he's figured out about you. But he's agreed to keep silent about our counter-investigation into your activity. Of course, I'm sure it will cost you in the terms of his employment." Wolf raised an eyebrow. "Sorry, but you reap what you sow there."

MacLean's chest heaved as he wiped his nose. "And what about you?"

"Me?" Wolf's eyes glossed over. "I have to take some time to mend things."

"Well, no shit. I mean after that, what do you want from me? You clearly don't want sheriff, so what do you want? Undersheriff? Money? What?"

Wolf dragged his eyes back to MacLean. "For now, I'd like you to go into my kitchen, go into the cabinet to the left of the refrigerator, and pour me a Scotch."

MacLean stood still, his eyes becoming blocks of ice.

"And then," Wolf said, "I'll let you know."

MacLean bit his upper lip, and with a shake of his head he marched into the kitchen. A few seconds later he slammed the bottle next to Wolf and stormed to the front door.

The hinges shrieked, and a shaft of light burned into Wolf's retinas, and then the door slammed shut.

As the sound of tires crackled into the distance outside, Wolf reached over and picked up his phone. There were nine missed calls from Rachette, Margaret, Patterson, Burton, and his mother.

He ignored them and pushed the voicemail button for the hundredth time.

"Hi, David. It's me." Sarah's voice was timid, full of tension. "I need to talk to you. Call me back. Okay?"

Need to talk to you.

Wolf closed his eyes and lowered the phone. He cursed the political game he'd been roped into over the past few months, because it was so clear to him now—Sarah was dead because of that game. If he hadn't been so pissed off about Chama's visit that night, Wolf would have answered this very phone call. He would have helped her. She would be alive.

Wolf reached over and picked up the bottle of eighteen-year-old Glenlivet he'd gotten from Burton on his fortieth birthday. A twinge of pain arced up his back as he twisted the cork, but the paper seal gave way and the stopper slid up with a squeak and then popped.

He poured a few fingers in the water glass and scrolled to Jack's phone number. He swallowed and stared at it, once again pulling forth the fuzzy memory.

He knew it was a memory now, but for weeks Wolf had thought it had been a bad dream. One of many of late. But now he was certain. Through the haze of pain killers and agony of healing wounds, Wolf had only recently realized that Jack had not once been to see him. And he wasn't answering Wolf's phone calls, either.

And then the truth had settled on him like a pile of rocks.

It hadn't been a bad dream. It was a memory.

After one of Wolf's hip surgeries in the county hospital, he'd cracked his eyes and Jack had been there waiting for him. Jack had gotten up from his cloth-covered chair, stood next to his bed, leaned over so close that he could smell his son's breath, and said those words.

"It's your fault she's dead."

And then Jack had left.

Wolf's breath caught at the vague recollection; then he gritted his teeth and pressed Jack's phone number.

After a single ring it went to voicemail.

"This is Jack, you know what to do."

Wolf inhaled and shuffled the right words in his brain.

When the beep sounded in his ear, he said, "Hey, Jack." His voice wavered. "It's Dad."

After a few breaths, he screwed his eyes shut, then opened them, staring at black and white credits as they flashed on the TV screen. He pushed the call-end button and dropped the phone on the bed.

"One of these days you'll answer," he mumbled to himself. "I'm not giving up."

With a numb motion, he took a sip of the warm liquid, feeling the burn slide down his throat. Sloshing a dollop onto the cart table as he replaced it, his body sank into the hospital bed as if he was pulling five g's in a fighter jet.

As his eyelids drooped, he saw Sarah's beautiful blues, and her wide smile. Then he saw Jack next to her with a big grin of his own. And then their images swirled and vanished.

Wolf would find justice for Sarah and his shattered family.

Through this whole ordeal, at least Margaret Hitchens had been right about one thing.

"I never give up," Wolf said, closing his eyes.

ACKNOWLEDGMENTS

Thank you for reading Cold Lake. I hope you enjoyed the story, and if you did, thank you for taking a few moments to leave a review. As an independent author, exposure is everything, and positive reviews help so much to get that exposure. If you'd consider doing so, I'd greatly appreciate it.

I love interacting with readers so please feel free to email me at jeff@jeffcarson.co so I can thank you personally. Otherwise, thanks for your support via other means, such as sharing the books with your friends/family/book clubs/the weird guy who wears tight women's yoga pants across the street, or anyone else you think might be interested in reading the David Wolf series. Thanks again for spending time in Wolf's world.

Would you like to know about future David Wolf books the moment they are published? You can visit my blog and sign up for the New Release Newsletter at this link – http://www.jeffcarson.co/p/newsletter.html.

As a gift for signing up you'll receive a complimentary copy of Gut Decision—A David Wolf Short Story, which is a harrowing tale that takes place years ago during David Wolf's first days in the Sluice County Sheriff's Department.

Two thumps ripped Wolf out of his sleep.

Or so he thought. The silence in his ranch house living room was absolute save the ticking clock. The walls flickered in the darkened space as muzzle blasts puffed out of an actor's revolver on the muted television.

With a slow breath, he tried to blank out the throbbing in his limbs. Every time he woke, the pain seemed to have multiplied anew from the previous conscious moment; of course, being drugged up on Percocet and a smattering of other pills, adding doses of Scotch to the cocktail of medication, made it hard to remember those previous conscious moments.

This must be what it's like to have Alzheimer's. How many times had he repeated that thought in the past few days? What day was it?

He craned his neck as crunching footsteps approached his house outside, and then a knock on the door echoed in his skull, making him cringe.

He cracked his lips and peeled his tongue from the top of his mouth. "Come in."

There was no response.

"Come in!" Pain shot through his pelvis.

The knob turned and the door opened, letting in a burst of light that assaulted his eyeballs.

"Mr. Wolf?"

"Yeah."

"My name is Special Agent Cumberland with the FBI."

Two men were silhouetted in his open doorway, holding square ID wallets in his direction. He lay back and closed his eyes, staring at their after-image burned into his retinas. "I'll have to take your word for that. Come in."

"This is the Assistant Special Agent in Charge of the Denver field office, Steven Frye. We're here to ask you a few questions."

Wolf reached over and grabbed the handle of the oversized plastic cup of water and sucked from the straw. He was vaguely surprised that it was so full, cold, and rattling with ice. He drew a blank trying to remember who had filled it. It could have been any number of people who came in and out of his house as of late. Probably the big nurse.

"Open those shades," one of the agents said.

His living room brightened and Wolf tried to straighten in his reclined hospital bed, sending another bolt of pain from his pelvis up his spine. He broke into a sweat and pulled off his sheet, letting the relatively cool air caress his damp gown.

Fumbling at his sides for the bed controls, he found the plastic box next to his leg cast and pushed the incline button.

As the bed whirred, one of the agents stepped in front of the television. He was tall and wide, and filled out his suit with muscle underneath. Holding mirrored sunglasses in one hand, his badge wallet hung in his other.

"Let me see those badges and IDs again."

The big agent glanced at his partner and handed it over.

The badges were real, and the ID cards looked genuine

enough. Cumberland was the tall guy in front of him, and ASAC Frye was the other man to his left that he'd yet to look at properly.

Both men had military cuts in their pictures and no-nonsense blank facial expressions. They wore white dress shirts and black ties cinched around muscular necks.

When Wolf looked up, the two men were identical in dress and presentation to their IDs. But from each other they were different in every way. Cumberland was tall and imposing, while Frye was short and wiry. It looked like Cumberland had to endure a grueling physical routine to hold his shape, while Frye had to eat to hold his.

He handed the wallets back. "What questions?"

Cumberland tilted his chin up. "We need to ask you about the night Sarah Muller and Carter Willis were murdered. Straighten up a few things."

Though he spent most waking moments thinking about Sarah and her gut-wrenching demise by the hand of an unknown coward, the mention of her by these agents startled him to the core. "Straighten up a few things? What's there to straighten up?"

Cumberland clenched his fists and spread his hands while gazing around Wolf's living room.

It was a reflexive move for the big man, Wolf thought, like the agent was trying to contain anger.

Agent Frye cleared his throat. "What were you doing the night of Sarah Muller and Carter Willis's deaths?"

Wolf took a deep breath, suppressing upwelling rage at the direction the conversation had steered. "I was out having a drink."

"With a woman who was a suspect in your murder investigation up at Cold Lake, correct?" Frye asked.

"At the time, she was a person of interest."

"Until what time were you two having a drink?"

"I don't know. Nine-thirty? Ten?"

"You're not too sure about this because?"

"I left under extenuating circumstances."

Frye blew air from his mouth. "And I guess what you mean by that is you were in a fight with a man named Carter Willis, knocked unconscious, and dragged out of there by this woman of interest?"

"Something like that."

Cumberland squeezed his hands into fists again.

"Have you heard that said woman of interest, Miss Kimber Grey, aka Rachel Kipling, has just committed suicide at County Hospital?"

"No, I haven't."

"Ah. Well she has. So, there goes your alibi right there."

"Actually, you don't have your facts straight. I don't think I was having drinks with Rachel that night. I think it was her twin sister, Hannah Kipling, whom I pulled off a cliff and killed. So, actually, my alibi was long gone before Rachel offed herself."

Frye smiled without teeth. "So, you have no alibi for your whereabouts for the rest of that night. We talked to the bartender at the Pony Tavern. You were dragged out of there at closer to nine p.m., so you had the whole night ahead of you to recover from your fight and take care of whatever you needed to."

Wolf ignored the bait.

"You've got motive like nobody else," Frye continued.

"What's this guy here for? To stand and flex? You mind moving away from the TV there, Hulk?"

Cumberland's face darkened, and then he turned and poked the off button.

The flat screen squeaked as it rocked back and forth on its stand.

Frye smiled again, this time displaying teeth that seemed to glow. Clearly a fan of whitening agents. "We've been checking on your recent movements, specifically before the murders of your ex-wife and Carter Willis. Turns out you and Carter had a little run-in at Antler Creek Lodge, the restaurant at the top of Rocky Points Ski Resort?"

"Is that a question?"

"And from what we've been able to gather, it looks like Carter Willis and your ex-wife hugged at that encounter, and you overreacted, causing a scene."

"I reacted the appropriate amount."

"Out of jealousy?"

"The guy was a sleaze ball. He was groping my date in front of me."

Frye nodded. "I'm just going to cut to the chase, maybe save us all some time here. Did you kill Carter Willis and your ex-wife, Mr. Wolf?"

"No."

"Because it looks like you did."

"Can't arrest someone for looking like they might have murdered someone. Listen, I've got some *Rifleman* to catch up on, so if you guys don't mind leaving and lifting your legs on some other tree? Thanks."

"What are these?" Frye slapped a manila folder on the plaster cast that covered Wolf's lap.

Wolf stared at it but didn't move.

Frye opened it and tipped out a stack of photographs.

They were photos of his deputy, Tom Rachette, and the girl they'd come to know as Gail Olson. They were familiar—Gail Olson handing Rachette a bag, Rachette hugging the woman, Rachette putting the bag in his car, Rachette and Gail driving their separate ways.

They were an innocuous set of photographs under normal

circumstances, but Wolf knew Gail Olson had been caught months earlier by the Ashland PD with marijuana and money in her car, lots of both, and these photos were supposed to implicate Wolf and his department in the smuggling of drugs.

When Wolf kept silent, Frye picked up a photo and studied it. "Sheriff Will MacLean of Byron County told us that he brought these photos to you. He knew all about Gail Olson's past and mentioned that he might make these photos public. He said you freaked out and dropped out of the race. He's done right by giving up the pictures to us now."

"Yes," Wolf said, "these photos were a blackmail attempt by Sheriff MacLean, who set up Gail Olson to make this fake drop while he took these pictures to make my deputy and my department look bad."

Frye straightened with a confused look. "MacLean set the whole thing up, which you figured out, and yet you dropped out of the race? So the blackmail attempt worked? I'm confused. You say it was a set-up, but you dropped out of the race to keep these photos under wraps."

"I dropped out of the race because I didn't want the job."

"And why's that?"

"I learned I didn't fit the job description. MacLean did perfectly."

Frye laughed. "That's an interesting angle."

"What's that supposed to mean?"

"It means that's not what we heard."

Wolf leaned back. "Heard about what?"

Frye smirked and walked away from the hospital bed. He picked up a sheet of paper and studied it, set it down, and moved on.

"Hey, why don't you take a look around?"

"Thanks, I will," Frye said, his voice coming from inside Wolf's bedroom.

Cumberland stood motionless, gazing at Wolf.

Engines revved and tires rumbled on the drive out front, getting louder as they approached.

Frye appeared next to Wolf and gestured to the window. "The rest of our crew."

"Why?"

Frye stepped to the window and forked open the blinds with his fingers. "Did you kill Gail Olson, Sheriff Wolf?"

Wolf frowned. "What? No."

Frye twisted and stared at him.

Wolf looked at Frye and Cumberland in turn. "Gail Olson's been murdered?"

Both agents held their stares.

Frye blinked first. "She's been missing since the night of Carter Willis and Sarah Muller's deaths. Vanished."

The vehicles outside came to squeaking stops and car doors opened and closed. Chattering agents and squawks of radio static filled the silence.

"You guys seriously think I shot my ex-wife, Carter Willis, and Gail Olson?" Wolf tried to counteract his escalating blood pressure with deep breathing, but it wasn't working.

Frye gestured toward Wolf's bedroom. "Could have been with that Walther PPK sitting in your nightstand drawer."

"The bullets that killed my ex-wife and Carter Willis were nine millimeter parabellum. Since a blown-off right hand isn't one of my current injuries, clearly, I didn't use the PPK to fire those rounds. You got a warrant inside that empty head of yours? If not, then get the hell out of my house."

"And your department-issue Glock 17?" Cumberland asked.

"My deputies already checked to see if my piece was fired the day we discovered the bodies."

"We discovered the bodies?" Frye asked. "They. Your

deputies discovered the bodies. You were supposedly here with a psychotic serial murderer at the time, doing hell-knows-what kind of sick things in that bedroom of yours—or at least, you say you were here. And when your deputy checked your weapon? We heard about that visual check and sniff. That's not going to cut it. We'll need to do some ballistics." Frye slapped a folded sheet of paper on his bed. "And here's our warrant. We're going to take a look around now. You just sit here and make yourself comfortable while we do." Frye pulled a radio from his belt. "All right, let's move."

Calls and responses echoed outside and the front door blew open. Two male agents entered in full stride.

"Go ahead, make my day." Wolf leaned back, his confident words sounding not so confident to his ears. Because the truth was, he remembered little of that fateful night a few weeks ago, when Sarah and Carter Willis were shot dead and left in a BMW sedan.

There were still unanswered questions about that night—as in *all* of the questions.

"Agent Frye."

Frye paused in mid-conversation with an agent and stepped close to Wolf. "What?"

"Carter Willis."

"What about him?"

"I've been looking into him. Who the hell is he? Aren't you guys worried about that? He's not in any of the databases, no public record, nothing. He doesn't exist. He's a ghost. And you guys are worried about me?"

"That's not your concern."

"Not my concern? He was found dead with my wife."

"Your ex-wife." Frye squinted and tilted his head. "Is that all, Mr. Wolf?"

Wolf leaned back and closed his eyes. "Is Special Agent Luke here?"

Nobody answered. When Wolf cracked his eyes open, Agent Frye was gone.

Wolf looked on his bedside roll-table for his cell phone but it, too, was gone. A young-looking FBI agent was dropping it in a plastic bag.

"Is Special Agent Luke here?" Wolf asked the agent.

The agent kept silent, but after a quick glance around the room he nodded.

"Tell her to come talk to me."

The agent ignored him and stepped away.

Wolf sat back and pulled up his bed sheet, feeling exposed in more ways than one. There was nothing he could do but breathe and remain calm.

He leaned back and racked his brain again, like he'd done in every waking moment between pill and Scotch-induced sleeps the past couple of weeks.

He'd relived every memory from the night of Sarah and Carter's deaths countless times, but the problem was that the memories were few. Wolf had been having drinks with a woman he'd thought to be Kimber Grey when Carter Willis had come into the bar with two of his cronies. It had been only a few minutes until Carter Willis had approached Wolf, leaned close, and told him his ex-wife was an *unforgettable piece of ass*. He remembered that clear enough. And then Wolf had attacked him without hesitation.

Wolf had gotten some good shots in, and taken a few, too. But the lights had gone out when he'd taken a pool cue to the head from one of the two men with Carter.

From that blackout moment onward, Wolf had been at the mercy of a woman who had murdered an unknown number of young men, mutilated their bodies, and dumped them into Cold

Lake, south of town. The rest of that night had been erased from his mind, if it had ever been there to begin with. He'd had more than a few whiskies at the Pony Tavern before the action ensued.

Then there were the memories of the past few weeks since his plummet off a cliff. Those were chopped and jumbled, and remembering anything in any order was like trying to put together a thousand-piece puzzle with the pieces turned upside down.

"David." The voice in his ear was feminine and full of concern.

Wolf opened his eyes.

"You look like shit," Special Agent Kristen Luke said.

Luke's brown hair was pulled back in a tight ponytail, her face chiseled, yet soft. Her wide cinnamon-bark eyes were bleary but still as stunning as ever.

"You look good," Wolf said.

She darted a glance toward the nearest agent and waited for him to move on. "I'm sorry I haven't gotten back to you. I can't really ... *talk* to you."

He nodded. "Deputy Baine has proof that MacLean was behind those photographs with Rachette and Gail Olson—a video interview Baine conducted with Gail. Which makes me think MacLean might be behind her disappearance. Get to Baine, and get that video file he has."

"Of course I ..." she stopped talking and stepped away.

A few seconds later she came close, this time avoiding eye contact with him. "Go ahead."

"MacLean also said he had photos of me and Hannah Kipling here at the house that night. Those photos might be my alibi."

She walked away as if he'd said nothing.

Agent Frye appeared next to Wolf, his eyes trailing Luke. "She tells me you're innocent."

"She's a smart agent."

"So am I. That's how I became ASAC. And I know that when emotions get involved, investigations go sloppy. So I'm not listening to a thing she says."

Wolf closed his eyes. "Let me know what you find. I'm confident I'll see you again soon, and you can apologize to me then, okay?"

When Wolf opened his eyes, Agent Frye had gone, back to the bustle of agents ransacking his home.

You can order Smoked Out (David Wolf Book 6) at Amazon.com to continue the adventure!

Made in the
USA
Monee, IL